CATWALK:
MESSIAH
A Leon "Catwalk" Caliber Story

Nick Kelly

COPYRIGHT

Manufactured in the United States of America

Cover by My Creative Pursuits
Interior Design by Stacia D. Kelly
Edited by Jennifer Parkinson
Cover Art by My Creative Pursuits© 2013

Published by:
CatKlaw, Inc.
www.catklaw.com
Virginia

ISBN 978-0-9852837-6-6
Print Version

DEDICATIONS

To My Parents, for allowing my creative side
to show, even when it meant holes in the walls,
and to my blushing bride, who has been my
Muse since we met and every day since.

Table of Contents

PROLOGUE

"Okay, Sweetie, open your eyes."

Leon "Catwalk" Caliber takes a long drag off of his cigarette. The voice on the vidscreen triggers the same sick taste in his throat as the first time he pressed the play button. The series of events on-screen remains the same: the awkward smile of the girl in the frame, the sweet and self-absorbed tone with which the man off-camera delivers his dialogue, the slight, excited shaking of the camera as she looks up at him. Once again he asks the young girl which hand holds the coin, even though only his left hand is extended. She's nervous. Her shoulders are pulled up, and her arms are tight to her body. She shifts to accommodate the tight fit of her school uniform. She blushes, the ghost of Shirley Temple, complete with pigtails and storybook innocence. She giggles and touches the back of the man's gloved hand with a finger. She's correct.

It's the right hand that wields the bone saw.

Catwalk stops the recording. The glass next to him is empty, the bottle of bourbon almost the same. The dull glow of the paused recording is the only light in the loft, save a few blinking sensors from the bay that hosts his motorcycle and gear. He stares mutely at the image on the screen. He already has the rest of it memorized. The girl survives for another two minutes and 17 seconds. She doesn't suffer long. Thank whatever God she believes in that she doesn't feel what happens next. This killer doesn't keep his victims alive along. He saves the mutilation and sex acts until after they're dead. He doesn't get off on torture, only the rush of ending a life, even that of an eight-year-old girl.

Cat takes a hold of his whiskey tumbler, mindlessly raising it to his lips. The lack of liquid distracts him from

1

the screen. The video was an unexpected test. Someone hoping to remain anonymous had paid a deposit for his services. The instructions were simple. Watch the video. Find the killer. Get vengeance for the victims. Get proof. Get paid.

His eyes return to the screen. His lips curl into a sneer. After watching the recording once, he was willing to do the job for free. That feeling amplified each time he watched the girl die.

Cat chuckles out loud. He's curious at his reaction. This chit never bothered him before. Why now? Why her?

He stands and walks away from the screen. He needs a break. He stands and stretches. The muscles along his arms and sides are sore. His legs and spine don't protest. They're hard-wired into his nervous system. Thanks to modern cybernetic technology, he can leap from the sidewalk to the top of an apartment complex and outrun most of the commercial vehicles on the market.

The benefits aren't without a curse. His immune system has never quite solved the riddle of his experimental cybernetics. Treatment is painful and expensive. He could use the money this job would bring in.

Catwalk stands in front of one of the windows, listening to the endless clamor of sirens, screams and gunfire in the distance. He's chosen a nasty part of Downtown. It's dangerous, but it's very private. As a professional hitman, that's worth the risk.

Running his hands through his hair, he ties it into its customary ponytail. He looks over his shoulder at the custom-crafted, armored helmet resting on the counter. The triangular yellow cat eyes stare back at him. Cursing under his breath, Cat walks toward the helmet and the armored motorcycle behind it with cold intent.

There's work to be done.

CHAPTER ONE

8 August 2033

"C'mon. It's just one drink. What could go wrong?"

His colleague's words reverberated in his skull as Catwalk took a sip of his bourbon. Plenty of lives had gone from promise to peril in the shadow of 'just one drink.' He'd managed to pace himself, offering empty smiles and courteous nods while Emory Blake, Esquire, ordered round after round, making eyes at their polite waitress all the while. Emory was in the mood to celebrate. Why wouldn't he be? He had just won a conviction on 'The Hooded Hooker' serial killer, thanks largely to the evidence and witness testimony Catwalk had dug up over the past few weeks. In Emory's mind, a killer was away for life. He'd rid the streets of a murderer, a menace to society, and a media target all in one.

Cat's perspective was understandably different. He had put away plenty of those predators during his years as a DC cop. Tonight, thousands of kilometers from his former law enforcement career, he studied things from a different angle. He recorded the look of satisfaction on Emory's face—every crease of the man's forehead, the giddy turn of his lips and the heavy-lidded look that indicated the drinks were shooting Emory's dopamine levels through the roof. A silent beacon flashed in the corner of Cat's cybernetic vision and his lips spread to a smile rivaling that of his host. The slick lawyer guaranteed Cat would be compensated for each witness he rounded up. The first payment just cleared.

He raised a glass and proposed a toast. "To the first of many big fish reeled in by the hard work a' the Nitro City Police Department, and Emory Blake, Esquire."

Emory's bleary eyes met Catwalk's as he raised a glass. Cat feigned ignorance of the man's condition and forgave all his overstated claims so far. Why should he hold a grudge? Emory had come through, delivering his half of the bargain they'd struck. Cat rounded up the eyewitnesses and got them to testify. In exchange, Emory ensured prompt, untraceable compensation. The blinking light in his heads-up display didn't lie. Cat smiled. His client's payment had cleared.

Emory ordered another round. He approached the barely legal, artificially enhanced brunette tormenting him from the bar with long lashes and crossed legs. A few awkward lines later, the pair began to dance in the center of the bar. Cat refused to celebrate the arrest of one more Nitro City thug. For every mass murderer the NCPD successfully put away, two more hit the streets, and a third escaped from custody. The smile faded from his lips, and Cat realized that was one thing that drew him to the West Coast and the former City of Angels. He'd left the world of law enforcement for freelance work. What better place than the city with an endless supply of murderers and thieves?

His cybernetic eyes stole a glance at his comm. A blinking light confirmed he'd chosen the right path. The 'message received' beacon notified him the warning he'd sent last night was received. Cat exhaled sharply, thinking of the little girl from the video. The twisted psycho from the recording had received, and read, Cat's warning.

"No prison cell for you, Hitch," Cat whispered aloud. "There's a special level of hell, and you have a reservation."

The brunette bent at the waist and ground her hips against Emory's. The lawyer stole a quick glance at Catwalk, feigning the motion of slapping his new playmate on the ass. Cat raised his glass in a mock toast, and the lawyer returned his focus on the heavenly body writhing against him. The ex-cop snuck a look at the clock behind the bar. He scoffed. If he could scrounge up twenty more minutes of feigned interest, he'd have no trouble escaping into the shadows and leaving the impromptu party. He shot a glance back to the dance floor. Emory and the brunette moved together in time to the music. Cat rattled the ice cubes in his almost-empty glass.

Twenty minutes dragged along like dental work. Catwalk tuned into Emory's unsteady gait and offered to hail a cab, pick up the check, and call it a night for their party. He succeeded in forging Emory's signature on the

4

bar tab and even improvised a short farewell speech. The brunette refused to leave until Cat forced her number into his buddy's palm and promised he would call as soon as he sobered up. He was still shaking his head when he noticed how quickly the bar emptied out.

Emory slapped a heavy hand on his shoulder, laughing loudly. "Now that was one hell of a party, Cat man!"

Catwalk agreed, steadying his weight and that of his colleague against his cybernetic legs. "We should do it again sometime."

"Soon," Emory answered in reply. "Sometime soon."

Cat nodded. "I can't wait."

Emory took a few unsteady steps to the exit, leaning hard on the exit door as he left the bar. Cat recognized the Auto-Taxi waiting at the curb and wasn't sure if his friend could make the eight steps to the awaiting door. Emory paused a moment, steadied himself and made the first six steps with no problem. A meter or two from his ride home, the lawyer stopped, his blood shot eyes looking back at Cat through the window.

Emory winked and raised his fingers, pointing them at Catwalk. He fired both hands like mock six-shooters, mouthing the phrase, "bang bang."

Catwalk chuckled, lifting the tumbler to his lips.

Then, the world went white.

The windows shattered inward. A fist of wind blasted into the bar, knocked over tables and chairs, and slammed Cat backward onto the floor.

A flash of fire followed the wind. Cat stayed low and watched the fire quickly rescind. Glass and wood rained down on him. He shook his head, growling a mechanical sound in return. He lifted his knees to his chest and kicked his feet out. Landing in a crouch, he reached to his belt and snapped the self-defense baton to its full extension.

Catwalk ran to the door. He attempted to regain focus, though his cybernetic eyes should never have lost it. His eyes were programmed to compensate for everything from low light to flash grenades. His lack of focus wasn't technical. It was mental. In the din and fluttering shrapnel, he made out Emory's silhouette on the pavement. Cat drew nearer then stopped in disbelief. His friend's body was hardly more than a skeleton.

One blink later and Emory's bones melted, leaving nothing but a puddle of liquefied flesh.

A mechanic roar shook through his body, and Cat

twisted with the force, skidding to a crouch back by the bar entrance. As the roar died down, Cat shook his head to clear the stars in his eyes and the ringing in his ears. The horizon became an orange-red haze of fires and explosions so close together that Cat couldn't tell where one ended and the next began.

Suddenly, a huge figure darkened the skyline. It was gigantic, inhuman and heading right for him.

Not waiting for introductions, Cat pressed back against the doorframe.

"Son of a bitch."

The approaching being lumbered on its arms more than its legs like a giant gorilla. It pounded the ground, sending mechanical vibrations in each direction. Its head pitched forward between its shoulders. The Titan roared and beat its chest, and the sound rattled Cat's teeth and shook through his body. This thing was enormous. From what he could make out, it was some kind of mechanized Titan, complete with an army of Corporate Security forces trying to put it down permanently.

From where he crouched, Cat could make out the percussion of gunfire and the wailing of sirens. These sounds were the soundtrack of Downtown, but now they were close and coming closer. An enormous Police Hovertank motored over the street, and Catwalk steeled himself against the force and sound of its engines. The Titan landed on the street just in front of the bar, crushing the remains of a taxi. No screams. Hopefully, the cabbie had enough sense to beat feet once the shooting started.

The Titan swept the taxi aside. Cat leapt backward as the car smashed against the front of the bar. Shattered glass and trashed bar stools clanked all around. A mechanical growl rose within Catwalk, and he knew his eyes flashed yellow. He looked out at the Titan. It was easily ten meters tall. The gunfire had torn away areas of its skin and flesh, revealing the unmistakable robotic skeleton of a MetaHuman. The mechanical primate slammed its fists into the pavement and then launched into the air, continuing down the street, away from the pursuing security forces.

The swarming Hovertanks continued to fire on it, and on anyone caught in the crossfire.

"Rest in Peace, Emory," Cat muttered under his breath.

He took in a breath and ran from the cover of the bar. Catwalk changed filters in his Cyberoptics and began recording everything he could. Explosions and muzzle flashes prevented him from getting a clear enough image to run against his databases. Another Hovertank raced overhead, and Cat braced against the side of a shelled-out delivery van to avoid becoming collateral damage. He focused on the Hovertank, able to snap an image for later analysis. It looked different than the first one that had passed overhead. That meant there was more than one corporate security team attacking the same target. Multiple Security Teams. Multiple jurisdictions. That could be a very bad thing.

Gunfire from the pursuing Hovertanks peppered the parked vehicles and piles of rubble along the street. Brick and mortar flicked into the air as the shells struck the walls on both side of the road. Cat dove back across the pavement. He rolled, landing on one knee. The sidewalk was hot, waves of humidity rose from its surface. The wind from the Hovertank engines tossed debris into the air. He was caught in the pure static that attacked sight and hearing. He pushed himself up to his feet, looking each way for a potential exit. He turned to the opposite side of the street. He needed to get the shock out of there. Now.

Cat bolted. He would have to cross the street, get between the two-parked cars and over the rusty fence to reach his ride. Another Hovertank came into view, auto-cannons firing thousands of rounds. Cat grabbed the damaged fender of the car the Titan had struck and slid underneath the vehicle. A plague of bullets rained down, peppering the asphalt, the vehicles and the storefronts. The pavement beside the car disintegrated under the hail of automatic weapons. He heard a Hovertank pass overhead, then another and a third. Faster, lighter buzzing followed, the engines of the media teams covering the event. The sound of the Titan's footsteps moved further away. It roared again, the sound audible above the cacophony of engines and gunfire.

The sounds died down—the calm between the newsworthy event and the combination of emergency teams and scavengers who would follow. Cat lifted his knees to his chest, pressing his feet against the bottom of the car. Grunting loudly, he kicked with both legs, and the car rolled off of him, landing on its hood like a desperate turtle. He watched the fading visions of the machine and the pursuing security forces.

Choosing self-preservation over curiosity, Catwalk leapt over the rusty fence and landed next to his armored motorcycle. He donned his helmet, and the bike roared to life. Cat needed information, and he wanted to see how this confrontation would end. As close as he had come, this wasn't his case, so a ringside seat wasn't priority. He sped out along the damaged streets of Downtown, his chest on the motorcycle's gas tank, the needle in the red. He wanted to get somewhere safe before the battle between the enormous beast and the hired corporate guns ended.

Cat swept the motorcycle across several lanes of traffic, taking an exit that offered him a higher vantage point. He slowed the H-S enough to triangulate the position of the mechanical primate through the lights, flames and explosions. His heads-up-display centered on the beast's silhouette, filtering out the white noise while recording the festivities. An instant later, the image turned to static, and Cat shifted the filters off. His helmet popped open, offering his Cyberoptics a direct look at the confrontation below.

Fire and shrapnel erupted a hundred meters into the air in a fireworks display that would make New Year's Eve jealous. Gas pumps morphed into oversized bottle rockets. The screams of civilians cut through the air. As the echo of explosions faded, they were replaced with a hollow groan as the service station framework cracked and gave way under the angered steps of the Titan.

The metallic beast rose to the height of its ten meter frame, batting aside an abandoned car and a dumpster with no effort. It pounded the ground.

Bullets rattled off of its chest as it leveled its red gaze at its assailants.

Figures scattered around behind it, panicking and fleeing the destruction. The Nitro City Police Department fired round after round of standard and armor piercing ammunition, with no effect other than shredding the fake skin of the cybernetic being's exoskeleton.

From this distance, Cat could safely start guessing at what he saw. Sure, it looked like a giant gorilla, but almost all natural animals were extinct on Earth, moved safely to off-world colonies. Someone may have constructed a giant, robotic gorilla, but that wasn't likely. This thing was chaotic and destructive. He'd seen this type of psychosis before. That murderous, mechanical being had started out human, but its human brain couldn't control the machine it had become. Cybernetics overwrote its ability to feel, to think, to relate – like a virus wiping away its very humanity.

Cat filtered out individual screams. He heard an old man with a thick accent, a woman's voice whispering soft, playful words, and a shaking voice betraying outright fear. Each was a different component of humanity executed at the hands of the mechanical behemoth. Cat wondered for a moment where exactly he tipped the scales. His own body was the marriage of human and machine, and he knew that marriage often ended badly. In his case, the jury was still out.

This particular gigantic war machine had crossed over the line, deciding in the process to let any normal human in its wake follow its sanity into the afterlife. Cat had seen it before, but never on this scale.

Impressed, Cat watched the manic MetaHuman grab one of the armored Hovercars in mid-flight and shake it violently then toss the inhabitants aside like unwelcome parasites on its last supper. The enormous war machine clapped its hands together, crushing the Hovercar like a beer can.

Enough was enough. The Titan couldn't last much longer, and the battleground was growing, and it was moving back in his direction. Cat gunned the motorcycle, racing out of the line of fire as two more armored vehicles approached. He flipped his comm to the open channel, listening to the media coverage and watching the proceedings in a small pop-up in his display.

The battle continued for another fifteen minutes. Cat made a note. There was no way that thing should still be moving, let alone raging and causing property damage and loss of life. No MH he had ever fought had sustained such injuries and remained upright. Finally, a combination of armor-piercing rounds and Electro-Magnetic Pulse attacks in succession caused it to slow and stumble. In an effort to escape, it leapt, and the camera lost the shot as the MH fell off of the highway overpass.

By the time the camera crew got the target back in frame, it was lying prone near an enormous building bathed in blue. Additional attacks came from the arriving security forces, leaving the magnificent machine, formerly human, nothing more than a smoking pile of rent flesh and decimated cybernetics. Cat smirked. Emory's ghost might take small solace in one fact: the city would save money on a trial.

Within seconds, the media covering the assault started in with a superlative-laden description rivaling the end of civilization. Ratings still ruled above all else, and the reporters were compensated by keeping viewers. Accuracy always played second fiddle to speculation when it came to such an event. Conjecture rolled forth like a tsunami, and Cat lost interest.

He pulled the H-S into the parking garage of his building, typing a few keys to disarm the warning systems, and rolled right into the freight elevator. As fanaticism outweighed the facts, Catwalk hit a switch, and the media feed went dead. He pushed the button for the loft, lifted his helmet and rubbed his neck. The elevator door opened, and a small confirmation indicated his residence was safe.

Cat drove the H-S to its customary spot. He powered down the engine and hooked up the leads to do diagnostic testing and repair. He mounted his helmet on its perch, connecting similar wires so it could download the images captured earlier. The hitman was sore and tired, and he couldn't figure out if he was more affected by losing a professional colleague or nearly becoming Nitro City's newest pothole.

He decided that the best pain medication, as usual, was intoxication. He walked to the bar, leaving the hum of the video feed to die in darkness behind him. He mentally replayed some of the old cases he'd worked on as a cop, thinking back to the most tumultuous period of his life.

Cat drained the first glass as quickly as he poured it. He spent four years, four dangerous and chaotic years that nearly drove him insane putting down MetaHumans gone rogue. He'd never seen one as big as the Titan who'd just stormed through Downtown. It was a bomb whose fuse had run out. He poured a second glass, catching the reflection of his yellow eyes in the glass, cold, artificial, inhuman eyes. He took a long drink, swishing the liquor around in his mouth before swallowing it. The liquor burned as it hit his stomach reminding him that he was still human. He could still feel.

Cat walked to the window. Downtown sang to him its constant symphony of sirens, screams, and gunfire. He raised a silent toast to Emory, downing the rest of the glass. Emory Blake, Esquire – esteemed Assistant District Attorney, successful prosecutor, rising star snuffed out by a MetaHuman out of control.

Cat poured a third drink. MetaHuman out of control. Maybe they'd carve that on his tombstone when he followed the Titan's path to insanity. He raised the glass to his lips, determined to drink until he stopped seeing himself as the next victim of cybernetics' conquest over humanity.

CHAPTER TWO

The morning ride to the local precinct was comfortable, downright soothing at moments. Catwalk twisted his wrist slightly, and the armored Honda-Suzuki motorcycle answered his every request, cornering like a gazelle, sprinting like a cheetah, and responding with the devotion of a hunting dog.

Cat had called ahead, getting Will to agree to meet him on the premises. Will was a paranoid forensic anthropologist and medical examiner who obsessed over the details of every case. He was also willing to take some very thorough and unethical steps, for the right price. Cat had very few allies in Nitro City, but Will was as loyal as they came, as long as the checks never bounced. Cat trusted him from their first interaction, seeing a lot of himself in the slightly strange death investigator.

For some reason Cat never figured out, the mortician used the name Will N. Testament for all his proceedings. It was an odd title, but then again Cat's own handle had nothing to do with his abilities. He was no male model. He couldn't sustain himself on crackers and nose candy. Some fool cop had labeled him Catwalk after seeing the acrobatics provided by his cybernetics. The name stuck ever since.

Cat never really decided if he should be grateful or pissed. He'd been labeled by a fellow officer during his first week on duty. Despite every attempt, Cat stood out, and the moniker followed him like cheap cologne. Eventually, he accepted it. He wasn't certain when, but he was relatively sure it was the first time one of his lovers had screamed, "Fuck me, Cat!" That was the sort of thing that made a man reevaluate how he was recognized.

When Cat arrived, he wasn't surprised to see Will chugging black coffee, even in a room full of human remains, somewhat human parts, and leftovers only scientists could define. Will's eyes were glossy, their undersides as black and leathery as the morgue's body bags. He was visibly upset at being called to action before sundown. His shaved head was completely covered in a tattooed mural and barbed piercings, and his mood was as fiery as the giant MetaHuman on last night's vid feed. Several parts of the Titan now covered the steel table.

Guitar-driven synth-rock filled the room loud enough to shake the steel trays containing forceps, scissors, chisels, and saws. Cat considered shooting the audio source, but thought twice when he realized it might be hardwired into Will's skull. Instead, he picked up a clean bone mallet from the table next to him and whacked Will on the shoulder with it.

The mortician hardly flinched, but the music magically dropped a hundred decibels. "Please, please tell me you brought me here for a reason, Cat man?"

Cat had little more than a hunch, but his gut told him it was enough to engage the ornery coroner he'd called a friend for the last few months. "I wish I could claim some Divine Vision, but, really, partner, I ain't got too much ta go on. That thing took out a friend a' mine, and almost put me on the next table over. I would have hated ta die without givin' you one last kiss goodbye."

Will flipped Cat an appropriate one-finger gesture in silent reply, as he pulled aside the tarp covering the corpse. The news coverage had been above average and with the pressure on the MH's manufacturer coming as a result, Cat was right, there would be little chance to investigate it without a badge very soon.

"As you're so fond of reminding me when I need something, Cat, you ain't a shocking cop anymore. So, what's with the sudden desire to play detective? Or are you the hired dick on this case?"

"C: none of the above," Cat replied, scanning the MH for markings not inflicted by the arsenal that finally took it down. "Rogue Metas pay a hefty cred load." He pried open the scorched and dented panel at the base of the skull, quickly snapping a digital image of the serial numbers. There were enough remaining digits that it could be tracked. "Rumors have this thing linked to three different contract companies. Any guesses?"

Will rubbed his neck, opening one eye and addressing Catwalk over the lip of his coffee cup. "It's too mish-mashed. Every time I think I've got it figured out, I find a different design algorithm that makes me second guess myself." He walked to one of the side tables and lifted a metallic plate wrapped in a department-issued bag. It was the size of his fist. "This was interesting, though."

The ex-cop stepped over. Will didn't think anything was interesting. The statement alone caught him off guard. "What's that, its forehead?"

"Not even close. This is the palm of its hand, before the swap-out to the Autoguns, but you saw that, I'm sure."

"Yeah, full-auto, air-cooled, 15mm, looked like a Czech origin from what I saw."

"Israeli, and it was 18mm, which is really rare."

"Well, cut me some slack, there was the little detail of duckin' Hovertanks and fallin' buildings."

Will nodded. "So here in the palm, I've never seen this design. I'm running it, and the numbers against the db and waiting on results. This artwork came close to a few gang symbols but not all that close."

Cat snapped an image of the artwork. It was a cross, with the base planted in stone. The left and right points ended in a flaming profile face and a grinning skull, and a set of scales hung from the top point. Silhouetted behind it was a pair of skeletal wings. He turned the image slightly side to side. Something about it was familiar, but he couldn't place it.

"Shockit," he cursed, "have I mentioned I hate religious fanatics?"

"More times than I can count. It's time for you to head out, my man. Press is already pounding at the gates for answers I ain't got."

"You're not the DI on this?"

Will shook his head. "Nope, jurisdiction went immediately to CorpSec for TransTechnica when they got the kill. That's odd, since they only engaged when it crashed onto their parking garage after three other companies wounded it. They've been fighting for the credit, which is how I got to sneak you in here."

"Much obliged, baldy."

"Shock you and your family. Now, get out of here before I have to toss you into a slab just to hide you."

Cat silently obeyed, rushing out with his newfound information. This thing came from a manufacturer Will couldn't identify quickly which meant a rogue company, a lunatic one-off, or the beginnings of something big. Hell, Will was a specialist in MH autopsy and analysis, a recent field added to the science of forensic pathology.

If Will didn't know, something very strange was beginning to unfold, and the images Cat had just snapped were going to open the first doors to its revelation.

CHAPTER THREE

"Shockin' son of a motherless whore!"

Cat chucked the wooden practice sword across the loft, wincing slightly at the sound of breaking glass when it impacted with his bar. He stared at the newsfeed, which seemed tailor-made to ruin his day.

"...and under the pressure of local Security Forces, Nanoengineering Institute, Inc., has immediately cut all funding to its Military Neurotechnology Research branch. This will mean layoffs of almost 200 highly educated and well-paid scientists. The Institute's legal representation has stated in clear and concise fashion that the margin for error with the research branch's experiments has cost far more than they had allowed in this fiscal budget, and therefore the risk had exceeded the benefits to the company's long-term business plan." The reporter droned on with a delivery usually reserved for test programs and Off-World terminal notifications about the "motorized walkway is coming to an end." Cat wanted to commit violent acts against the face on the Holoscreen, but deep down, he knew that would forfeit more of a paycheck than he wanted.

Instead, he followed the path of the wooden projectiles to the bar, happy to clean up any unceremoniously opened bottles of indulgence. The news broadcast confirmed what he'd found from the serial numbers. The NII was certainly the official manufacturer of the rogue Meta, but there was something screaming at him about the nature of its sudden rampage. And, despite three days of media coverage, no one save Will himself had even mentioned the rather unique artwork on the MH's palm. That led Cat to believe this wasn't a test subject gone bad, rather, it was an anomaly, something meant to stay off the record.

He cursed, shooting a glance over to the H-S. He wanted to ride, to clear his head, and get the hell out of the loft. The research part of the job wasn't his passion. He had a partner for that. Correction. He formerly had a partner for that. He made a note to confirm a meeting with the new candidate. He preferred investigating first hand. It was, after all, where the excitement was. With a snarl, he picked up the comm. There were some headhunters on his contact list. The first step was to start scrubbing the database for the suddenly unemployed RII scientists.

The scientist stared at the Holoscreen. The image of the MetaHuman—his MetaHuman—filled the screen as the news replayed the destructive scene from downtown. The reporter's polished voice went on about funding cuts and layoffs at NII, responsible for the rampage that killed.

He switched off the sound and watched the MetaHuman fall after armored vehicles and security forces unloaded a barrage of ammunition, enough to take down a small army, into it.

Impressive.

He scowled at the screen, a sneer crossing his scarred lips.

Too bad NII shut down his department. He'd like to try again—soon. He replayed the disaster again, keeping the sound muted. He'd use this incident to learn and do it better next time. The sudden psychosis of the MetaHuman occurred far earlier than he postulated. This miscalculation meant another setback and once again re-routing his financial sources. Without the NII lab at his disposal, he'd have to secure alternate laboratory facilities, something he'd researched in case this type of unfortunate event occurred.

There was no lack of investors for what he had planned. Many in the underground clamored to be the first to use his research, and he'd learned to be discreet. He had spent years on his pet project, all right under the nose of NII. The corporate snobs were so interested in profit margins that they never had a clue about his real work, the work that would change humanity itself. While his colleagues scattered from negative press like rats from a sinking ship, he had already secured a new stream of income to fund his research.

He narrowed his eyes and paused the image on the screen. Tiny yellow triangles caught his attention in the corner of the frame. He lifted his hand into the air and pushed his thumb and forefinger apart to expand the screen. The small yellow lights came into focus.

"Catwalk," he whispered and smiled. His eyes trailed over the man who would be contributing to his next project.

Fortunately, for the scientist, Catwalk had no clue about his impending contribution.

He raised his hands, and the holograph scrolled upward until Catwalk's cybernetic legs were at the scientist's eye level.

He ran his hands over the image of Catwalk's armored cyberlegs. His lips felt dry, and he licked them instinctively.

"What a shame. You will help herald a new era but won't live to see it." He lifted his hands above his head. Catwalk's body filled the screen once again. The scientist waved his arms back and forth, the image of the hitman wavering back and forth with his every movement.

"Just be a good boy and let your conscience be your guide ..." He nearly fell over laughing at his joke. "... straight to hell."

The scientist snapped his fingers, and Catwalk's image disappeared in an instant.

He flicked his hand and pulled up several bank registrars listed under various aliases. The down payment for Catwalk's services had gone through. Catwalk accepted the assignment the scientist had hired him to do. He'd take out the pederast known as Hitch.

Not that the scientist particularly cared one way or the other if Hitch lived or died. He was a disgusting pervert, but he was a means to an end. An end that wouldn't implicate the scientist, because once Midas—Hitch's master and the most notorious and powerful pimp in the city—learned that Catwalk killed one of his own, he'd retaliate. And Catwalk didn't have enough lives to stand against Midas' very experienced team of assassins.

Midas would kill Catwalk, and Catwalk's body would be up for sale. Then the scientist could swoop in, lowball the butchers for Catwalk's corpse, and finally have his hands on the only existing prototype of his mentor's cybernetic research.

By the time they all realized how he'd played them, it would be too late. His children would be leading the path to a new world, and he would be their Savior.

CHAPTER FOUR

The voice on the recording belonged to Hitch. Catwalk was certain, even before he saw the man's crooked frame crowd the lens. Hitch had a rap sheet longer than an only child's Christmas list: five counts of possession, four counts of intent to distribute, one count of attempted rape, one assault with a deadly weapon, and half a dozen counts of disorderly conduct. California's penal code didn't include a charge for necrophilia, but if it did, Hitch would have qualified for the state's frequent flier program.

Physically deformed from a botched cyberleg implant, the creep couldn't fight. The surgery had left Hitch with a limp and a permanent feeling most closely resembling sciatica. The painkiller addiction and bouts in prison had cooked his brain. If there was anything left of his conscious mind, it was controlled and manipulated by his employer. On any night, Hitch would be an easy hit, if not for his connections. The limping miscreant was well known as a handyman and occasional lab rat for one of the more demonstrative criminals in all of Downtown, the character who called himself Midas.

Tonight, Hitch was up to his old tricks, scouring the worst parts of town with the seediest of unspoken appetites. Usually he killed anyone innocent, stupid, drunk, or high enough to join his company. It was after they were dead when he chose to violate them, able to perform any of the variety of sick acts of sodomy, which drifted through the cobweb-filled rafters of his brain. Given his limited strength, death would ensure success and eliminate any witness testimony outside of the sordid story he created. His modus operandi, combined with bribes and crooked cops and lawyers, had held up so far. For all the charges against him, Hitch only served a combined three years in prison over two convictions. Midas held that kind of power in Nitro City.

Nick Kelly

Cat didn't like the setup. It was too easy. Hitch tried to copy his boss in the game of flash and reputation. His attempts to appear rich and famous made him an easy tail. Any competent investigator could track the weasel down. The fact someone had been willing to pay him to retire such a waste of flesh was either a bonus or a trap. From Frame One, Cat's gut told him that Midas himself was hiring him to either off his Renfield, or using Hitch as bait to draw Cat into the open. Either way, it could be a fatal mistake. Midas had more connections than an international telecom switchbox, but Cat made a mission of tracking his transactions for almost three months. He knew more about the pimp-turned-godfather than Midas knew of himself.

Cat wasn't moved by the idea of Midas targeting him. He'd had hits taken out on him in the past. That was the ante if you wanted to play the game. If you didn't have someone aiming to put steel between your shoulder blades, you weren't really a player. Cat learned to sleep lightly, shoot straight, and cover his tracks long before he came to the former City of Angels.

Hitch's rental limo was the cheapest Cat could remember tailing. The obvious kit-car was little more than a four-cylinder under the hood, with a fiberglass cover-up. The engine could hardly drive a scooter uphill. It clearly couldn't handle the weight of an armored, professional escort service. It was held together with the cheapest of materials. Cat scoffed. The same could be said of the passenger's sanity. When the driver eased up to the corner of Ocean Park and 4th, it was a welcome relief. He'd followed them so far west they'd run out of land, nearly reaching the polluted Pacific Ocean itself.

Cat slid his motorcycle into a parking lot, sliding a chip into the meter with a quick and silent payment acknowledgement. He armed the anti-personnel alarm and traversed the thirty meters between his vehicle and the opposite corner from Hitch's limo in seconds. From the camouflage of a vacant newsstand, he watched the working girls approach the limo. One after another, they walked away, rejected by the disfigured man inside.

Finally, a slight man, his hair dyed blacker than an eclipse, approached nervously. Even across the intersection, Cat could read the surprise on the young man's face. A one-sided conversation followed, with Hitch offering the stunned man a myriad of treasures. The youngster hardly remembered to negotiate price. Catwalk cursed under his breath, turned and ran back to the motorcycle as the pale male prostitute was led into the limo.

"You gotta be shockin' kiddin' me," he mumbled, the tires burning as he ripped into gear and after the limo.

Hitch had his victim and a head start. If Cat didn't act fast, it would be the wrong inhabitant of the limo who'd be without a pulse by dawn. The four-banger limo was no match for the Honda-Suzuki in acceleration or handling, but Cat wasn't certain how far Hitch would go down the highway before committing his murder and dumping the body. He didn't fear for the young man, but he didn't need the death toll piling up due to his lack of insight. Pissed at missing a clue, he pushed the throttle harder.

Cat's motorcycle roared through traffic, avoiding the armored taxis and limos. Armored escorts cost a little more, but as dangers like the Titan became more common in Downtown Nitro City, these vehicles began to take over. Riding in something that couldn't buy you a few extra seconds to scatter was becoming a death-defying risk. The roar of the motorcycle's engine frightened off the few courageous pedestrians trying to cross against the street signals. Cat raced through more than one light as it blinked red, but none of the NCPD showed up to pursue him. Either he was lucky to avoid them, or they bet against catching up.

After a few minutes, the signature taillights of the limo appeared, growing larger against the increasing heat of the asphalt. Cat was closing the gap, laying out multiple courses of action as he did so. Offing Hitch meant one paycheck, but did it take away from the odds and ends he'd picked up as peripheral business from tailing Midas and his crew?

It didn't necessarily make the best financial sense to eliminate Hitch. The most intelligent business decision would be to scare him into inactivity for a few months, collect on the bounty as if Hitch was dead, and then let him resurface, only to start collecting on his accomplices.

When he first arrived in Nitro City, Cat would have done exactly that; let the smart business decision override all other options. After months here, he was willing to listen to the other, more human parts of his psyche. Letting Hitch live meant letting others die. The image of the innocent eight-year old girl from the video ripped through his skull with the vacant cries of a poltergeist. Cat gritted his teeth; a bead of sweat slipped down the side of his face. Given the predatory nature of the crippled miscreant's crimes, Cat was willing to forfeit a few creds to see Hitch ushered into the Church of the No-Longer Living.

With a twist of his wrist, he accelerated, intent on fulfilling that goal.

Hitch caressed the back of the young man's neck with a meaty paw. At first, his new prey had seemed distant, even frightened. Every advance pushed the boy away. Hitch sighed in response. He didn't enjoy his prey's fear or lack of intimacy. He wanted acceptance and hoped for desire. If neither could be received, then a motionless, still-warm body was preferable to one who would resist him. Hitch had met with rejection throughout his entire life. He wanted more.

"What's your name, pet?" he asked. His hand brushed the pale skin of the slender young man.

Bright eyes heavily framed in black eyeliner met his. "Jesse, sir."

Hitch smiled, showing his discolored teeth. "Don't call me sir, Jesse. We're here to be friends, after all."

His hand trailed over the young man's collarbone and pushed his thin shirt open. His fingers caressed Jesse's chest. The dark, sparse hair on Jesse's upper lip and the trail down his stomach that disappeared into his jeans told Hitch that Jesse was probably of age, even though the softness of his slender arms and legs and chest made a drag queen look butch. His skin was the signature pallor of those unfortunate Downtown dwellers that had never seen the sun. He represented little challenge, and that alone was an aphrodisiac to Hitch. The other women in the area were older, calloused, more experienced and more likely to point out his shortcomings. He would have none of that.

Jesse was silent, evidently intimidated by the man who gave off an air of wealth, despite his physical atrocities.

Hitch continued. "You have beautiful eyes, Jesse."

"Th-thank you, sir."

"Tsk tsk."

"Thank you."

22

Hitch grinned. "Your heritage is something foreign. Something exotic. You are from Turkey perhaps, maybe Syria?"

A wordless nod was his only reply. Hitch grinned wider. He offered a brief phrase in Hebrew, roughly translated to mean, "Every hole is black in the night." At the end of his statement, Jesse raised his frightened eyes to meet his gaze. He addressed the man who paid more than his normal price. "How can I serve you, sir...uh, not sir?"

It was more temptation than Hitch could stand. He raised his hand to the boy's throat, gripping it with a frenzy driven from the heat of his loins. The sooner he murdered Jesse, the sooner he could claim dominance over the bright-eyed youngster.

The sound of thunder near his head made Hitch jump back against the seat.

The limo driver's brains splattered against the Plexiglas screen that separated him from the passengers. Hitch boggled at the sudden shift in direction, forcing him to release Jesse and grab the sides of the maneuvering vehicle to steady himself. The sunroof shattered inward and he raised his arms upward to cover his face from the rain of glass. He heard a scream and turned to look at his would-be victim. Jesse's eyes met his. The youngster was screaming in sheer horror. A moment later, the scream was gone. Jesse's shocked form disappeared upward through the broken frame of the sunroof.

Hitch heard a muffled voice, and suddenly the here-and-now drew him to a reality his brain had covered with dementia. His prey was gone. His escort was gone. He turned his gaze upward and met face-to-face with a pair of glowing inhuman yellow eyes.

"I told you that you'd burn, chitbag."

The thing with the yellow eyes grabbed Hitch before he could scream and ripped him from the limo. The shattered sunroof tore through his clothes and cut into his flesh as the creature dragged him onto the roof. The limo careened out of control; the dead driver's foot still pressed against the accelerator.

A second later, all the cobwebs and shadows hiding his psyche dissipated, leaving him vulnerable to the cold recollection of every one of his crimes. Without the comfort of the shadows, his eyes opened wide. Clarity of thought tore into his mind like a scalpel, and he prayed that the vision before him would disappear into a nightmare. Centimeters from his face, yellow eyes stared back at him. The recognition petrified him. It was the Cat, the one who'd sent him the vow of revenge following his last conquest. The threat had seemed so innocuous at first, until the would-be avenger had spelled out detail after detail. Now, it was evident. His throat constricted. He couldn't swallow or cough or beg for his life. Stars and spirals invaded the edges of his vision.

The Cat gripped him hard. Its claws ripped through his cheap suit and into his skin. He felt his flesh tear as he struggled to avoid its grasp. It stared into him…through him…like some inhuman avenger. It wasn't human; couldn't be human. He moaned in agony. Its claws made him remember the sting of his father's belt – submission through pain. But this thing wasn't his father. It wasn't even human.

Hitch felt a greater threat, even as his mind splintered. Tearing his focus from his assailant, he looked beyond the Cat and saw the outline of something large...an ominous, formless shadow somewhere behind them. In the dark, he couldn't decipher what it was or how long they had before impact. A desperate voice tore at his temples, scratching like rats on a sinking ship looking for a way out. He even thought for a second to warn his captor.

Words from the yellow-eyed assassin brought him back to consciousness. "This is for Amber."

The avenger placed a piece of fabric into Hitch's hand. Suddenly, he was gone from sight and touch. Hitch looked down, through the blood trickling from the cuts in his arm, long enough to read the name tag attached to a blood-soaked piece of a school girl's uniform.

When he looked up, it was too late. The giant shadow began to reveal details, bricks, windows, markings. He recognized hoses, then a swarm of small, glowing lights. In an instant he understood.

Fuel pumps.

Hitch's reality erupted into flame and cinder. His screams were never heard above the explosion.

Cat launched on cybernetic legs as the limo exploded behind him. He felt the heat of the flames all around him. Felt the air blowing all around him. It singed his hair and lapped at the few parts of flesh his armor revealed. He flipped and spun in the air. He landed hard; the impact of his armored boots cracking the asphalt. He shifted his gaze side to side to ensure no uninvited guests were filming the event.

Cat watched the limo burn for nearly five minutes. Hitch's wail made him chuckle. He pictured Amber's face on the recording one final time, and nodded in satisfaction. The distant sound of sirens registered in his ears. Hitch's cries had long been replaced by the crackling of flames. He gauged how soon the emergency crews would arrive, and then gazed once more at the burning husk of the limo. At first he questioned his own sanity for sticking around. Then he shrugged it off, considering the emotion justified given how many innocents the disfigured pederast had claimed in his time. He shouldered the shotgun he had drawn. He knew he wouldn't need it, but a small part of him hoped the necrophiliac would somehow scramble out of the wreckage.

Cat considered it all as he carefully made his way back to the Honda-Suzuki. There was more to be done. There were defenses to prepare. If Midas had hired him to off his disfigured henchman, it was part of a larger plan. If someone else had paid for Hitch's long-overdue date with the reaper, there would be a price to pay. Cat smiled. As powerful as Midas was, he welcomed the challenge. It was a risk he'd calculated when he chose to take the hit on Hitch. Either way, he had just put out the welcome mat for a new enemy, right in the middle of investigating the Titan that killed Emory, and hiring his new partner. Cat scoffed. The dancing flames reflected in his yellow eyes and he felt that fate be damned, it was all worth it.

He heard the sound of his laughter before he realized he was laughing. "Damn, Leon," he said aloud, "since when do you give a chit about kids?"

With a twist of the wrist, Cat turned back east toward Nitro City, and the unavoidable wrath of the Fixer known as Midas.

CHAPTER FIVE

9 August 2033

Cat knew better than anyone that he needed the right resources to survive, let alone turn a profit as an odd-jobs man. The same technology that made him powerful threatened his very humanity. Every ounce of machinery he accepted came with a sacrifice. If the scales tipped too far, the human he once was would be deleted and overwritten by a sub-routine. The man who was once Leon Caliber would be extinct. Only the machine would remain.

To prevent that, Cat had hired several cybertechnology specialists as business partners. In his line of work, they tended to have very short careers. He'd been both fortunate and ignorant in his past choices of technology consultants. With Midas likely on his path, and the curious case of the raging MH looming, he needed someone he could trust if the chips came down and his system flat out rejected his cybernetics. The last thing he wanted was to follow in the giant MetaHuman's footsteps, down the road to madness.

Cat had conducted the interview process twice since arriving in Nitro City. His first partner, Renaldi, tried to go rogue and turn him in to the Seven Sisters coalition for assassinating their Vice President of Murders and Acquisitions. Cat rewarded Renaldi's efforts with an 11mm bit of gratitude, then sold his parts to a shady transplant service that paid cash up front. No questions were asked, and Cat was convinced that organs from the whistle blower had saved the lives of transplant candidates across the state. The details weren't important.

The second specialist, Fiona, was more technical then medical, and had nearly killed the hitman out of ignorance by overdosing him with anesthetic. She became apologetic and overly courageous, attempting to shadow

Cat downtown during a sabotage job. The cyber-enhanced guard dogs were still fighting over Fiona's limbs when her screaming subsided.

Cat exhaled. Tonight's work was stressful. He should be meditating and preparing escape plans and assessing just how big an army Midas was going to throw at him. He stared at the glass in his hand and smirked. He deserved a drink for putting Hitch in the dirt, or at least into a fiery ball of four-cylinder destruction. His victims would have wanted the necrophiliac cremated after all, wouldn't they?

Catwalk raised a silent toast to the memory of his first two prospective partners. He wasn't proud of their departures from the realm of the living, but he knew better than to keep barking up a tree that had only brought him trouble. He put the call out for a partner through the usual channels, and this time, the response was different. The unidentified resource reached out to him, claiming to have researched his past work and holding a very deep interest in a potential partnership.

Cat swished the liquor around in his mouth. He had met the other resources in isolated, silent surroundings. Tonight had to be different. Anyone who had the time and tools to dig into his background deserved careful consideration. If this new candidate was worth his time, he would prove so, and he would do so in a crowded club, complete with dancing patrons and deafening music. This time, Cat lounged in one of the private alcoves of the crowded club known as Liquid Chrome.

The mix of synthetic instruments and human vocals pitched in together, creating a maelstrom of sound that rolled forth from the stage with velvet intoxication. Pulsating lights flashed over the bodies on the dance floor. The patrons below boasted every color and material on the popular market, and a few available only through the technology underground. Kevlar, neon, leather, and metal writhed together as the performers drove the debauchery to new heights.

The vodka filling Cat's glass was every bit as unnatural as his armor-plated legs. He'd had the real stuff on rare occasions, and not since he left DC, but at least the synthetic version was tolerable. He wouldn't let some of the other artificial liquors near his lips after tasting the original, but vodka could pass. Bourbon or sake, no chance. A taste of the authentic was an eye-opening experience, entrance into a world that couldn't be wished away or forgotten.

A man stepped quickly into the alcove. Either he was here for the job, or he planned to drive something in the neighborhood of an explosive projectile through the hitman's chest. Cat merely held his glass before his mouth, watching from behind black shades. He raised an eyebrow. "Can I help you?"

"If you're Catwalk, you can."

The tall man had dark hair, graying slightly at his temples, and a neatly trimmed moustache and beard. He was thin but not unhealthy. He wore sensible clothes, the kind scholars wore, but not so upscale that he would draw unnecessary attention. He was, in a word, practical.

Cat could abide with practical. It beat the hell out of a partner with delusions of fortune and fame. He studied the man again. His eyes were obviously not natural. The way the light caught them at certain angles betrayed their artificial nature. His tone provided no hint of nervousness or fear. His body language was stable, especially for someone in a club vibrating at the mercy of the music. This man was focused and well prepared.

Cat tilted his head slightly and pushed one of the faux leather chairs toward the stranger. The man sat, comfortably folding his legs as he did so. Cat drew the pack of cigarettes from his jacket pocket, offering one. The man waved a hand in denial.

"You mind?" The hitman asked as he pulled out a lighter.

"Not at all, though that tells me something of your nature when it comes to caring for your health. You will start me at a bit of a disadvantage if you're going to be poisoning yourself regularly."

Cat nodded and lit the cigarette anyway. The man's simple statement revealed that he was here for the interview as Catwalk's biological and technical consultant. It was an odd mix, but one that was growing tightly intertwined as mankind embraced machine in a symbiotic relationship.

"Touché. So, I read up on you, sounds like you ain't no stranger to some a' the seedier elements in town."

"I have constructed my professional career in accordance with my goals. There were a few…mistakes amongst my acquaintances, to be certain. But, that is why we're here, isn't it? Each of us wants to ensure that this is not another mistake?"

"What do you know about cyber-surgery?" Cat replied.

The man brushed a bit of ash from his cleaned and pressed pant leg. "If you've read up on me, you know already." He paused and then leaned forward. "I understand that your cybernetic enhancements are somewhat unique. I admit that I carry a professional fascination with unraveling the mysteries of your internal workings."

"You think I'm a puzzle ta solve?"

"I think you're an interesting case on the biological level, Mr. Catwalk. I have no delusions of being a psychiatric professional and no desire to provide you with such an analysis today, or ever."

Cat downed a slug of the vodka, "Smart man."

A silent nod was his only acknowledgement.

"You already know how I pay, then," Cat continued. "There's a commission on completed jobs, plus an ongoing rate for my maintenance. I can handle my own gear."

"Are you saying I'm hired, then?"

Cat took a drag from the cigarette. "Don't get ahead a' yerself. There are a few more things that factor in. First of all, there's a bit of a trial period. I'd love to hear how yer 'professional fascination' digests the in's an' out's of my gear. Secondly, there's a little matter a' professional courtesy, meanin' you disclose the right info to the wrong parties, an' you get scrapped for parts. Third, I'm gonna need ta know what ta call you."

The man smiled the faintest of grins. "For your first condition, I'm as enthusiastic about diagnosing you as you are to hearing my analysis, but you know that already. To address the second, I would not carry the longevity in my career working with your particular brand of professional if I did not respect that level of privileged information already. Third, I've used many handles in the past, though I've had to retire them due to conflict with a former client who is still seeking to partner my testicles with jumper cables. Hence, my need for employment."

Cat nodded, downed another mouthful, then gestured, glass in hand, "Why the eyes?"

The question caught the tall, well-dressed man slightly off-guard. Cat noted the first time he had succeeded in doing so. "I overcame a rather debilitating disease which threatened many of my biological processes when I was young. It was the result of a misdiagnosis from a public servant medical practitioner. I nearly lost my eyesight, as well as my kidney and liver functions. My eyes never fully recovered, making me quite sensitive to bright light and flashes. When I was a teenager, I opted for full replacement over generic chemical enforcement. I've never, as they say, looked back."

Cat grinned at the level of humor suddenly shown by the previously stiff conversationalist. "Gimme an address an' I'll meet you tomorrow for an initial scan."

The man nodded, betraying his self-satisfaction slightly at having passed the initial interview. He slid a card across the small glass-topped table to Catwalk. Then, he stood, "Is 10am acceptable or should I make it later for you to fight off the effects of that vile drink?"

"Ten's fine, doc," Cat replied. As an afterthought, he slugged the remainder of the vodka. As he placed the emptied glass on the tabletop, he looked up at the stranger. "I'll see you then, Delambre."

The man raised an eyebrow then smiled his slight grin again. "Hmm, then à demain, Catwalk."

He turned and exited, fading into the crowd of swirling bodies and pulsing lights. Cat watched him as he left. Without a word, he crushed his cigarette. He looked the man's card over again. It offered a contact number with no name. Cat grinned, signaling the waitress for another drink. He stared at the card, filtering through the first interview, and weighing the abilities of his potential partner.

CHAPTER SIX

"This...is...unacceptable!"

Midas slammed a golden fist through the glass coffee table. Shards filled the air, then dropped like glittering rain to the carpeted floor. A handful of yes-men and concubines scattered to the corners of the room. Hitch was dead. His body had been discovered burnt to a crisp inside his limo. The initial reports said he was trying to claw his way out as he was burned alive.

The only lead was the presence of some inhuman thing that had appeared out of nowhere, according to the eyewitness testimony of a drugged-out, underage streetwalker. Midas stood up, straightening his collar. Shards of glass fell as he brushed his silk dress shirt.

Long ago, Midas had undergone irreversible cyber-surgery, giving his skin a glowing hue, while his eyes become two imposing golden spheres. He'd converted masses with the simple message that "Everything he touched turned to gold". Hitch had been no exception.

Midas provided the pathetic necrophiliac with all the attention and affection that Hitch's broken psyche constantly craved. As a result, Hitch was an obedient, if flawed, dog.

Midas' slightest gesture kept him in line for years, providing him an outlet for his inhuman sexual advances while leaving him a productive member in the trafficking of weapons and drugs through Midas' empire. Hitch was a henchman, and despite his flaws, he provided Midas something he needed. Hitch had been the sales pitch to many of the drug runners in Nitro City. If a limping, disfigured scavenger could rise to the right hand of the Golden King, anyone could. Now, Midas would have to hide the disappearance of his Renfield before the same impressionable scum began pissing themselves over rumors of some vigilante.

The fool who had lashed out at Midas' empire would have to suffer, if only to send a message to the competition. It wouldn't be hard to find the chitbag who'd pulled the plug on his disfigured errand boy. Midas stared at the footage from the limo's security camera. He lifted the golden goblet to his lips and took a long drink.

He beckoned with a finger to one of his guards. The armored man, large enough to fill most of the entrance to Midas' quarters, stepped forward with programmed obedience. Midas gestured, and the screen froze. The scared face of the scrawny male prostitute filled the screen. "Put the word out. We have a new target."

"Bring me the boy…alive."

CHAPTER SEVEN

The H-S reluctantly cut to silence as Cat parked it on the top floor of the parking deck. He stole a quick glance around. The building wasn't exactly upscale. There were no armored guards or wired fences, but it boasted reinforced concrete walls, and the doors were solid enough. If Delambre had put his lab here, he'd done so with a great deal of consideration ahead of time.

Cat armed the explosive theft-prevention alarm on the motorcycle and stepped off. The wind made his pony tailed hair feel ratty and had blown up one side of his collar. He ignored it. He left the shotgun and SMG's under lock and key, opting for the baton and pistol as he entered what was supposed to be friendly territory. Punching in the key Delambre had provided, he was whisked downward by the elevators. He slipped the plain brown envelope from one hand to the other while he waited for the descent to end.

Several floors below ground, the doors opened to a room of artificial light with a pale blue glow that reminded Cat of hospitals, morgues, and his old PD. He recognized medical equipment in organized fashion along the walls, and the steady hum indicated more computers than were readily visible.

The figure that greeted him wasn't Delambre. Instead, the click of heels and startling, warm tone of a voice caught him by surprise. "You must be Mr. Caliber."

Cat raised his gaze to the hostess, his mind instantly in spin-cycle. Her features betrayed a heritage that was equally African, Latin, and American. Her skin was a light, mocha brown. Her straight, black hair was pulled up into a bun with ebony chopsticks keeping it in place. Her brown eyes were framed with black-rimmed glasses. She wore a white, clean lab coat over a black pair of pants and black shoes. Cat recognized that he was staring, but couldn't stop until Delambre's voice drew him away.

"It's admirable that you found us, Catwalk, and early, too."

Cat replied, still unable to take his eyes off of the surprising new person in the equation. "I always aim for a few minutes ahead a' time. Gives me some leeway in the event of an undisclosed road closure."

"Ah, and were there any today?"

"One. But I jumped it and left a few shells behind ta assist with rush hour."

Delambre grinned. "Such a humanitarian." His eyes trailed to Cat's hands, "something in the envelope I should know about?"

Cat nodded, tossing the brown envelope to Delambre. "Sure. Passport and ID ta match up with yer cover here in Nitro. Might as well have you able ta shop an' walk among the legit crowd if yer gonna be helpin' me out."

Without opening it, Delambre placed it on a table. "Passport and ID only? What about an Off-World credential? If I'm a legitimate scientist, I'll need an Off-World registration. Scientists are in-demand in the colonies, after all."

Cat's smile stretched across his face. He reached into his jacket pocket and tossed the card into Delambre's hands. "Nicely played."

The geneticist's smile mirrored the one he had displayed in the club. He was again grateful to have passed the hitman's unspoken test.

Without a word, the woman who had been studying them both spun on a heel and left the room. Cat knew his eyes were on her figure as she left, but he didn't bother to be discreet.

"'Ta' assist with rush hour?" Delambre asked.

"Huh?"

The geneticist squinted, studying Cat. "You said 'ta' assist. Hmm. I was curious last night if your definitive east coast accent was the product of alcohol, or if you always had it. I think I've had my question answered."

Cat scowled. "You suddenly my vocal coach, too?"

Delambre shook his head, his eyes confirming the younger woman's exit.

"You must forgive my daughter," he said, thickly accenting the last two words. "She hasn't learned the necessity or promise of dealing with someone in your less-than-legal profession."

Cat chuckled, acknowledging the inflection of a concerned father. "I've been on the legal side, hombre. I like where I am now a shock-of-a-lot more."

Their eyes met briefly, the geneticist and the killer. Delambre spoke first, gesturing to a clean, metal table before him. "Shall we begin, then?"

CHAPTER EIGHT

The scientist's laugh crept in pitch and volume until it grew to a cackle bounding off the laboratory walls. He laughed until breathing became a chore. He nearly regained composure, but one more glance at the news feed sent him into another bout of uncontrollable laughter. When he finally regained composure, he wiped the tears from his eyes and stood upright. Reaching for a small airbrush, he painted a five-pointed star atop the forehead of a metallic skull resting on the workbench. He placed his hand under it, cupping it, and raising it until he was eye-to-vacant-eye with the inhuman face.

"We want to ask you some questions regarding the disappearance of a local resident." He furrowed his brow and gave the severed skull a tone of authority.

Feigning surprise at the voice he'd given the skull, he replied, "I'm happy to assist, officer."

"Have you ever seen or met this man? His name is Hitch."

"Oh," he mocked, almost spitting out a laugh. "I'm afraid we've never met, officer."

He tilted the skull as if it was lost in contemplation. "His limo was found burned almost beyond recognition out at the old airfield. You know anything about that?"

"Oh, no, sir," he swooned, "I've never even been there."

"Anything else you'd like to add then?"

"Yes, officer, I believe you can rule out aneurism when determining cause of death." The scientist fell on the floor, clutching his stomach as he laughed. The skull clattered to the floor, landing on its crown, facing him upside down like a disapproving metallic bat. It took almost a full minute for him to brace an arm against the workbench and rise to his feet. Even then, he doubled over, still breaking into fits of laughter.

36

"Master, you called for me?"

The words ripped through his glee like a scalpel. He turned, eyes still wet from tearing, cheeks hurting from smiling so wide. "Yes, my dear, indeed I did."

The figure who addressed him was a mix of natural and surgical perfection. Beautiful to the brink of description even before his expert hands had adjusted her, she now boasted a superhuman sensuality. Her dark hair was straight, barely touching her shoulder, centering a face with high cheekbones and full lips. Her bright eyes were permanently framed with dark lashes, designed to project temptation.

She wore a leather sleeveless top, displaying her defined arms and tanned skin. Her full breasts filled the leather, which followed her hourglass curves over her slender waist and supple hips. Her long legs drove downward into heeled boots. Her lips pursed slightly before she continued. "You have need of my services?"

He grinned at his magnificent creation. She wasn't his first, but certainly one of his proudest accomplishments. "Yes, Angelyka, I do."

CHAPTER NINE

Cat reveled in the freedom the Honda-Suzuki provided on the highway, partaking once again in the open wasteland that had once been I-40. There were plenty of evils still afoot out in the desert sands, but he had driven this stretch dozens of times since his arrival in Nitro City. It was therapy. The ride was one sacred release he had from partnerships, caseload, and potential enemies. It was a perilous ride for the uninformed, but Cat's growing reputation kept most threats at bay.

The new armor felt strange. He'd been accustomed to a black leather jacket and pants with the armored fittings for his legs and hands, but Delambre had insisted on more. For a geneticist, he showed a knack for military engineering that simply didn't jive with his background. The armor, similar but lighter and more composite, still required some breaking in. Cat's first test was to see how it felt on the H-S. If it failed that, it wasn't worth even walking in.

The more he drove, the more he pondered. Delambre was strange, but instinct said he was reliable. His daughter, well, who really knew what made her tick, but Cat wouldn't mind adjusting her gears to find out. Hitch was on a slab. Payment had been received for the job, and Midas hadn't sent anyone after him yet. There was something seriously wrong with that part of the equation.

As if on cue, the comm buzzed inside his helmet. "Cat."

"How's the armor feel?"

"Yellow."

Delambre chuckled in reply. "I'm not certain I've ever felt yellow. Can you describe it?"

"Sure, grab some binoculars, take a trip uptown or to the sim-lab and stare at the sun for an hour. Then get back to me."

"You seem edgy. How can I assist?"

Cat rolled his eyes. "Just tryin' ta put together a few loose ends on some cases. The armor's better'n I thought so far. Ain't had cause ta try it out yet, but the night is young."

Delambre paused before replying, as if seeking a second opinion. "You have my assurance it will meet your needs, Catwalk."

"I'll keep ya posted." Cat clicked the comm dead and twisted his wrist, burning more kilometers beneath him. The price tag on the armor was more than he had anticipated, and he would demand a back-up suit, given the pace of some of his investigations. He was going to need to cash from a few other outstanding jobs.

Fortunately, there was one he'd been trailing for a while, and tonight might prove the perfect outlet for a little recreation.

The Paradigm Shift was founded by two lifelong virtual world gamers who had decided on a permanent meeting place for those who logged more minutes in a fantasyland than reality. A neon display above the entrance boasted a myriad of colors, and the doors flanked by eight-meter high guardians. A red dragon reared on its hind legs on one side, perfectly crafted from reinforced steel. Opposite the dragon, a large robot with chain-guns instead of hands faced off against it.

The bouncer and his correspondents inside sported some formidable armor. After all, the clientele here was only half composed of meek gamers playing dress up. The other half had the resources and funds, usually through gaming, to undergo surgery to closely resemble their in-game personas. Everyone in the place represented some sort of fantasy rendition of reality...a character.

The main areas of the club weren't potentially hazardous. It was in the VIP section where the real money flowed. The inhabitants there were revered by the common crowd. These virtual power brokers often decided on a whim how to change the very dimensions where hundreds of thousands clung to every imaginary facet of their lives. In this restricted area, the wardrobe ranged from custom tailored suits to armor and shields. Each player had their own idea of how to represent the money in their deferred off-world accounts.

There was a portion of the gamers who chose to represent their investments through appearance. They sported uniforms identical to what their avatars wore in the virtual world. Some did so by choice. Others were so physically altered they'd become the very character they'd once invented.

Cat grinned to himself at the notion. He'd been no different, really. The surgery he'd undergone made him into the character he'd become. The difference was that when he killed an opponent, they didn't get to reset somewhere. They flatlined, regardless of what game they thought they might be playing.

He set the half-empty glass of bourbon on the small tabletop. Sweat dripped from the glass to the rectangular surface, dripping onto the chessboard set into the mahogany. The chair across from him was empty. There would be no opponent tonight, merely a job to be done and a paycheck to collect.

He had pieced together the backstory, a high-level rivalry amongst the gaming companies. The man who called himself DoB, aka Descendant of British, had jumped ship to start his own firm, leaving one of the leading gaming companies without a head designer. Then, DoB decided to show up at Paradigm to celebrate with a few of his close friends.

Cat grinned at the irony. There was a benefit to identifying your friends solely by virtual renderings. It meant that in real life they could look like anything. In this case, they could even look like a scarred and tired ex-cop who'd moved west to make a living in theft, murder, extortion and other odd jobs.

DoB was a slovenly man, who clearly chose indulgence over self-preservation. His dirty blonde hair was unkempt, and the cheap suit he wore had been tailored for him long before he'd put on the excess weight of sloth and greed. His skin was a mess and his tie looked as if he knotted it together with his teeth.

The developer was the kind of man Cat took pleasure in hurting before the kill. There was simply too much self-satisfaction evident on the fat man's face for Cat to let him go quickly. From here, he had a clear shot, which had never really been the hitman's best exercise of assassination. Even after years as a cop and now as a killer, he was far from a marksman.

Instead, Cat had gone a different route, following DoB's limo to the Paradigm on the HS motorcycle. Once DoB had gone inside, Cat bugged the limo, then went back a second time and wired it. The detonator rested nicely in one of the compartments of his new prototype armor that Delambre had crafted. For now, Cat could pick the cocky gamer off up close or blow him into a few million pieces later. Which option he chose would depend on how his night went.

Bored with the supposedly rich and powerful clientele, and nearing the end of his glass of underwhelming bourbon, Catwalk looked out to the main room through the one-way mirrors down at the "regular" folks. There were grinding bodies, plenty of misfits to be certain, and a lot of liquid courage creating flirtation and lousy pick-up lines. Elves danced, wrapped around vampires. Golems and cyborgs exchanged heated glances across the dance floor. Orcs and werewolves were heavy petting in the corners. A knight of the round table had his hand halfway up the wicked witch's dress. A mermaid was riding a unicorn in a manner that should have been anatomically impossible. The entire place was a buffet of dream-driven fantasies. Cat chuckled to himself, pulling out a cigarette and lighting it while scanning the outside bar.

Several women appealed to him instantly. He ruled out two after seeing their profile and identifying Adam's apples. He shook his head, took a drag and double-checked on the loudmouth developer he'd been sent to retire. The man hadn't moved, still holding audience at the far end of the VIP section, boasting about past accomplishments and future triumphs. In one hand, he held a glass of something that glowed an unnatural blue, with the other he was typing code into a virtual keyboard, changing the worlds he'd created without thought to the lives he affected.

Cat returned his gaze to the outside bar and felt a paralysis wash over him when he caught the form of one woman near the end of the bar. She wore a manly outfit, almost exclusively urban camouflage and Kevlar. Beneath her hat, her deep auburn hair was pulled into a tight ponytail, and her otherwise flawless face was marked with dark eye shadow and eye black.

Try as she might to hide her identity, Cat could pick her particular face out of an adrenaline-fed riot throwing Molotov cocktails at his face. He'd seen her face before on billboards, vidfeeds, digital stills, and in his own drunken lust.

That woman, as much as she would deny it, was fashion model and designer Delilah DuPree.

CHAPTER TEN

Cat headed out of the VIP section immediately, the cigarette dangling from his lips. He strode with purpose through the writhing crowd on the dance floor, making an unnatural slice through the drug-fueled incarnations of warriors and wizards. He emerged on the opposite end, confirming in a split-second what he'd originally thought or hoped. The subject of a thousand photo shoots, five hundred interviews, and an immeasurable number of his own fantasies, was sipping from a tumbler a few meters away.

He watched for a moment as she looked just past the brim of her faded cap and caught the unsteady advances of a potential suitor stumbling up behind her. Taking a drag, he let the drunken man get closer. The man wore a full-fledged ogre outfit, dyed his skin green and wore a torn shirt, leather kilt, and boots. He reached to tap the woman on the shoulder and instead landed a hand on the bar next to her. She shifted to her left, revealing more surprise than she had intended. The man belched involuntarily and then asked her to slow dance with a crooked, awkward smile.

The woman graciously thanked him for his offer, stating she was waiting for her other half, and patted his cheek. That alone satisfied the would-be ogre, who eventually regained his balance and stumbled away. Relief was evident on her face as she exhaled a deep breath and reached past the ice-filled tumbler for her cigarettes.

"Le Courvoisier, I presume," Cat offered, lighter in hand, faux accent on his lips.

The woman looked up at him, startled for only a fraction of a section. She smiled and allowed him to light her cigarette. "Thank you," she stated with a note of dismissal.

43

Cat smiled back, with no intention of letting so little a tone dissuade him. "The pleasure is mine, Miss?"

"Mrs.," she replied coldly.

He nodded. "But of course," he said, leaning closer. "Madame Dupree, as it were."

The woman's insightful green eyes flared slightly then settled with a deep breath. "It's Mrs., as I said. Mrs. Raul Azuria."

Cat smiled. "Of course it is." He dropped the accent, going back to his own delivery, "Listen, Mrs. Razawhateveryouthinkyouwannacallit, you've got at least six separate parties in this particular little chithole of a bar who are infightin' over which of them is going to come over here an' get you to dance. So, how bout you an' I either entertain ourselves over a nice glass a' real-world natural liquor in the VIP section, or you let me escort you safely to whatever transportation you swindled inta gettin' you into this joint?"

Her eyes flared with the challenge as she blew smoke in his face. "And why should I trust a yellow-eyed stranger like yourself?"

"Because," he smirked, "despite the fact I share their appreciation of that body a' yours, I'm the only one here who knows yer technically still married to a multi-billionaire off-world investor."

Delilah's face didn't betray the change in her emotions, but her body language shouted profanities at him. "How sweet, I believe I've had enough of your banter." She reinforced her statement by suggesting he perform a self-servicing sexual act.

"It's Leon," he said confidently, leaving a small card on the bar near her drink, "Leon Caliber. Payin' parties call me Catwalk." He took a step away, paused and leaned back toward her. "By the way, when the vampires in the corner start stalkin' you tonight, feel free ta call me." With a smirk, he disappeared into the crowd on the dance floor.

How long had it been since she left the bar? A minute? Two?

The shadows shifted behind her, filled with mechanical catcalls and laughter. She knew those voices. They belonged to the vampires from the bar. She pulled her coat tighter around her. No one was supposed to follow her. This was a research trip. Damn it, where was her driver?

She rushed forward on quick steps, heading east on Rampart for the brighter lights of Beverly Blvd. She'd be safe there, hidden among the tourists and fashion-famined crowds who walked those streets all hours of the night.

Voices spoke, no, howled in the distance behind her. Delilah's pace picked up, though she told herself to maintain the façade of control. The boots had barely any lift. They were comfortable and warm compared to the heels she wore the majority of her typical week. She stepped up her pace, walking quickly, fighting the urge to break into a run. Her breathing quickened. Even in the cool air, she was sweating openly. The snap of leather trench coats joined their caterwauling. She knew they were closer than she'd thought. She spun, bearing pepper spray in her right hand. "Stop right there."

The four vampires moved as if in slow motion for a few moments before laughing in unison. The tallest, with his blonde hair cut in a Mohawk, grinned from behind his dark sunglasses. "Pepper spray? I've never had a meal that came with its own spice rack before." His supporting cast broke into a laughter as uniform as their black leather apparel.

Delilah backed away slowly, as two others circled her. She couldn't get between them and onto the main road. They would be too quick. The open pavement to her right led to a small, ruined community park. That would only provide more privacy for their attack. To her left, there was an alleyway between the buildings. It was dark, pitch black, except for a flicker of light.

No, not a flicker at all. Delilah's breath caught as she saw the faint outline of two yellow triangles meet her eyes and then disappear.

She blinked and the vamps picked up on her suddenly focused attention. The blonde turned his gaze to the alley. A brick slammed into his face, shattering his glasses and breaking his nose. He grabbed his face, howling in pain.

The others raged quickly. The one closest to the blonde, a dark-skinned black man, moved to help his fallen leader. The other two, dark-haired and donning the typical leather trench and pants, moved toward the alley. In appearance and action, they could have been clones.

The slight glimmer of metal rolled from the alley, a

simple cylinder that looked like a soda can. Three meters past the alley's edge, it erupted into brilliant white light. Delilah tried to avert her eyes, falling to her hands and knees, facing away from the illumination. Even squeezing her eyes tight, the brilliant light flashed in her brain. She could only imagine its effect on the vampires.

She struggled to make out the shapes. Everything was a blur. Her heart was in her throat. To her right, she saw three figures, heard a scream, and then could find only two. She blinked repeatedly to clear her vision. There was a loud snap and then only a solitary figure remained upright. The other fell, its silhouetted head gone from its body.

The remaining figure leapt in her direction, and she prayed it wasn't attacking her. She squeezed her eyes tight. Every breath felt like forever. She wanted to scream, but couldn't. The combination of shock and fear paralyzed her.

She opened her eyes again. The brilliant light was gone. She could make out figures, but her head still shook with fading fireworks. What had happened and was it over?

"This is all your fault, you shocking cunt!"

She swung her attention to her left, getting a foot under her and standing up, disoriented and afraid. Though the stars and flashes still pounded against her skull, she saw the bloodied, angry face of the lead vampire. Fangs bared, he screamed as he approached.

Raising her hands in self-defense, she realized she still had the pepper spray. In a fury, the vampire batted it away. One quick shove and she fell backwards. As she struggled to sit up, the blonde vampire was atop her. He made a sound, half hissing, half growling, his mouth open just a few centimeters away. His face had been punctured by the glasses, the blood filling the creases of his skin.

Suddenly, he was gone. His sound was cut short as he was yanked backward. There was a sickening sound of flesh impacting something solid. It was repeated, with interspersed cries and howls.

Finally, there was silence.

Delilah told herself to breathe. Her chest was tight. She could still smell the foul breath of the vampire on her skin. She had regained her ability to see, but wasn't certain anymore that she wanted it. Forcing herself to exhale, she turned in the direction of the sounds.

The blonde would-be vampire lay dead in the road, his skull cracked in several places, leaving a mosaic of blood and grey matter to cover his jacket and the pavement. Standing above him was a black and yellow figure. As it turned to face her, she stilled in the glow of its yellow eyes.

These were the eyes of something mechanical and feline all at once. She gulped in the potential fear that she'd just seen the frying pan murdered by the fire. The figure approached, snapping something on its hip loudly.

The figure knelt on one knee so they were face to face. With a flip, the face of the Cat disappeared.

Delilah blinked again, her gaze met by the man who had approached her at the bar, calling himself Catwalk. He smirked slightly. "Bon soir, Madame Dupree."

CHAPTER ELEVEN

Delilah was two cigarettes and a tequila shot in before she remembered to thank him. She was three cigarettes and three shots in before she gathered the courage to start the interrogation. Before that, it was simple, short, nervous sentences about her attackers. She stared at her glass for most of the conversation during the rare moments she opened her eyes.

Cat had witnessed shock countless times before. In the past, he had watched it manifest in the form of Post-Traumatic Stress Disorder, like when one of his fellow officers had to shoot someone, or when answering the occasional domestic dispute that ended in bloody violence. He'd take PTSD over its cybernetic equivalent, Post-Cybernetic Episode Disorder. With the right treatment, a person could be treated for PTSD. PCED was the equivalent of cutting the last chord to humanity and succumbing to the subject's technological implants. The only cure was permanent incapacitation. That was his career back east, respond to acute incidents of cybernetic psychosis, and terminate the target. Retirement. Termination. Assassination. He shook his head. They were one in the same, and the only end he could imagine for himself.

Delilah brushed a strand of red hair from her forehead, tucking it behind her ear. She began to ask another question, paused, and took another drag from her cigarette. She had asked a dozen questions. Cat's answers were short and informative, letting her digest everything she'd seen. He had his own questions to ask, but it was too soon.

"Who were they?" Delilah asked for the eighth time he could recall. She had even mouthed his answer along with him the last time, but once again the acknowledgement failed to reach her conscious mind.

Cat exhaled the smoke from his cigarette. "Well, it wasn't Robin Hood an' his merry shockin' men, but it wasn't anyone who really knew who you were. It was a small, tight-knit group of gamers who want desperately to be the walkin' dead." He chuckled internally. He'd granted them half of their wish at least.

She took a swig of vodka, the best that the cheap hotel bar had to offer. It wasn't the preferred spot for either of them, but it was close, and it was safe. There was one other couple in a booth nearby, an obvious affair with twenty years age difference between the participants. A quiet man sat at the bar, contemplating his life with imported beer as a unit of measure. The bartender was washing glasses, silently praying for an early closing time.

Delilah looked up with an attempt at courage. "You killed them."

Cat nodded. "Three. I let the other one go to tell his buddies at the Paradigm."

Her look was a question that didn't cross her lips.

"In case either of us winds up back there. I want a little rep so we're left alone."

"We? Oh no," she was already shaking her head. "I'm not, not ever."

Cat grinned. Staying away was the proper decision. It was a shame it took an attempt on her life to crack her bravado enough to realize she was completely out of her element. He saw the small flashing light on his comm. "Excuse me a moment." He stepped away from the clean vinyl booth they occupied, and Delilah pulled her coat tighter around her shoulders. She was still shivering.

"This is Catwalk."

Delambre's voice replied, "I have confirmation of payment to your account. Apparently, there's one fewer member of Her Majesty's service walking our streets?"

"Her what? Oh, British! Yeah, I almost skipped on that too, had a side project come ta my attention." Cat chuckled, thumbing the used detonator in his jacket pocket.

"Ah, well, one fewer limey bastard won't depress me any. Nice work. Did the armor meet your initial field testing?"

"Got an unscheduled test drive tonight. I'm really likin' some a' the extras, the spring-loaded Asp, grenade assortment, etc. If I didn't thank you fer takin' the initiative on that, remind me ta do so."

"It was my pleasure. Actually, my daughter shares some of the credit."

"Really? Well, tell ya what. Instead a' the 40 I owe ya for British, take 40 fer you an' 40 fer yer kid, provided I get ta thank her in person someday."

A chuckle led Delambre's reply. "Thank you immensely, Catwalk. I'll ensure you get to display your gratitude to my daughter, as long as I'm present. Your reputation precedes you."

"Thanks, man. Get some rest."

"You as well." The link flashed dead, and Cat returned to the table. Delilah had regained more of her composure than he'd expected.

She was gone.

Jesse tried to breathe. Fear squeezed his lungs. He clenched his eyes shut, feeling the others in the room, though the bag over his head kept him from seeing them. He sobbed, clenched his teeth, and tried to take in a full breath. He froze completely when he heard the man's deep voice.

"You have something for me?"

The woman's response ran chills down Jesse's spine. It was her, the one who had taken him off of the train. "I've got a gift for my king."

Footsteps echoed around Jesse. Someone paced slowly around him. The steps were soft. The floor pressed against his side. The stone was cold and wet. Jesus, what was he lying in?

The man spoke again, scaring Jesse back to the moment. "You always come through for me, dear Silver. When will you accept my generous offer and join me? I have use for someone with your unique talents."

The woman was quick to answer. "My sword is my own, my king. I will serve you. I simply put a little more value in free will than your offer outlines."

The man tsk'ed in reply. "My offer stands. In the meantime, you will be rewarded for your efforts. Fifty thousand, as promised."

The woman replied with something other than words. Jesse heard her steps echo in the distance, followed by the closing of a door. The familiar click of the lock scared him as never before. The bag was suddenly pulled from his head. He squinted against the light. He blinked the stars from his eyes.

A man stood over him, staring down. Jesse blinked several more times. The light played tricks on him. The stranger looked like he was made of gold.

"You recently spent a rather memorable evening with one of the members of my organization, son. Tonight, you're going to recount every memory of that night, no matter how painful." With the last word, the man struck. Jesse screamed as the knife went through his hand, pinning him to the floor.

Golden eyes stared down at him.

"Now, where shall we begin?"

CHAPTER TWELVE

Cat had intended to take a ride south, across the open expanse of desert and debris. Maybe he'd even head out toward the armored religious settlement of Mission Viejo, one of the few remaining centers of 'Holy ground'.

He'd barely escaped the confines of Downtown when they were on him.

There were four in the pack. Each displayed similar skin jobs, a mix of green and chrome, blatantly synthetic, and well armored. They sported neon green hair in different fashions ranging from double Mohawks to straight dreadlocks. Their uniforms were tight fitting and silver, providing another lair of inhuman appearance. If the description was accurate, Cat had wandered into the Sirens territory.

Everyone on this side of Downtown knew about them. The heads-up display on the H-S beeped warnings about the road ahead. The Sirens had destroyed most of it. His only options were to try to jump some gap he couldn't measure, or to ditch the motorcycle. He spit out a string of profanity. Then, he cut the handlebars hard to the left, kicking out the back tire with his weight. The motorcycle skidded along the road, digging a trench through the asphalt.

He finally stopped. Planting a foot in the ruined pavement, he used the strength of his cybernetic legs to push the armored bike off of him. He looked behind him. Broken asphalt tumbled into a deep gorge. Rebar jutted through the walls of the deep chasm. A few more meters and he and his bike would be buried in an unmarked grave.

The roar of engines resonated in his ears. Company. Cat crouched, snapping the baton to its full extension in his left hand. His right hand gripped the 11mm H&K pistol. His eyes flashed yellow, and a deep, electronic sound resonated from somewhere within.

Two attacked him immediately. One brandished a pair of sai, the other a glowing katana. Cat managed to parry and evade with the baton and his armored forearms. Their blows were coordinated and precise, and he had to admit that if he was still in the old jumpsuit instead of the new armor, he'd be sliced to pieces by now. Thankfully, if his attackers had done their homework, they'd been misinformed.

They stayed too close for him to raise the pistol. He countered with a series of baton strikes and a flurry of kicks. The Sirens managed to evade him, timing each attack in perfect coordination. One attacker struck his side as he was late on a parry, but failed to cut through his new Kevlar underbody. Instead of puncturing his lower ribs, the sai clattered uselessly away. Delambre and his daughter had certainly earned their paychecks tonight. Had he been more stubborn and Delambre less persuasive, Cat's internal organs would resemble a well-used corkboard by now.

As the sword-wielding foe went for a thrust, Cat flipped over its head. The other warrior trapped the blade with the hilt of his sai. They turned and met his gaze, one fully extended with a sword thrust, the other cross-armed in defense. Cat unloaded with the pistol, 11mm bullets tore through the Sirens' skulls. Cat snarled a grin as their bodies dropped.

Two Sirens down, he spun, seeking the others. He heard the clank of a canister nearby and leapt without looking. The fragmentation grenade exploded, sending the remains of an abandoned supply truck erupted skyward. One extra moment of contemplation and he would have been a mist of flesh and bone. Instead, he shrugged off the dust and debris that struck him in the aftermath. He switched through his cybernetics' visual filters until he made out the movement of his enemy.

He caught the single pair of green glowing eyes on the far side of the attack and opened fire. Unfortunately, his marksmanship was as well versed as his handwriting, and he succeeded only in forcing the assailant to duck for cover. Before he could locate the fourth enemy, it tackled him. The Siren slammed his side, forcing the breath from his lungs.

The repetition of punches against his face and body was a whirlwind, the clang of metal fists against metal armor repeated so quickly that it caused a ringing in his ears. He felt himself growing in rage with every blow that struck him. Finally giving in to the anger, he drew his legs upward and kicked the pugilist in the chest.

The attacking Siren landed on its back on the far side of the street. As it shook itself to awareness, Cat was on it, slamming the baton repeatedly against its skull. Cracks appeared in the metallic sheen. Liquid followed. Soon, the Siren's skull was concave, its body motionless against the ground.

Feeling the last attacker approach, Cat reached into his fallen enemy's helmet, gaining a solid grip on its skull. With a howl, he swung wide, the dead Siren's body acting as a bat as he rolled. The unsuspecting assailant tried to pull back, instead catching the brunt of its dead colleague full force. The two Sirens slammed into the pavement.

With the weight of its dead colleague trapping it, the last Siren struggled for freedom. Cat approached angrily, stopping only briefly to pick up his pistol. The Siren mumbled something resembling a plea in a language the hitman didn't comprehend. Cat pressed his thumb above the clip handle, catching the emptied ammo clip in his free hand. Tired of the useless voicing of the Siren, he slammed the empty clip into its mouth.

Standing above the last of the gangers, Cat reloaded the 11mm. The Siren's eyes grew wide, and its vocalization switched to outright begging. Scowling, the hitman emptied the fresh clip into the Siren's face.

CHAPTER THIRTEEN

With a crushing blow indicative of his namesake, Midas swung a fist, shattering the one-piece mirror that ran the length of his bedroom. Glass shards rained through the room like a plague of locusts. He roared. The anger of Nitro City's Golden King shook the walls.

The hired whores who'd earlier been writhing in his satin sheets fled in any direction they could find, praying that his violence found only inanimate victims. His golden eyes stared at a few hundred of his own reflection, varying in shape and size, each occupying a fractured portion of the mirror. The shards of his image fell to the carpeted floor. Midas waited a few breaths, regaining his posture. He brushed a few flecks of broken glass from his shoulder.

Watching his assassins overcome so easily demanded a reaction. Had he thought it through, he'd have simply choked one of the whores in his bed. Each of them was chump change compared to the value of the mirror.

He turned his eyes to the nearest woman. She didn't even realize what a lucky little cunt she was tonight. He beckoned a gold finger, and she approached, unaware of the glass cutting into her feet. She disrobed and moved to the bed as he gestured.

Midas reached a hand to the nightstand, his metallic fingers gripping the bottle of Courvoisier. Shrugging off etiquette, he took a swig of the cognac directly from the bottle. He barked into the table-mounted comm. "Get me a line to this assassin. He'll be one of mine soon." The pimp took another deep gulp, staring at the frozen image of yellow eyes on the video feed.

"He'll be mine, alright, or he'll be dead."

It was all wrong.

Cat blew out a quick breath. Sweat rolled down his temples and the nape of his neck. He shook off a chill, impossible for how hot it was outside. He squeezed his eyes and shook his head, careful not to lose control of the motorcycle in the process. He stared at the wavy horizon, focusing on his breath. Finally, the feverish symptoms began to wane. His head cleared enough to process the attacks.

Cat knew it before he even got close to the confines of familiar territory. Someone had tried long and hard to make sure he was a corpse, and that the Sirens got credit. Only whoever had organized this missed on two key definitive areas. First, Cat had new armor, armor that only he and Delambre knew about, which meant his newfound acquaintance had been trustworthy after all.

Secondly, the real Sirens were equipped with sonic weapons surgically implanted to imitate the mythical creatures of the same name. Several also opted for cybernetic controls for their intercostals and diaphragm. Popular rumors circulated that a coordinated attack by two Sirens in harmony caused more damage than an earthquake registering 6.0 on the Richter scale.

The four beings who'd attacked him had anything but vocal attacks. Two were martial artists, the other two a cleanup crew. That composition was far more conventional, common to hostile takeovers, assassin teams, or even his old cop squad in DC. This team could have made up a small infantry band in the last territory war, or a Fixer's eraser squad. Cat let the logic play in multiple directions.

First of all, he had to thank Delambre, or rather, his daughter, for the design of the composite armor. Without it, he'd have been punctured like balsa wood in a hailstorm, left to bleed alone in the desert outside of Nitro City. Second, someone had just sent a squad after him. Midas was the obvious candidate, since Cat had converted the pimp's sidekick from Original to Extra Crispy. If Midas had shown a willingness to kill him, it meant either an escalation in his enemies' talent level or the pimp's tenacity. Sooner or later, Cat was going to need to eliminate the power broker. It was a scenario he'd wished to sidestep, but one he knew was coming when he offed the crippled pederast.

Third, there was the matter of Delilah. The simple

thought of her brought a scent to his nose and a taste to his lips. He wanted to protect her, if only for the absolute selfishness of having her skin pressed against him. He wanted her mouth at his mercy, her body his to conduct like an orchestra. He could certainly overlook the fact that she was married, since her dinosaur husband had been declared missing Off-World for well over ten months.

He'd love the chance to tap into her brain and to see if she was willing to put her morals on hold. Cat was thirty years closer to her own age than the fashion tycoon, Raul Dupree. The old stiff might as well be dead, and Delilah should be on the back of the motorcycle, nervous arms wrapped around her new rescuer, or better, legs wrapped around his waist. At the moment, she was just plain gone. She'd fled his presence as quickly as that of the vampires. There was some rebuilding to perform with her.

If he was lucky, he'd find the chance.

If he was a lottery winner, she'd find him first.

The scientist struck the keyboard again and again, sending letters into the air like rain. He screamed a torrent of syllables, if not complete sentences. Trailing a stream of vandalism in the air, he gritted his teeth. He could not allow the symbiotic relationship of the pimp and the hitman to come to pass. Midas had made an uncharacteristic switch in his plans. Instead of doubling his forces to kill Catwalk, he planned on offering the yellow-eyed ex-cop a job. The thought of Midas and Catwalk working together drove the scientist to a point beyond reason, causing fire around his temples, blindness in his eyes, and lightning in his brain. The two simply would not be allowed to align against him.

When the pulsating brightness against his temples subsided, he leveled his gaze. The anticipating eyes of his finest subject met his own.

"Ah, my dearest Angelyka," he stated, as a trickle of blood dribbled from his lips, " the time has come, at last, for you to do away with our former ally. At last we shall claim power for our own, and Nitro City, the embodiment of Sin it has become, shall taste the wrath of its new Messiah."

"Go. Make me proud."

A smile crossed Angelyka's black lips. "I will fulfill

your desire, Master."

The deep crack of leathery wings split the night sky as his Dark Angel left the lab, heading skyward. As her humanoid form lifted into the darkness, the scientist sneered. The cybernetic enhancements that made her something far beyond human would serve as an alert to anyone close enough to bear witness. With Midas and Catwalk brushed aside, he would continue to develop the next generation of MetaHumans. Though his creations had been imperfect in the past, Angelyka was different. She symbolized the new dawn in human cyber-genetic evolution, and her superiority over his enemies would prove that.

He pictured her dark claws ripping Midas' heart from his body, and he began to laugh. The scientist thought of his enemies' death, careful to depict every satisfying detail. Soon, but not soon enough, he would eliminate the few obstacles that had dared to obstruct his path to glory.

CHAPTER FOURTEEN

"He's a reckless, careless idiot."

"That is quite enough!" Delambre's tone was enough to send his daughter spinning on her heel out of the lab. From Cat's position, strapped to the cold, steel slab, he couldn't judge her reaction.

"I'm sure she took that well."

Delambre frowned, "Don't be an ass, Catwalk. My job is to enable your success, not facilitate your suicidal tendencies."

Cat smirked. He wasn't certain if the geneticist or his daughter was the one with most expertise, or greatest interest, in his health. He coughed to one side as an exercise, receiving no reaction from Delambre. "Sorry, Doc. I'll take blame for the vamps, not this whole bout with the Sirens. I didn't go callin' fer that."

Concentrating on the diagnostics, Delambre offered only a grunt. Cat's grin drew broader as he realized that just as the geneticist's daughter had designed his new armor. She was the one who maintained a watchful eye on its functionality. Eventually, she could be an outlet for some serious education, or a great deal of fun.

Without intent, his mind brought up another woman he'd met recently, and forced him to ask why he hadn't tried to track down the fashion model. He wanted her near. He had developed a desire for her from the first glimpse of her on the vid screen. It had only grown more intense when he met her in person at the Paradigm. There was more to it, though. Something kept him from chasing after the redheaded off-world goddess. He couldn't put his finger on it.

"How soon til I'm up an' about?"

Delambre scanned the diagnostics he had been running for the better part of an hour. "The damage you've sustained is minimal. We're almost done here."

"Good, I could use a smoke."

"Smoke any more and I can't promise you'll be able to avoid heat-seeking missiles."

"Hmm, so I'm guessin' you don't have a light?"

Delambre leveled a wordless gaze. Cat shrugged, deciding against asking if the geneticist's daughter had any interest in lighting his fire. He wanted to get out of the sterile and stuffy lab, hit the open road and do a little wrenching of his own. Last night's inventory of upcoming conflicts hadn't lessened any. It had only inched closer to the inevitable deadline. He'd been fortunate that two of the Sirens had records, and that meant a little bonus money. It also meant more money that Midas would be putting on his tab. Half of the hitman wanted to smash Midas' shiny dome into the pavement. The other half tried to make a rational assumption of the extent of Midas' power. The rational half usually came out on the losing end.

The cleaner watched Delambre scour the diagnostics. "You two are close, then, huh?"

"What do you mean?"

"You an' your daughter. Seems like even when you hate each other, you ain't so far apart."

Delambre stopped for a moment before responding. "We don't have anyone else, Catwalk. We have only each other."

Cat nodded with a smirk. "So, she has ta put up with you…and me?"

The elder man chuckled.

Cat swung to a seated position, then dropped soundlessly on the lab floor, still grinning. "I dunno, doc. You ask me…she's gotta be some kinda angel."

By nightfall, Cat had put a few hundred more kilometers on the H-S, tweaked and tuned it for a few hours, and snagged a short but deep period of meditation before cleaning up and hitting the streets again. Midas loved metal, both visual and aural, and he had a few familiar hot spots. Liquid Chrome was one, but his sphere of influence there was limited. The owners had spent plenty of time and money cleaning up. If they were dealing with crime lords, they were very, very good at keeping it a secret.

Instead, Cat headed slightly uptown from Chrome, to a district called The Cell Block. The Block housed three separate industrial factories, closed down almost twelve years ago when the majority of chipset manufacturing had been moved Off-World. Purchased by a music mogul and sports agent called DJX-Machina, the factories were overhauled, walkways were built between them, and the buildings were fit with enough bars and speakers for the party to be heard kilometers away.

The exterior looked like some twisted version of a storybook castle. The old smokestacks reached skyward, begging the past to return to the earth. Walkways crisscrossed, some open to the air, others enclosed. Silhouettes moved and overlapped stories above the ground. Lights pulsated in perfect synchronicity with the punishing guitars and synthesizers. The Block itself seemed to beat with the music, feeding the lust and thrill of its inhabitants.

Cat ran a series of scans around the exterior of the factory. The results were as expected. Snipers occupied each corner. A few other warm bodies found their way to the assumed privacy of outside for some mutual satisfaction. He knew his decision to play bait would draw out some attention at The Block. It was virtual suicide to walk into the spider's web, but he was tired of looking over his shoulder. If Midas was going to come after him, it might as well be head-on, instead of sending half-a-dozen amateur goons every few days.

The first factory was a perfect marriage of wreckage and treasure. The interior had been shelled out, an arson job started on the inside by workers furious at rumored layoffs. Most of the machinery and the foundation were impervious to the intense heat, but the flames had charred the majority of the walls and the flooring, and left a faint hint of smoke that clung to the inhabitants' clothes, hair and throats. It was a dance party inside an ashtray.

The factory-turned-concert hall was three floors high, with the ground floor a tsunami of writhing bodies. While the DJX commanded the tones in the next building, this was ruled by a psychotic-themed live band. A stage extended out from the second floor, making the band three dimensional, with fans both above and below them. The front man had a commanding presence. He was several kilograms overweight, evidenced by his heavy breathing and profuse sweating between belting out murderous lyrics. Cat caught himself staring for a moment at the gyrating vocalist. Cop nostalgia nibbled at him. He scanned the singer's face and ran it against a database of high profile cases. It took only seconds for a hit.

Cat shook his head for missing it at first glance. The stage performer had undergone cosmetic surgery and now permanently bore the smile and mask of a children's party clown. Not just any clown, Cat noted, but Pogo the Clown, the character behind which the 1970's serial killer John Wayne Gacy hid. Gacy was famous for sexually assaulting and killing 27 people. Cat wondered what twisted phreak would elect to wear that face for the rest of his life. He wondered how many skeletons Pogo had in his closet. The other band members also donned the faces of serial killers. Gary Ridgeway, the Green River Killer, smashed the drums. Aileen Wuornos played bass. Dennis Rader, aka BTK, whipped out a guitar solo.

As the Gacy clone howled and writhed through his set, rolling on the plexiglass and neon stage that protruded above the bodies below, bartenders on each side doled out fluorescent drinks to a buzzing crowd, bees to the alcoholic hive. Each floor had two bars, one each to stage right and stage left, and each had a swarm several victims deep waiting for the next round. The VIP area on the third floor was the least crowded. It was designed for security and sound-dampening to promote business networking. Things inside The Block were just as in Nitro City, rising above was as literal a term as it was figurative.

Cat downed two doubles of synth-vodka and burned through two smokes while he took a mental inventory. He was thankful for his cybernetic eyes every time he scanned the swarm of bodies writhing beneath the strobe lights. The band continued its torrent of blistering guitars and pounding drums, with Pogo half-screaming, half-squealing above it all. If Sodom had a soundtrack, it may very well be performed by the clown and his supporting cast.

He hadn't ventured upstairs yet, but the first two floors met his every expectation. A small portion of him was bummed he didn't suddenly find Delilah's radiant figure attempting to hide among the crowd. With no luck in the out-of-place supermodel category, he moved to the next portion of his mental checklist. Midas was somewhere in the complex, and if his resources were worth the cost of a can of cheap spray paint, the pimp would know by now that Cat had come to visit.

It took zero effort to gain access to the third floor. When Cat told the giant-framed bouncer that there was a couple performing all-out sodomy in the stairwell (and that the female half of the couple had 38 DD's), the bouncer gave him a cursory warning before moving past him to investigate. The fact that there really was a couple performing was icing on the cake. He might have exaggerated about the girl's artificial breasts, but not by much. Cat strolled past the bouncer's evacuated seat, moving to mingle with the well-to-do crowd on the top floor.

His new armor was hardly visible. The metallic plating of his legs could easily be mistaken for the modern, fashionable Kevlar-mesh combinations. By removing the padding planted in the motorcycle jacket, he'd created room for the armor. His straight, black hair was pulled into a tight ponytail, and he wore square black shades in front of his softly glowing yellow Cyberoptics. The cigarette between his lips and the glass in his hand gave the impression that his goal was to enjoy the night for what it was.

Had the Pogo look-alike fronting the band taken a few more vocal lessons, Cat might be willing to forego business tonight and relax. The superhuman tap on his shoulder squelched that line of dreaming. Glancing back, the cleaner saw the familiar form of the bouncer blocking out most of the light of the room.

"Your presence has been requested," the bouncer stated with a metallic timber to his voice. Stepping aside, the enormous security guard pointed to a pair of double doors. The doors, frame, and hardware were made of solid gold. An inverted eye of the Egyptian god, Ra, was engraved in each door. Cat smirked. The Golden King showed no humility, and no weakness, in revealing his presence.

Catwalk stepped inside the lair behind the doors. Furnishings of scarlet velvet covered leather furniture around the room. A plush red carpet draped its way to the far end of the room. Along the walls, figures mingled in whispers and moans in the shadows. He heard dozens of voices, each seemingly driven by pleasure and oblivious to his presence. He shifted his view across the room, to a series of adjoined couches.

A figure sat in the center, clad in a top-dollar suit, complete with a few very friendly ladies as garnish. The silhouette rested a golden chalice on the table top, raising his view to meet Cat's. The Golden King's gaze met the hitman. He wouldn't need to find Midas after all.

Midas had found him.

CHAPTER FIFTEEN

Midas said something and the escort to his right scattered like a cockroach. The pimp waved a shimmering hand at Catwalk, beckoning to the plush, empty seat by his side. "Care for a drink?"

He took a few, slow strides forward, eyeing the shadows to both sides. He stepped closer, but he stopped before outright accepting the offer to join the festivities.

Midas studied him for a long moment before addressing him. "My invitation surprises you, cleaner?"

"Not as much as the fact I'm still breathin', but, yeah, a bit."

The glimmer of his golden skin made Midas' emotions harder to read, but from Cat's best guess, the pimp had rehearsed this speech and its every potential direction ad nauseam. Still, Midas was known to lose his metallic cool from time to time if things didn't go as he'd planned them. Maybe he was just going to hand Cat a bill for the Sirens, and then, try to kill him.

"Your sense of humor is well-known in the industry." Midas took a slow drink from his golden goblet. The small area around them was a mix of faint smoke and unending music. The women surrounding Midas were oblivious to their conversation, ebbing and flowing around the pimp. Their liquid movements made Midas seem even more like a living statue than testimonies Cat had reviewed.

Midas' gaze remained unchanged for several long, quiet moments. Cat took a drink and a drag on his cigarette. He stole a quick look around the place, confirming as many targets as possible. With the security of his new armor, and the increased draw speed of his holsters, he could still get the drop on the bouncers and the pimp. He eyed Midas, wondering what the hell would make a man try to appear solid gold. At least he wasn't trying to be a human shocking clown. Midas was either greedier than a career politician or insane. Insanity didn't usually come with such business acumen, so Cat was willing to bet on the former. His speculation was interrupted when Midas spoke again. "Tell me about Hitch."

Cat grinned, "Bad skin, yellow teeth, below-average height, unmistakable limp, ugly as a burn victim. He liked to fuck dead kids, coz then he had a fightin' chance against 'em." Cat surprised himself with the inflection of his words. He hadn't intended the edge that he revealed, but Hitch's behavior struck something inside of him. Him, he'd killed people for a ride home in his past.

Midas nodded. "So, this was some sort of street justice for you, cleaner? You took it upon yourself to erase a vermin that hunted the streets of Downtown Nitro City suddenly? That does not fit the profile I've got on you. You're better than some petty foray into heroism. You're a killer. You make people disappear for a paycheck. Why so different with Hitch? What made it personal? Did he remind you of your childhood? You don't strike me as altar boy material."

Cat chuckled at the pimp's attempt to strike a chord. "Oh, my feelin's don't even enter into it. You said it yourself. I offed him coz I got a nice sum a' money ta do exactly that." Cat sipped his drink. "The fact that he was a bottom-feedin' skinbag did provide a little personal satisfaction."

Midas' face remained unchanged. "Who paid you?"

"You don't really think I'm gonna tell you."

"If you don't, you're a dead man."

"If I do, I'm worse than dead."

Midas stopped and stared. He took another long drink from his goblet then set it on the ornate table. Crossing one leg over the other, he leaned back in his chair. "Why do you think you're here, Catwalk?"

Cat drained his glass. "Near as I figure, it's one a' two things. Either yer the kinda guy who just has ta see someone face ta face and kill 'em yourself, or yer willin' ta double my check ta off the guy who hired me ta kill Hitch."

Midas leaned forward. His stare pulled Catwalk inward like a magnet. After a brief a pause, the pimp stood, brushing away his female slaves like lint on his collar. He picked up the golden cane that rested against the chair and looked down at Cat.

The stare down between them lasted forever, yet only a breath. Midas finally turned his gaze to his side and nodded. Two figures stepped from the darkness behind Catwalk. Cat reached for his weapons, but the men didn't attack. Instead, they lifted the corners of the long, scarlet rug that led from the door. They began to roll it up. He had to step aside as they neared Midas. He caught the scent of the liquid on the floor even before he saw it on the underside of the carpet.

Blood.

The men reached the space in front of Midas, lifting the carpet on their shoulders and disappearing into the darkness to his left. Cat scanned the floor. A drain was set squarely in the center of the room. Traces of blood, some old, some recent, colored the stones. He lifted his gaze to Midas, who beckoned from his right. One of the guards tossed another something off of his shoulder on to the cold stone floor. Cat caught the form. It wasn't something. It was someone.

A yelp of terror left the person dumped on to the floor. Cat clenched his teeth. The body on the floor was frail and pale. Scabs covered the ankles and wrists. It curled in the fetal position, facing Midas. Cat fingers clenched into fists. He gritted his teeth. Words couldn't find the way through the rage running through his muscles.

The Golden King made his way down to the body on the floor. "Now, now. Let's not be ungrateful hosts. Say hello to our guest of honor, won't you?" He struck the hobbled figure with his cane. A wordless moan left his victim. Midas sneered. "What's wrong?" he shouted, kicking the figure hard enough that it rolled over, "Cat got your tongue?"

The victim's head bounced off the concrete floor, in and out of the light. Cat froze. Ice seized his fingers, crept along his arms and paralyzed everything he still considered human. As soon as he saw the young man's face, he halted. His heart seized in his chest.

The boy's eyes and mouth were sewn shut. Scars covered his arms and legs. His fingers were broken in unnatural angles. He whimpered against the damp floor.

Cat staggered forward. The room disappeared.

"Jesse…"

An eternity passed before Midas' voice registered in his head. "Join me for a walk, cleaner. I have a proposition I believe will interest you."

Somewhere below, Pogo's band broke into a new song, screaming about "The Best It's Gonna Get", accompanied by pulsing electronic drums and strobe lights that matched the rise in rhythm and adrenaline. The crowd shouted. Apparently, this was a fan favorite.

Midas led the way onto a walkway out of the club, with Cat a few steps behind. The hitman wasn't stupid. He was aware of the multiple sets of eyes, and probably a few laser scopes, on him the entire time. He hadn't quite figured out what the fixer had up his shiny golden sleeve. Delambre would offer some 'I told you so' to his daughter once they realized Cat had confronted Midas and wound up with his organs sporting a few dozen holes. He concentrated on breathing. His human muscles were tight, almost to the point of seizure. If he couldn't flex, his body was useless.

Spotlights and occasional fireworks erupted above the factories. The disharmony of crowds hollering and the cacophony of multiple bands and DJ's all met outside the confines of the industrial buildings. It sounded like a full-throttle orgy in Hell. The wind somehow managed to bite at the fog of guilt that numbed his senses. Words began to make sense. The reality around him became less like the nightmare that surrounded him.

Even through the half-dozen audio sources, Cat could identify one in particular. One of the DJ's was spinning the new cover of "I'm Too Sexy" by Bootie and the Holefish. He rolled his eyes. There was a line in the song about "doing a little dance on the catwalk" that drove him insane every time he heard it. Maybe Midas would excuse him for a few moments just to torture and maim the idiots enjoying that particular song.

"So, here we are," Midas stated from the center of one of the walkways, bringing Cat back to the matter at metallic hand. Midas gestured around him, against the wind, standing midpoint between two of the gigantic structures. Cat switched on his recorder, feeding the view from his Cyberoptics to a storage bank on the H-S and replicated back to the lab. If the snipers were going to blow him to bits, the least he could do was have evidence. NCPD would never bother to investigate, but maybe he had a crazed fan who would attempt vengeance in his name.

Cat gazed around, noting the faint lights from the buildings, the debris floating by on the wind and the spotlights disappearing into the heavens. "So, here's where you retire me an' further yer good name?"

"On the contrary, cleaner, I have no desire to let you die, now or for as long as I can imagine."

"So, why exactly are we here?" Cat wanted to feign ignorance, but Midas' last statement made everything agonizingly clear.

Midas' grin provided enough of an answer. "You left a void in my organization by murdering my assistant, Catwalk. That's a void I need filled."

"Goddamnit…" Cat muttered under his breath.

"You eliminated my Renfield, cleaner. You left a void in my organization, and in doing so, proven yourself worthy of that post. You have a very specialized skill set. Clearly, what you have to offer is different from what Hitch brought to my organization. I'm intrigued at the opportunity available here. Let's say I want to evolve from the mangy old cur I could kick to a panther I could unleash on my competition." Midas gazed intently, as if he could force his power and sphere of influence on Cat with a single thought. "I brought you here to hire you."

Cat nodded silently, turning over every possible response and its repercussions in his mind.

Midas grinned broadly and then broke into open laughter. "You had no idea this was coming, did you?" He slapped himself on the knee, laughing louder. He leaned on his cane and shook his head. He rose back to his full height and returned his gaze to the hitman. "And here I thought you prepared yourself for anything, cleaner. Now, join me. I'll even let you put the bullet through that worthless little hooker inside to seal the deal."

Cat opened his mouth to voice his best response when a flash of light pierced his peripheral vision. From Midas' left, something broke into view, something with the speed and accuracy of a laser. Sparks erupted as metal met metal on the walkway. Cat tumbled backward, adjusting his direction and coming to a stop in a Krav Maga defensive posture. He looked at the bridge where he had just stood. He focused his view in time to see Midas' headless form crumble to its knees and fold like a cheap suit.

Shocked, Cat looked the direction of the source, finding nothing. Something deep and distant registered in his ear. He dropped to the surface, feeling the rush of air above his head. As he spun and drew his pistol, he saw a humanoid form moving…no, flying, away from him.

Cat fired a handful of random bursts in the attacker's direction. Barely visible against the night air, he caught its silhouette as a pair of the spotlights chanced to cross its path. It was humanoid, and feminine, with a set of enormous leathery wings. Worse, it was heading in his direction. Instead of checking on the corpse of his recent would-be employer, Cat sprinted back towards the factory. His cybernetic legs accelerated with superhuman speed.

The winged assailant sliced into the area where he recently stood, missing by a few meters. Sparks erupted as the thick steel railings holding the walkway in place split apart. Cat crouched, waiting for another pass from his attacker. The walkway creaked as the weight tugged on the final metallic threads keeping it in one piece.

The feminine form split the spotlights, visible for barely a second before she was on him. Cat spun aside, not realizing until she'd passed that she had even succeeded in cutting him. From his cop days to his barbaric surgery, Cat had enough scars on his back to mimic the constellations. This bat-winged bitch wasn't going to provide any more.

When her form disappeared against the sky once more, he recognized the familiar sting of severed flesh. He was stranded in a losing proposition, and he knew it. That meant his enemy probably picked up on it as well. The creaking gave way to the moaning of shifting steel, and the walkway gave way. Cat stared over his shoulder long enough to watch the far end of the bridge bend towards the earth. Midas' headless form slipped from the steel and plummeted below to the courtyard and its unsuspecting inhabitants.

Cat turned and sprinted to the building where he and Midas had met. He extended the pistol before him, firing round after round. Instead of hitting the door, Cat aimed above it, perforating the stained glass. A change altered the air behind him. He heard the singing of her wings cutting the night sky. He leapt forward, crashing through the window. Every ounce of oxygen left his body upon impact. Each shard of glass magnified the pain a thousand times as he landed in an unceremonious heap. Gunfire filled his head. Midas' goons had arrived, too late to save their master, but in time to provide cover fire. Cat gritted his teeth, dropped several floors below to the dance floor, and joined the masses flooding to the exits.

Above the din of shock and amazement around him, he heard the passing of leather wings. If he'd have gone for the door, things would have ended differently. Screams and shouts filled the room around him and echoed as metal, glass and one of Nitro City's most recognizable celebrities rained down on the crowd. The result was chaos. Bouncers sought control. Patrons flocked to the exits. There was no telling how many of them would be injured, mauled or trampled.

Cat rose to a knee, lifting his pistol at the backlit frame of the emergency exit door. Panicked forms crossed his vision, rushing to the exits, or to hiding spots. They were all a blur. He stared at the door, watching, waiting. The socialites seemed to move in slow motion. Their screams were distant. Their fear was a fantasy, something in a dream.

He concentrated until his pistol stopped shaking. He stared through the passing bodies back to the creaking walkway and the echo of leathery wings. He thought of Midas' headless form, recalling an old joke about losing 10kg of ugly fat and smiled. He'd killed Hitch, drawing the attention of Midas. Now Midas was dead, from dealing with him, and there was a short list of those who had the stones to kill the powerful fixer.

Whoever it was now had a bull's eye squarely on his…or her…back.

Cat turned from the door. He chose a pattern of chaos. He would be shadowed by the figures running rampant for safety. Less than a minute later, he was astride the Honda-Suzuki heading away from The Cell Block.

Nitro City's biggest pimp was dead. Cat had been set up, and he'd been lucky to survive the night. He was luckier still that he recorded Midas' assassination. Someone was making a power play big enough to kill Downtown's golden child. As he raced back to the freeway, Cat sent a confirmation message to the lab. He wanted to make sure the recording went through. He began to formulate the list of power brokers who would take a run at Midas. That list was short. A light in his Cyberoptics confirmed that his recording had reached the lab. Delambre and his daughter would have access to it. Maybe they could shed some light on the situation he had just escaped.

Cat banked a hard right and joined the flow of traffic on the freeway. Hitch's murder had led him to Midas. Now, the pimp was dead, and someone or something else had tossed its hat into the ring.

Things were about to get very, very interesting.

CHAPTER SIXTEEN

4 March 2022

Artificial light provides the only comfort from the darkness. The air smells fabricated. He can taste the chemicals in the air. There is no warmth. There is no heart. Everything here is a sterile, inhuman construct.

All he wants is something, anything with emotion, a feeling.

His throat is dry. Words barely escape his mouth. He would plead for water if he had the voice. The separation of his dried lips pulls from the exterior of his teeth. It adds another layer of slow agony. When his eyes gain focus for the first time, he clicks on the call button. It is a century of measured breaths, inhaled and exhaled with practiced efficiency, before the uniformed nurse arrives.

She is an angel, light-skinned, hinting at an African-American heritage. Her hand graces the bare layer of his arm, and he cannot resist the attraction at the feel of her fingertips. He mouths the request for water, though he never realizes if the words cross his tongue. His attention is solely on her, his new savior, the embodiment of his physical improvement. She represents a life away from the wheelchair, from the paralysis.

He lies here in the hospital bed, a young punk who willingly hit the streets to find quick and easy money and sex. He had been the feet on the streets, the delivery mechanism for the latest and greatest in chemical satisfaction. It occurs to him, numb and distant, that the drug runner is all the nurse sees on the bed. She has no inclination of his life, no desire to find out who he is. She tends to him because she is paid an hourly wage to do exactly that.

The angel reads the chart and sneers, her words thick with contempt. "You'll never walk again, Leon."

Hope dies in his throat. The vision of the wheelchair is

a slap in his face. He chokes on his own breath, the frozen emotion of hopelessness. He struggles to draw air in defiance, but her words crush him. Leon swallows, memorizing the instant for eternity. He remembers every wrinkle of her face, some caused by age, others by disdain. He remembers his own response, and how it isn't defiant enough.

The time will come soon enough to return that venom.

"Oww!"

"Don't be such a baby." Delambre fought off a grin as he addressed the man accustomed to murder and mayhem as a way of life.

"Pulling glass out of me shouldn't involve putting metal in its place. I've been through that before, remember?"

"If you're such a hardass, why didn't you take out one insane woman who envisions herself a bat?"

"Shock you, Delambre." The medtech had hit close to home with that comment. Why hadn't he been able to even mount a countermeasure against the winged attacker? Cat had been caught so unprepared he'd barely managed to survive intact. Now, his newly hired partner was pulling shards of glass out of his unarmored neck and hair. He had no answers regarding Midas' killer, and nothing to go on, save the brief video feed he'd snapped while running for his life.

Delambre's confident and chiding response interrupted Cat's mental assessment. "One of Nitro's highest conductors just found himself the recipient of sudden, and rather drastic, cosmetic surgery. Any leads?"

"I gave you the video feed. That's the best I got. I'll do a search on his allies and enemies, but you know how long that'll take."

"Hmm, I already have Angela working on it."

"Did you have her include the keywords for leather wings, razor sharp claws, and the ability to decapitate shiny pimps at will?"

"Of course, Catwalk. I even had her use the filter that protects her backside from drooling ex-cops with a blatant desire to fondle her, regardless of her father's presence."

"Hmmm, subtlety's never been my strong suit, Delambre. Next time, have yer old lady push out an ugly kid with a huge ass an' you won't have to put up with me so often."

Delambre twisted the scalpel in a way that made Cat flinch. "Somehow, Catwalk, I doubt it would even slow you down."

Cat's response never escaped his gritted teeth. Instead, he focused internally, centering on his breath and the ability to fortify against his pain. The medtech could have continued the procedure with less agony, but they hadn't yet reached a level where they truly knew or trusted one another. For now, he would suffer the probing metal of a protective father and counter it with meditation.

Shock it. It was worth it just for the line about Angela's backside.

CHAPTER SEVENTEEN

There were six messages waiting as Cat stepped, tired and sore, into his loft. Three were solicitations or exotic off-world travel packages targeted at the financial group he was in as a front. The fourth was a concerned mother seeking to restrain her estranged husband. The last was the same woman, openly crying and confessing about dumping the body of the man previously identified as her missing ex-husband. That case was easy to close, but Cat doubted he'd get a commission or reward for it.

It was the fifth message, which caught his attention. Delambre's daughter spoke with a tone of emotional absence and analytical precision. When she stated there was material Cat 'needed to see', an alarm rang in his head. Angela hadn't exactly radiated calm the first few times they'd met. He grabbed his helmet and bounded toward the Honda-Suzuki. Creeping back into her shell meant something had triggered her. Cat needed to know if it was a threat, a change or a break in the case. He also needed to figure out if he could trust the crafty medtech, and what extent exactly Angela played in his work.

The quick ride through Downtown was as uneventful as things ever got in Nitro City. Cat pulled the motorcycle into an empty parking space. He had run through a handful of possibilities on the ride over, but few had any real substance. Still, it was better to come off cocky than to let his partners know he was completely at a loss. He stepped into Delambre's working area.

"What's the verdict?" He asked.

Angela, as Delambre had referred to her, dropped the control to the video feed on the table and walked away. Her brown eyes offered no depth, a conscious attempt to hide any hint of her internal anguish. It didn't take an empath to read her concerns. Cat cursed silently for not checking for other telltale signs. It was too late to check her eyes for redness or tears, too late to monitor her hands or posture for signs of stress. Instead, he had a black screen and a remote.

Deciding to pursue her behavior before the video feed, he called across the open room. "I'm gonna grab a drink. You want anything?"

Angela slammed the door behind her.

It took almost four minutes to track down any alcohol worth imbibing and another two to find an empty glass clean enough to drink from. By the time Cat sat down in front of the monitor and cracked his neck, Angela was locked away behind who-knew-how-many doors. He wasn't sure if her feelings towards him were fear or distrust. Either way, she'd called him here without dear ol' Daddy D to look out for her, which meant he probably had wasted crucial time before viewing the video.

He sighed, poured a tumbler of cheap whiskey, and flipped the monitor to 'play'.

Instantly, he recognized his own video feed, an eerie out-of-body method of witnessing his recent near-death experience. It was as if he had actually died and was watching his spirit pull away from his physical form, only he hadn't been graced with the invite to the pearly gates. He was quite alive and dealing with the dizzying images dancing in the frame. It was annoying at first. Before he knew it, he was becoming entertained at the experience.

Angela had slowed the footage, filtering it for clarity. As a result, Cat watched the words mimed on Midas' gold-tinted lips. Instead of a surprising blur, he was able to track the assassin's attack movement-by-movement. Midas' eyes engaged him with the self-important smugness, unaware of the airborne murderer. As the flash entered the screen, Cat witnessed the tearing of the platysma and scalyne muscles, the severing of the jugular, and the separation of the spine from the base of the skull, clear step-by-step features of Midas' decapitation. He raised a glass to Midas' cadaver just before it dropped.

"Bottom's up," he chided the video feed.

The video returned to standard speed for the next few moments. Cat recognized as he picked up the target, acknowledged its speed and reflexes, and moved in counter-measure. It was just before he turned and leapt through the window that the feed returned to frame-by-frame super-slow motion.

As he backed up, the attacker entered the screen, her

figure obviously female, and (just ask Midas) homicidal. With several slow clicks, her aerial form filled the view, growing closer. The video feed paused. Cat stared at an outlined and detailed shot of her face.

Staring back at him from the screen was an artificial image of Delambre's daughter.

Cat had kicked through two doors, unhinging one of them completely. He pounded on the third, demanding some answers from Angela but receiving nothing. He pushed back from the door far enough to line up a sidekick. The door crashed open from the force of his cybernetic leg. His blood was boiling at his new endangerment and the result of the recent discovery. Angela wasn't a masochist and had stashed herself away far too well to be the real assassin on the case. Instead, she was ripped apart from within that the murderer wore her face. She simply wasn't prepared to discuss that fact with a violent and self-important business partner on the outskirts of the law.

Cat's calls for her had gone unheard or ignored. His best guess was that Delambre's quiet daughter had ducked out of another exit and was long gone. If she had anything to contribute to the fact that her look-a-like had murdered Midas and nearly added Catwalk as a side dish, she wasn't prepared to volunteer that information. Deciding against chasing her or searching her private quarters, Cat instead clicked on Delambre's ID on his comm, summoning the medtech.

"Please tell me this is urgent, and you're missing at least two limbs, Catwalk."

"No such luck, D. Close, though. You seen my upload that yer daughter scoped out yet?"

Delambre's voice changed so suddenly the comm might have developed whiplash. "Where are you?"

"Relax, doc, your daughter ran outta here after tossin' me the remote. I'm guessin' she's not very cool with somethin' she saw on the feed."

"What are you talking about?"

Cat paused a moment for effect, long enough to draw in a breath and resist the temptation to verbally badger his new partner. "Get yer ass down here to yer own lab, an' let's talk."

Delambre was silent.

"An' pick up a bottle a' better booze. Yer cheap whiskey is like formaldehyde with food coloring." Cat clicked the comm dead, picturing Delambre's mind jump-starting into high gear. He wanted answers and forcing the medic to switch from scientific genius to concerned father provided him with a better angle for an interrogation. He tossed the comm into the air, at first willing to let it drop, but before it was past his face, he swung a roundhouse kick, shattering the small device into pieces. He caught himself gritting his teeth as he stared at the broken device.

Cat blew out the air in his lungs as if it was responsible for the frustration and hatred he bottled up inside. As he released the tension, clarity returned. Delambre's daughter couldn't be the winged assassin, and if she was, why would she reveal that to him? That was either stupidity or a challenge, and Cat had no reason to believe the prim and proper technician would suddenly take flight and behead crime lords.

He pressed his fingers against his temples, going over what else had changed. He had hired Delambre, and apparently Angela, worked out the kinks in his new armor, had a run-in with the fake Sirens, and what else? There was that little matter of killing Hitch. Offing Hitch had caused a reaction in Midas, but it also had to be related to whoever killed the golden-skinned pimp. So, what was the connection?

Cat tapped into his cop days and began drawing up motive scenarios. Midas kept Hitch around as an example, but didn't approve or finance the sidekick's underage habit. Cat had learned that from the source who sent him the recording. Hitch was paying for innocent flesh on the side, and when those payments dried up, his source went right after Midas. It was a desperate move, the kind committed by panicked amateurs or raving lunatics. Of course, Hitch was both.

Cat knew insanity like a boyhood chum. He'd fought it at arms' length since his surgery, countered it with booze, chemicals and violence during his police years, and distanced himself from it since going freelance. In the end, it would find him, but for now, he maintained control and separation. Still, the signs were as legible as the neon advertisements that graced Nitro City's skyline.

He picked up the desk line and dialed a number from memory.

"Will's Meats, you can beat our prices but you can't beat our…"

"Will, I need a favor," he said calmly. "Get yer boys, an' do a search on the followin' account." Without another word, he uploaded Hitch's account number. He'd followed it secretly for so long he could recite it in his sleep. "If you see any trends, lemme know…an' if you see anythin' more than four times, poison it."

Will's chuckle on the other end was an acceptance and an invoice all wrapped into one. Cat didn't have the disposable income to pay the coroner's highly talented phreaks. Then again, tearing at the foundation of the pederast's trustees was enough to make him take up a few extracurricular jobs to pay for their services. He shook his head in an effort to focus again, and to break from the tempting picture of tracking and disemboweling Hitch's business partners. Instead, Cat slipped from the precipice of reason, if only for the slightest moment, as the past, present and projected future overcame him.

10 May 2022

The dark-haired girl who enters his plain room is a bundle of cheerfulness. Her smile is wide, and there is a bounce to her step despite her simple shoes in the dusty doorway. She holds a metal tray in her hands. Each compartment bares a serving of something claiming to resemble an edible material, smoked or steamed. Leon looks up from the rainbow of synthetic chow and catches the girl's eyes. She is Asian, with straight, eclipse-black hair that touches her collar. Her eyes are bright, matching her smile.

"Morning, rookie. Here's breakfast!"

Leon sits up, feeling the muscle soreness and a resistance he'd never been accustomed to. It's as if his legs had been replaced by those of a statue, cold, stone limbs as dead as his ancestors. The wave of reality rises above him, crashing down with more than enough gravity to crush his hope. He hadn't dreamed of his accident at all. The Security Force Hovertank really had flown so closely overhead that he'd felt the heat. He really had ducked under the overturned car. The stone building that had once been Tank's Armory really was destroyed in the crossfire.

His legs were crushed and mangled as a result of some rich stranger needing his own emergency rescue. He went through the hours and hours of surgery. He watched the doctors banter about his future. With no money, cybernetics are not an option. Human organ replacement, natural or synthetic, is expensive. It requires wealth, money he's never had. He has been fixed up, healed to the minimum requirements set forth by the government. He has been wheeled into St. Patrick's Orphanage. The drugs and disorientation have expired.

He is a paraplegic, with a pair of useless extremities currently buried beneath a neatly quilted blanket. His response is torn between two combating forces inside his head. One voice wants to reach to the dark-haired angel, beg her to hold him and allow him to show his vulnerability and grief at suddenly realizing what he's become. That voice, the passive one, loses out. Instead, the aggressor takes hold. Anger at the world, hatred of his physical condition and venom at having no one else to blame combines, reaching his lips in the most chaotic and violent manner he can gather.

Leon isn't even certain of the words he screams. He doesn't know the exact vocabulary he spits at the girl. By the third or fourth sentence, he is short of breath, coughing and struggling for air. He collapses backward, the victim of his own hatred. He struggles to draw oxygen back into his lungs.

With an unchanged smile, the girl approaches, reaching Leon's gaze, blurred through the tears he is unaware he's shed. She touches his cheek softly, her hand warm and soft. "It's okay, rookie. I understand."

Leon's field of vision decreases, disappearing entirely. The last thing he remembers is the warm touch on his cheek, and the feeling that hope is not entirely gone after all.

"Alright, Catwalk, let's have it. What's the sudden shocking development?"

Delambre's frozen words sliced through the solace of Cat's inviting memory. The combination of exhaustion and cheap liquor had steered him directly to his first encounter with Mi-Young, just another instance where he wished he'd behaved differently. Time was up on remorse. Now came the time for a much more direct type of interaction.

Cat didn't even open his cybernetic eyes. "What did you bring me?"

"I didn't. Sobriety should be a welcome change for you."

"You're fired."

"That would mark the third time this week you said that, Catwalk. Now, let's get to business." Delambre spoke with an edge, a clear 'tell' that his concern for his daughter overcame the more objective path of scientific reasoning.

Cat smiled. That was exactly his goal. With an exaggerated motion, he clicked the digital feed onto the screen.

The image was a still shot, pristine and perfect. The face in the screen was a light-skinned African-American woman with high cheekbones and slightly pursed lips. Her black hair framed her face with ideal symmetry, drawing out the best of her features. Her eyes would have been normal if not for the slight glow to her blood-red iris. The face was a very similar, yet obviously imperfect, portrait of Angela.

There was an audible 'clunk' as Delambre dropped the bottle in his hand. Protected by the store's budget paper sack, the bottle survived the fall and rolled in Cat's direction. With a smirk, the hitman leaned down and lifted it, removing the paper. His face widened in a sudden, overstated gratitude. "Blevins' Blend...12 years....this musta' cost you."

Delambre didn't answer. For all Cat knew, the medtech was no longer aware he was even in the room. He'd expected as much. If his newfound partner was faking, he'd know exactly how to act. Instead, the concerned father was magnifying every pixel on the screen. The hitman released the hammer on the pistol he held in his right hand under a synthetic goose-down pillow, holstering it again.

Cat stared a few extra moments before stretching and flipping backward out of the comfortable chair. His gaze returned instantly to Delambre. "I'm gonna get a glass before I explain what it is yer seein'."

The geneticist turned his gaze, meeting Catwalk's artificial eyes. The pale light from the screen made him appear older and more fragile than any other time Cat had seen him, exaggerating every wrinkle and crease in the process.

Delambre's voiced cracked slightly when he spoke. "Better make that two."

CHAPTER EIGHTEEN

The bottle was drained past the name on the label by the time Delambre gathered the strength to explain. "Have you ever witnessed a person driven past reasoning and moral comprehension? Someone driven to the point where all they comprehend is madness?"

His eyes weren't on Catwalk at all. Instead, he stared at the inhuman image burning in the monitor.

Cat chuckled into his glass, wondering if Delambre had completely forgotten his background. Before his freelance work, Cat was a detective in the DCPD, on the unit responsible for putting down any being who became so obsessed with cybernetics that it effectively burned out empathic reasoning. He had spent nearly half a decade retiring formerly human individuals or robotic creations gone wrong. He was accustomed to the exact type of threat Delambre referenced. It was his bread-and-butter before his contract expired, and he headed west.

Some might say he'd become one himself. They were wrong...so far. "Try me," he replied.

"I've had many colleagues in the field of bio-genetics and MetaHuman development in my time, Catwalk. There have been dozens, hundreds, who have attended my classes and lectures or have worked by my side in developing cybernetic enhancements. I've mentored students who displayed every level of aptitude. I've shared offices with professors willing to offer their own opinion, distant or devoted. I've resided over test subjects, prognosticators, even those outside of the education field who have felt they had greater expertise on a subject. In truth, MetaHumans remain a recently developed and somewhat undecipherable field of research. They, you, are a young science."

Delambre continued, entranced in his own words, without the need for recognition or acknowledgement. "I was younger then, just graying at my temples when my path crossed with a man who, at the time, I considered a visionary. That is not to say he saw the empowerment of mankind, the expansion of technology as the means to the greater good. Instead, he wove two very separate theologies to work for his own intent. MetaHumans exist outside of the realm of traditional human beliefs, wouldn't you agree? Men combined with machine have no place in the doctrine of our past generations?"

"Meta's are uncharted waters when it comes ta prophecy, I'll give ya that." Cat tipped his glass in agreement. Religion meant as much to him as fanaticism. In his experience, they were often one in the same.

"Suppose then that the very inhuman creations borne of our testing and experimentation became the deliverers of religious penance."

"Um...sorry, D, ya lost me." Cat slugged the rest of the Scotch, eyeing the bottle for a refill.

For the first time, Delambre leveled his gaze to the artificial eyes of the hitman. "Suppose that form you'd just escaped was designed by her maker to serve a single purpose. A single role defines her creation."

Cat blinked again. The pale light from the vid feed enhanced every crease of age and worry on Delambre's face as he stared down his partner.

"Imagine you just escaped the Angel of Death."

CHAPTER NINETEEN

Cat escaped the congestion of Downtown and headed northwest on I5 under the welcome acceptance of moonlight. Meditation was one way he fought off the chaotic and violent tendencies, which resulted from his cybersurgery. The other was to find open road. The feel of the engine beneath him and the twist of his wrist brought him a sense of peace. Instead of a microscopic introspection, riding provided a greater focus on everything around him. It was as if he could drink in every detail, in light or darkness, while every other being on the planet moved in slow motion.

When he was living on the streets as a teenager, he'd never found a place he could call home. Once he was dumped in St. Patrick's, it became his shelter and center of care for years, but it was a home, which had been forced upon him. Even the loft he occupied now was more functional than personal. If Cat knew anything he'd call home, it was here, the pure adrenaline and addictive feeling of absolute peace.

His comm sounded demanding his attention and shattering his tenuous peace.

"Catwalk."

"How's it feel to be one of the city's leading, uncredited civil servants, m'man?" Will's voice bit through the comm so strongly Cat could practically taste the black coffee and smell the formalin.

"Other than that part where I don't get paid, it ain't bad. What's the good word from the morgue?"

"Pick a number."

"You bein' all mysterious fer a reason, Will?"

"Pick a number."

"What are you askin', Will?"

"Ok, Cat, the number of missing kids cases you just solved by runnin' old pegleg into an airline hangar."

Cat questioned himself. He'd issued the inspection on Hitch's account to find one particular supplier. He wasn't thinking about the total number of interactions the pederast had in a week, or a month, or ever. He had no idea how deep or for how long Hitch had been preying upon children in Nitro City, protected under the watchful, golden gaze of his recently beheaded master.

"Shockit, Will, I dunno. Ten?" He asked.

"Eighteen and countin', cleaner."

The number caught Cat off guard. If he'd still been able to consider hope an asset he could muster at Will, that number would have surpassed his optimism. He wouldn't have imagined closing six cases. Closing eighteen brought a bittersweet image of murdered children. At least this might bring closure to their concerned parents. To hope for a higher count was to extend optimism and misery equally. Cat fell mute while he digested the situation.

Will brought him back to the present by clearing his throat loudly. "So, before you getting' all guilty or heroic, dependin' on your mood, let me drop the following on you."

"So much for my award ceremony."

"You weren't celebrating, Cat, you were killing yourself. You haven't seen a silver lining in your entire life."

"Back on topic, Will. Before I make it personal and add a few more blowholes to your skull."

Cat's slight insult succeeded in anchoring the mortician to the matter at hand. "Here's the story in a nutshell, Cat. There were 24 total transactions recorded by my network from Hitch to the same account. So far, eighteen have matched up within 24 hours of a missing child report through the NCPD. You want to wait for the results on the last six, you can, but I think you're just as willing to play the numbers as I am."

Cat nearly broiled on the newfound information. "What can you tell me on the destination accounts?"

"Account."

"What are you sayin'?"

"The first pass indicates the other six payments were all to the same account."

Cat hissed between his teeth. "Can you get me info on that account?"

"Not without a deposit."

Cat nearly choked on the sudden collar back to business-as-usual that Will implied. If the mortician and his network knew anything else, they expected payment, big payment, for the delivery of that information. He nodded to himself, upping the ante' again as he spoke.

"Confirm the last six transactions for me to that destination account. Then, block all transactions from that account to anything from Hitch's last known digits, and those from Midas. If I can cut this maniac off from getting' into ol' golden' boy's dollar bills, it might be enough ta draw him out. God knows there are enough other sources goin' after Midas' coffers."

Cat could practically hear Will smile across the comm. "Bill you the usual?"

"Yeah, the usual."

The comm went dead, and Cat allowed himself a slight smile. The person in charge of killing Midas might not have the courage to challenge him face-to-face, but he would at least send his latest and greatest MetaHuman. That would mean a chance at redemption, and one more slap in the face of his adversary. It may also mean another excursion to the brink of death, and most likely one that wouldn't pay him a dime. He was going to need to raise some funds and to do so quickly if he was going to keep the trail as hot as Will's network had made it.

Cat pulled up the positioning interface and programmed a route to the next exit from the freeway. He'd need to check his motorcycle, armor and weapons. Things were about to ramp up, exactly as he wanted.

4 June 2022

'I testify to everyone who hears the words of the prophecy of this book, if anyone adds to them, may God add to him the plagues which are written in this book.

'If anyone takes away from the words of the book of this prophecy, may God take away his part from the tree of life, and out of the holy city, which are written in this book.

'He who testifies these things says, "Yes, I come quickly." Amen! Yes, come, Lord Jesus.
'The grace of the Lord Jesus Christ be with all the saints. Amen.'

Sister Mary Cassandra turns to her class, finding the

universal response of disinterest. "Questions, class?"

No hands are raised, only eyes to the clock. "Angie, can you tell the class the fate of the false prophet?"

The blonde responds with a practice of feigned innocence. "Umm, I'm sorry, Mother, I left my notes in my room."

The nun shakes her head in disapproval. "Do you at least remember how many horsemen there were?"

"Four!"

"Yes, dear. Though I imagine you'd be hard pressed to name them."

Angie's eyes drop to her desk with the admonishing statement. Sister Cassandra moves across the orphans before speaking, "How about you, Leon?"

The dark-haired, wheelchair-bound orphan never even faces the orphanage matriarch. His eyes stare out across the rain, through the courtyard outside. "Pestilence, War, Famine, and Death, in no particular order."

His last comment gets a chuckle from his classmates. The nun manages to smile slightly. "Correct. And since the group has provided such disinterest in what may very well mean the end of all mankind, there will be an essay assignment."

The class groans as one as she turns and begins to write on the board. The children aren't interested in the potential entities that may descend from the heavens and destroy all humanity. They're interested in the weather outside, and when a hopeful set of parents might come for them. Instead, they get a writing assignment.

Leon is no different. His thoughts are far away from the classroom, back to the computer. He's long since killed any hopes of being adopted. He simply wants to load up the motorcycle simulator again and fall in love with the feeling of riding fast and hard on the open road.

The chime of the comm was alien and unfamiliar, a piercing siren's scream that flashed a white light inside of his eyes to nearly drive Cat off of the road. He gripped the handlebars tighter than he'd intended, leaning in counterposition to the sudden turn in the freeway. With the motorcycle nearly parallel to the asphalt, he managed to regain control, even as sparks from the pegs, and the exterior of his armored kneecap, erupted behind him.

Within seconds he was upright. It took several more for him to exhale.

By the time he realized he was holding his breath, Cat had slowed from his pace of 180 kmph to under 80. After another few rings, and a number of profanities, Cat answered the comm.

"Catwalk."

"We have a situation." Delambre's voice was curt.

"You're late for your cycle?"

The geneticist brushed aside Cat's sarcasm with practiced efficiency. "There is a MetaHuman on the loose, melting tourists and local security forces from the inside out."

"Where?" He asked.

"Slightly south of San Fernando. I shall forward coordinates."

The news was a curse, save for the location. San Fernando was north of Downtown, between Cat and the congestion of the city. He might even beat the media to the scene. "How long till CS is engaged?"

"Not long. I'm guessing with their collective hard-on following the last incident, you've got under ten minutes."

The sparks erupted once again as Cat slammed the H-S into a power slide, changing direction. He opened the throttle, pressed his chest against the tank and exhaled. When he found a familiar stretch of straightaway, he switched on the Nitrous to increase his pace. Every second meant the possibility of being the first on the scene. That meant exposure to the media, and more importantly, answers. If this incident was related at all to the oversized Meta he'd seen on the slab at Will's morgue, he needed every millisecond of advantage.

Catwalk raced to the heart of danger, shrugging off his own safety in the name of fortune and closure.

"I trust that brief static was an indication you're on your way, then?"

"Don't get yer hopes up, D, I didn't scrape my entire leg off changin' directions."

"From what I've seen from the pirated feeds, I'd worry more about the human portions of your anatomy than the technological additions."

"You holdin' out, Delambre?"

"I told you what I know, Catwalk. From the feeds, and they're not the best I've seen, this MH appears to be fond of barbecuing civilians while they're still alive. It's rather reminiscent of tossing a live lobster into a pot of boiling water."

"Whoa, you've seen lobsters? You *are* old."

"With age comes wisdom. Try to learn enough to keep your heart from erupting out of your chest. My expertise is in cybernetic organ adaptation, not organic organ replacement."

Cat couldn't help but grin under his helmet. "Alright, so how many pieces can I be in for you to slap me back together?"

"Keep your vital organs intact, and I should be able to handle the rest." Delambre paused a moment then added smugly, "though, if this particular Meta has a setting for neutering sociopath hit men with overactive sex drives, I may switch affiliations."

Cat laughed loudly at the older man's tongue-in-cheek warning regarding his daughter. "Really, D, I'm shocked. I'm not a sociopath. I've got people skills."

"Stay alive long enough to pay me, Catwalk. I'm certain I'll see your efforts on the news soon enough."

"Yeah, 'don't touch that dial'."

The comm went silent. Cat was tightrope walking between a scientific genius and a protective father. When he got back, he'd have to talk to Delambre about giving his daughter a professional moniker. Using her real name was a grave mistake, the kind that usually resulted in an actual grave.

Cat slid the Honda-Suzuki around other vehicles, drifting by some, drafting by others. He counted the exits and the km markers, while savoring the adrenaline of the ride. The comm rang, and he debated answering it. Figuring Delambre had an update, he tapped the communication channel to life. "What's the latest on our bad guy, doc?"

"Uh...I..I...is this Catwalk?"

The voice on the other end was less technical and far less masculine than his business partner. Cat tried to reposition himself in the conversation without changing his position on the bike. "Yeah, yeah, this is me. Catwalk. Who's this?"

"It's...It's Delilah. Is this a bad time?"

"No, no," Cat replied before he considered the correct response, "We're good. I mean, I'm good. I didn't expect you to call."

"You told me to call."

"Yeah, right, yes, I did. How can I assist you?" Cat voice hitched with an unexpected key change as he forced the bike between two delivery trucks.

"Are you sure this is a good time?" She asked.

"Hell, yeah. Never better."

Delilah paused for a few seconds. Cat wondered if he hadn't convinced her through his banter that he was getting a lap dance, tied up in an S&M club, or torturing some innocent soul in a crawl space. "I'd like to see you, Mr. Catwalk, about, well, about a few things. Can I ask you to meet with me tomorrow night?"

Cat considered pinching himself, but doing so would result in wrecking his trusted, expensive motorcycle. "You can ask, an' I'll be there. Shoot me the time an' place, an' I'll be there ta answer anything you wanna ask."

"Anything?"

"Anything," Cat replied, feeling a grin cross the comm.

"Hmm, how intriguing. I look forward to our next meeting. Au revoir, Catwalk."

Cat never returned the farewell wishes. He darted to the emergency lane and back instead, narrowly missing an oversized family van and a construction barrel. He centered once he found the fast lane and engaged the Nitrous again. Delilah had called him, while he'd been fidgeting with pimps, gangers and MetaHuman threats. At least now he had a real focus on surviving the fight with the mysterious enemy Delambre had described. Cat tried to force logic into his encounters and eventually shrugged it off. First things first.

The cleaner concentrated on his next threat. Hell, heaven, and even the arms of a beautiful redhead had to wait. This headline stealing thing had to be returned to its maker before he would gain a shot at rest, and maybe a payday.

He caught a glimpse of the scene mere moments after he'd split the route between San Fernando and Mission Hills. After the first visual, he needed no further clarification. Smoke obscured the stars, moon and neon of the night sky. When the acrid smell of burning flesh reached his filters, it was more than he needed to verify the situation. Delambre was right, as usual. Someone, human or otherwise, was burning people alive.

There was notoriety and, more importantly, information at stake if Cat could bring in the perpetrator before some Corporate Security force did the same, backed by a staff of professional public relations. In the grand scheme, he was a one-man show trying to outpace a well-organized and overly paid task force of goons intent on the same goal.

San Fernando hadn't embraced architectural development with the hunger of Nitro City. Instead, the citizens unleashed a huge backlash at the thought of destroying historical buildings to advance industry and high tech. The city, which was home to the original San Fernando Mission, as well as Los Encinos Rancho, the Andre Picos Adobe and Bolton Hall, had far more indispensable history to defend than its celebrity-obsessed sister city.

Cat ripped the bike sideways in a skid, viewing the scene up close for the first time. An armored shell, which had so recently included a living human being struck the asphalt before him, broiling from the inside even before contact. The dead man bounced once before finding his final resting place. The corpse's head dropped to the side, and Cat stole a glimpse at its face. The skin was bubbling, melting into a puddle of pavement, revealing the bones and teeth. The eyes had sunken inward, or exploded, leaving only vacant gaps. What had once been the man's face was now flowing from his skeleton on to the dirty asphalt. Cat exhaled through his teeth. Corporate Security had beaten him to the scene, a fact verified by the growing body count on the street.

As the second uniformed security agent dropped at his feet, Cat poured over Delambre's warning in his head one more time. It was time to take advantage of any and all means, which would keep him at a distance, while hoping to get close enough to uncover the missing key that would unlock the next stage of the investigation. From where he stood, the chaos of smoke, shrapnel and fast-moving security forces obscured his view. Safety be damned, he was going to have to get closer.

Cat cursed under his breath. The last thing he wanted to do was get near the MH that was cooking its enemies from the inside out. The first insult he directed mentally was towards Delambre and his mysterious daughter. They would certainly play a part in this entire endeavor until its resolution. The second insult was directed inward for not chasing down Delilah for some sweat and excitement. If he was lucky, he'd have the chance to follow up on that missed opportunity. The third, and most violent, was at whoever had designed the MetaHumans, the original behemoth whose corpse he'd touched in the morgue, the winged Angel of Death, and the one he was about to face.

Cat had little reason to estimate the three Metas had come from multiple sources. Delambre's scotch-soaked confession tied it all together. There was one mind driving this entire end-of-the-world strategy. When the time came, he'd have to serve as the roadblock between that self-serving lunatic and success. Given that most would classify him as a madman, what chance of success did he really have?

Catwalk ditched the high-powered motorcycle, snapping his Stinger baton to its full extension. The time had come for face-to-face confrontation. A growl rose inside even before his form left the comfort of the motorcycle.

It was time for combat. With a lick of his lips, Cat focused his attention on the MetaHuman in his sights. Time to prove his value.

Time to Play.

CHAPTER TWENTY

Cat tossed a cylinder from his bandolier and watched it rattle on the cracked pavement near the strange Meta. Within seconds, a pulsating flash ripped skyward all around the combat scene. The electro-magnetic pulse released an energy pattern designed to cripple cyberware and render artificial organs useless. If it had any effect on the MetaHuman, it went completely unnoticed. As the targeted MH cast aside the remains of a recently murdered soldier, Cat got a clear view of it. The image sent warning flares burning brightly in his mind.

The MetaHuman, if it was human at all, bore a slight and acrobatic frame, just under two meters tall. It moved with an inhuman agility suggesting that its core muscles were more fluid than structural. Cat watched in fascination as its knees bent forward or backward, allowing it to counterbalance and fend off assaults from multiple directions. Security forces advanced and it swiveled and turned, fending off hand-to-hand and close-range attacks.

Combat MetaHumans generally fell into two classes. Cat's cybernetics put him in the boss killer class – plenty of skills, designed for concentration on a single target. Boss killers ranged from physically invulnerable to untouchable. One on one, they were nearly unstoppable. Against a swarm, they displayed design flaws and eventually met defeat.

That led to the design of the second class – crowd control. That class was built to level armies. The military had toyed with the idea first. MetaHuman teams were often dropped into hostile zones to suppress uprisings, enemy governments, protests that had gotten out of hand. They could be tanks, destructors, or…or whatever the hell this MetaHuman was.

Cat tried to figure it all out, but adrenaline surged up

his spine, crept over his shoulders and ignited his extremities. This thing escaped normal programming. Humans regularly turned to chips for quick learning. That was fine when the combat was against another human. This insectoid MetaHuman did anything but what was expected. The chip-driven actions of security personnel were useless. It read the actions of its attackers as pre-determined conclusions. The MetaHuman waited with killing strikes before the security forces ever began their assaults.

Cat studied the MetaHuman, uploading his feed to the bank of computers in the loft. It wore a humanoid exoskeleton. The being's arms were abnormally long and had it been standing upright, they may have reached below its knees. Both hands sported elongated claws instead of fingers, long needles as sharp as a fencer's foil.

The MH's entire frame was covered in a grey reminiscent of storybook battleships or the smog-covered sky. When Cat caught a full view of its face, he dropped out of its sight. Its eyes were round like that of a fly, maximizing its ability to see attackers before they could strike. It had only a single line to represent its mouth. That line curved downward where its lips would have been, giving it a permanent grimace.

Whoever built this thing did so to portray a being enveloped in, or evolved from, pure hatred. Cat shook his head, snapping a shot through his cyber-optics. "There's yer sociopath, Delambre."

A would-be CS vanguard landed to the right of the MetaHuman, taking slightly more than a second to gain his equilibrium and raise his automatic rifle. The MH needed just under a second to adjust to its new attacker. Its weight shifted unnaturally on its legs, rotating the knees on ball joints. As it reached forward, it reversed the barrel of the rifle 180 degrees. Before the soldier realized what had happened, he pulled the trigger, turning his own skull into a violent spray of blood and grey matter.

Cat watched and took note of variables he hadn't factored in. For instance, how would you 'kneecap' a being whose knees rotated 360 degrees, or how would you blind someone whose eyes seemed hard-coded into their skull? A well-armed group of soldiers failed to overtake the single, sentient, inhuman being. EMP had proven ineffective. Dismemberment and blinding would be useless. The cleaner took a deep breath, and engaged the one plan, which had never failed him.

Let it ride and go on instinct.

Catwalk leapt skyward as he exhaled, mentally considering himself a dead man before his feet kissed the pavement. Just as he made contact, he swung the Stinger in an arc behind him, rising to the balls of his feet. The reinforced baton made contact but not with his target. Instead, the Meta raised the most recent corpse of the overachieving Corporate Security guard as a means of defense.

Cat expected as much. He launched into a back flip prescribed by his own logic rather than reaction. His theory had proven correct as the MH swung an overgrown arm, filling the space he had just occupied. Cat landed in a crouch. He squeezed the trigger, firing round after round at the MH from close range.

Nothing seemed to affect its exoskeleton as it evaded by cowering into its own shell. It crossed its arms over its face and collapsed. The posture allowed its armor to cover any exposed areas. Cat retreated slightly as the rounds he emptied at the Meta ricocheted around him. He stopped firing, finding sanctuary behind an overturned car. A new harmony of screams and cries confirmed that his bullets had found alternate targets.

The acrobatic form returned to its feet just as Cat landed on his. Their gazes met, barely-human eye to inhuman eye, the intent of mutual hatred coloring their brief interaction. Cat was accustomed to fighting the cybernetic-enhanced population after four years with DC's MetaHuman Engagement Force. This thing was far less human and far more demonic than anything he'd encountered during that career.

A normal MH would react to EMP. Cat had already tested that idea with less than stellar results. He opted instead for a more direct approach. He flipped a grenade into the air. The MH tilted its head, following the grenade as a potential threat. Cat batted it with his baton, something he'd learned from his childhood years playing stickball. The grenade erupted in smoke just as it reached the MetaHuman's face.

Bullets had drawn no reaction. EMP attacks had provided even less. Every logic in the world stated that a direct confrontation would mean instant suicide. So, Cat leapt forward, dove to a shoulder and rolled to his feet to engage the MH toe-to-toe. It was a suicidal move.

It felt right to Cat, so it was the path he chose. If the old geneticist was right, their enemy was a scientist, slave to the numbers of scientific method, theories and proofs. What better method then to go with gut instinct and shatter every analysis in the system. He pictured Delambre and Angela screaming protests. He tuned them out the same way he tuned out every other ambient sound other than his own breathing.

Inhale. He batted aside the claws of the lithe and lethal MetaHuman. Sparks flew in every direction, flashing in the corners of his optic filters.

Exhale. He struck the skull of the MH. His attack was minimized by its inhuman ability to shift its center of balance and defensive posture.

Inhale. He created distance through acrobatics while the enemy struck at his last location.

Exhale. Catwalk drove his cybernetic limbs with force as a countermeasure to the MH attack.

Inhale. The MH remained functional despite the damage to its exoskeleton. The damage it received was not entered in any controls. The programming had not accounted for this level of resistance. The MetaHuman calculated the most reasonable response. In accordance with its programming, it doubled its efforts, specifically targeting the heart of its attacker.

Exhale. Cat countered the leverage of the Meta overextending to create a newfound vulnerability. While airborne, the hitman changed his angle, driving the baton point-first into the MH's back. With its claws outstretched to catch him cowering, Cat instead had flipped above the MetaHuman. The elongated form revealed ports just below each of its lowest ribs.

An opening.

Catwalk saw exactly what he needed to switch his strategy. He leapt backwards, swinging on the extended pole of a streetlight and landing on an abandoned car. The insectoid eyes of the MH tracked him the entire way. He had almost no time at all when he felt the shift in wind behind him.

Without a thought, Cat dropped flat against the roof of the car as the heavy armored vehicle flew in low and tight above him. Corporate Security had called in massive reinforcements, nearly beheading him in the process. Explosions and shells erupted around his target, which swiftly evaded and moved to a covered position.

"Catwalk, I'm scanning for vulnerabilities," came the surprising voice of Delambre's daughter.

Cat wasn't sure what tactical advantage a forensic scientist could offer, but he didn't want to completely crush her optimism. "Yeah, thanks…"

Delambre's voice interrupted any further awkwardness Cat would stumble over. "You'll want its eyes."

"Why? Did you see something vulnerable there?"

"No, cleaner. However, if you're able to feed its image to us, then it's most likely doing the same to whoever made it."

Cat cursed Delambre for the three hundredth time in recent memory. The geneticist was right, and every time he was meant that Cat's chances at survival and success took a nasty hit. "Thanks, Doc."

"How about a few words for the camera?"

Cat swung his attention around. The voice was neither Delambre's nor his daughter's. Before him, in flex armor with a complex video feed helmet stood 'Scoop' McEwan, one of the most famous broadcasters in Nitro City. While most news teams involved an interviewer and a camera jockey, Scoop always took things solo.

Cat shook off his awe at being in the lens of the most-famous newsfeed in Nitro for a moment. Delambre was right. Even if he found a way to beat the MH, which was not a given, its boss would know who he was. Still, the chance to make headlines tickled his ego. Scoop's question was like a beautiful woman crossing and uncrossing her legs to give him a peek.

"Just keep shootin', Scoop. Yer about ta see a real fireworks display."

CHAPTER TWENTY-ONE

Craters filled the sidewalk and storefront where Cat last tangled with the Meta. A new smattering of armored corpses contributed to the scene. Trying not to appear distracted, he scanned for his enemy. Just before he could react, he caught something flying in his direction. He managed to turn the slightest amount, and the projectile slammed into Cat's shoulder and collarbone instead of his head. He rolled with the impact. The momentum took him to the ground. Using his cybernetics, he tumbled backwards and quickly found his feet.

The projectile was the helmet from one of the Corporate Security forces. From the stinging at the base of his neck, Cat could judge the weight. A slight glance down confirmed that the helmet still included the head of its host. Blood trickled from the base of the decapitated cop. Cat raised his glance to see the insectoid attacker launching itself in his direction. He dropped and countered with a Judo shoulder toss. The Meta's momentum carried it forward. The insectoid crashed through the barred window of a liquor store, shattering the glass and bending the gate.

Hatred ignited his senses. He dove at the disoriented being, trying to find junctures in the being's exoskeleton. The Stinger baton clanged time and time again off of its armor plating. The Meta began a series of moves to increase distance, but Cat stayed close. Fury flowed over him. Some piece of logic told him to stay close and tight. That reasoning fed the Machine. Cat pounded with blunt force, blow after blow. The assault kept the strange MetaHuman from using its claws with any velocity. Several times, he felt the tearing of his own uniform and skin as it nearly achieved its desired grasp.

Bottles of cheap booze shattered and colored the walls and floor. Steel racks bent beyond repair or toppled over as the two enemies battled. The duo exchanged blows of metal on metal. They concentrated on one another with the heat of lovers. Cat's yellow eyes reflected a thousand times in the insectoid's face. He growled. The low vibration filled his body, unnatural, mechanical.

Before either could react, the back wall of the shop exploded, showering them with debris. Cat slammed against a broken shelf of liquors. The insectoid was tossed across the shop, out of view. The Corps had fired in explosives. The building erupted in flame, and depending on the alcohol, which was spilled, it might just burn forever.

Disoriented, Cat managed to get to one knee. He concentrated on his breathing until he could think clearly. The battle had reached the point that the Corps didn't care about his life and were willing to detonate entire buildings to rid themselves of the troublesome MH. The next level of escalation involved leveling the entire block. Things were getting complicated fast. He needed to finish this thing before Corporate Security or the NCPD wrote off the buildings, and those inside, as collateral damage.

As his thoughts focused on his primary target, he felt it. The inhuman creature had finally managed to latch its claws into his left leg. The pain was intense and immediate. Cat gasped. His chest burned. He was drowning in fire. Liquid heat surged through his bloodstream, setting his body aflame, and beginning its journey to overtake his entire system.

He looked down, still trying to breathe. One broken insectoid eye stared up at him from beneath a few hundred kilograms of debris. Maybe it was going to die, but it was intent on taking him with it.

Cat concentrated. His solitary goal to keep his eyes from rolling into his skull. Its grip had his left foot planted in place. Perfect. Catwalk fired his right foot forward, then swung it backwards with every ounce of power he could muster, catching the Meta just below its jaw line. Even through the din of burning flame and distant screaming, he heard the snap of its neck.

He dropped to the floor, lying in the sewage of broken liquor bottles and slowly trickling booze as the MH released its grip slightly. The being's single working eye seemed to stare at him. Apparently, the severed vertebrae hadn't killed it after all. Suffocation would have to do the rest. Even with its lightened grip, Cat struggled to fight off the spread of heat within him. He wanted to think of the breath, to center, but something in the dying MH refused to allow him.

He had no choice but to outlast the inhuman. One of them was going to die from lack of oxygen. Bile filled his throat, and his eyelids felt like sandbags as he struggled to stay conscious. The smell of mingling alcohol was bitter, and it dried in his nose and mouth.

Cat rose to one knee again, reaching into his belt with agonizing effort. He drew forth a laser scalpel stolen from one of Will's tests so many months ago. Nearly falling forward, he reached down, concentrating on the exposed wrist joint of the MH. He blinked away stars and sweat from his vision. Unsteady and shaking, he severed the right hand of the MetaHuman at the wrist. Blood pushed outward from the artery of the dying form and mingled with the alcohol soaking the floor tiles.

The pain began to subside. The liquid heat running through his body began to cool, but lava coursed through his veins. He coughed and choked out the burning in his lungs. He tore the insectoid being's hand from around his leg, staring at it for just over a second before stuffing it into a pouch on his bandolier. If his theory was correct, the additional few seconds would be worth the effort. The Corps was closing in. He choked at the rush of oxygen in his lungs. Swatting at demons and smoke nightmares, Cat rushed to the back of the store.

30 seconds.

He couldn't even steal a glance to determine if his hunch was a pay off. He needed an escape. He struck the emergency exit with the efficiency of a drunken sailor, collapsing through the doorway. His helmet bounced off the pavement. He felt the impact of the alleyway, the splash of the puddle on his exposed skin.

20 seconds.

Cat struggled to his feet. Fire burned in his lungs. It spread across his back, claws of a phoenix. He wanted to drop to the cool moisture of the street. He wanted the sanctuary of death.

10 seconds.

A light struck him, something from a humanoid form, its lights burning into his skull.

5 seconds.

It was humanoid after all. It was a face he'd seen before but couldn't quite place.

4…

3…

2…

Was that a wink?

1…

CHAPTER TWENTY-TWO

13 July 2022

The taste doesn't strike him as much as the impact. Dirt collides with Leon's face with the force of a brick wall. He shakes his head to clear his airway as it strikes again. His eyes open wide in dismay at the force. He's being buried alive. He screams, inviting dirt, mud, and water into his mouth and throat. He coughs, praying anyone can hear him before they shovel him under. Oblivion awaits, and his screams of protest go unheard.

"Oh calm down, Leon, you're not dying."

Bobby's voice bares its eternal self-importance. The strongest and most charismatic of the orphans has always been accepted as superior, so why would he hide that in his tone? His grip is firm on Leon's shoulder as he lifts the paraplegic upward.

Dirt and muck escape Leon's throat as he coughs at the rush of fresh air. He realizes the dirt wasn't being thrown on him from above. Instead, he rushed into it face-first, another drop of the rusty Kawasaki motorcycle. He shakes off Bobby's grip, leaning on a shelled-out microwave in the midst of the junkyard.

"C'mon, kiddo, care to try it again?"

Another attempt is all Leon wants. He's been dreaming of riding a motorcycle every day of his stay in St. Patrick's. He knows the in's and out's of every simulator program the aged computers can support. The Kawasaki isn't a program, though. It's mechanical, responding with a sensitivity the programs can't replicate. The potholes and mud puddles of the junkyard are unlike the smooth curves of the simulators.

Leon isn't willing to give up any time soon. He spits out more of the mud, though plenty still sticks to his taste buds, caked in his gums. "I can do this."

Bobby nods, "I know, Leon. That's why I worked on

this thing so long. Heck, I even modified the shifter for your left thumb instead of your foot. That way you get to love this thing beyond the foreplay of one gear. C'mon, you can make this happen."

Disgruntled, Leon looks past Bobby to the pair of girls whispering to one another atop the wreckage of an old Freightliner rig. "Then shut her up." The blonde hasn't stopped poking fun at his misfortune, despite the lack of reaction from the Asian girl next to her.

"Angie's gonna have her fun any chance she gets, Leon. If you want to shut her up, ride rings around her."

Bobby's confidence is infectious. Leon manages a muddy grin, presses the starter with his thumb and twists his right wrist. This time, he's going to keep the Kawasaki upright until none of them can laugh at him anymore. He's meant to move again, and fast. He's not an invalid. He still has a chance to leave the wheelchair behind.

The undersized orphan breaks his own record, keeping the bike up nearly six minutes and through four gears before the rain makes Bobby call him back in. If the orphans don't get back, there will be hell to pay. The burly blonde jock gives Leon a rough pat on the shoulder as he sits him back in the wheelchair. For a while, the love of speed and adrenaline is enough to keep the paraplegic content and hopeful.

Leon smiles at his accomplishment. He's not meant to remain in one position his whole life. He's meant to move.

CHAPTER TWENTY-THREE

Light.

Sound.

Forms are moving around him. He is aware.

As he pierces the first layers of consciousness, Leon Caliber, Catwalk, the orphan, the hitman, recognizes that there is a world around him. He simply isn't a part of it. He is what he once was.

Imprisoned.

Alone.

He tries to raise a hand in protest of his sore muscles and dry throat. His body offers no response. He was paralyzed. He is paralyzed. The child and the man blur together. His muscles won't respond. He is a soul trapped in a corpse. The ending he has always expected has arrived. He is left as a witness, not a participant.

He should panic. He should care. He should be concerned, desperate. He isn't. He closes his eyes, shutting off the outside world. Numb to his own end, he returns to the dream.

Auburn hair traces the outline of his face as he pulls her closer. Her soft skin engulfs him once again, the full lips of his lover meet his own. He is content in his own sacrifice.

For once, the darkness isn't cold…it is comfort.

He is Home.

CHAPTER TWENTY-FOUR

"Any time you'd like to join us, cleaner, you are welcome to."

Delambre's tone was the sterile and sharp intrusion of rubbing alcohol in a fresh wound. It was the piercing reality that instantly dissolved atrophied thought processes and muscle movements. It was as unwelcome as it was necessary.

Cat pried one eye open, his optics instantly adjusting to the familiar lights of the lab. A silhouette perched above him. When he gained clarity, he was surprised to recognize the face of not Delambre, but rather, his daughter. "Well, hello Nurse."

Delambre's voice slapped him from just out of his visual range. "Quite the tango you decided to engage in, cleaner. I'd ask what on Earth made you decide on a frontal attack, but you've always had a preference for full frontal, haven't you?"

Cat tried to laugh. He coughed instead. His body violently aching from every pore as a result. The muscles of his back constricted and breathing became a concentrated labor. When he regained his breath and realized how dry his throat was, he barely voiced his reply.

"Shock, that was funny..." There was probably more moisture in his eyes than in his throat as a response to the joke. "I guess I ain't dead after all, huh?"

Angela made a derisive sound and walked away as Delambre stood and entered Cat's field of vision. "No, you're quite alive, thanks to a marathon of attention and deep well of knowledge from your MetaHuman biological experts."

"An expensive marathon?"

"Quite."

Cat could still make out Angela's silhouette in the

distance. He took another risk without calculating the responses first. "So, I guess I make the check out to Dr. and Evil Angel?"

Angela stopped in her footsteps. Delambre shook his head, brushing off the hitman's comment. "You're in no position to slap labels on anyone, Catwalk."

"No chit, Doc, but as long as we're chattin', I'm havin' a real hard time believin' you ain't tied to whoever's behind all a' this. I seen way too many coincidences, unless you wanna start a three-way conversation with you, me, and little Evil over there."

A glance was exchanged between father and daughter before Delambre broke the silence. "I'll handle our mutual partner, Angela. Go get cleaned up. It was a lengthy procedure. You did very well."

Angela's brown eyes moved from her father to the man on the table. She studied them both, not speaking a word. Cat felt the gravity behind her stare. She was more than he had bargained for. He hired her father, yet there was so much they provided together. He couldn't belittle her value, or the danger her presence brought to his partner, and his business.

"Angela, please," Delambre repeated. His daughter turned on a heel, leaving them to their discussion. Her father's gaze lingered on the closed door long after she was gone. "That was a brash and dangerous move, cleaner."

"She needs ta know, an' she needs a new handle. I was tyin' ta take care a' both."

Delambre lost his cool for the first time Cat could recall. The geneticist grabbed his neck and leaned forward. "If anything happens to her, so help you, Leon Caliber, I'll hunt you until the stars burn out."

Cat nodded with a smirk. "Good. Let go, Doc. I'm not tryin' ta hurt yer kid, an' I ain't tryin' ta have my way with her. She's bright, probably brighter than either of us. I'm tryin' ta teach her what else is out there. If she's here in my world, she needs ta learn exactly comes with the job." He tiled his head slightly. "Book smart may get you a scholarship, but Downtown, it'll just get you killed."

Several moments passed before the geneticist released his client. With an admonished look, he softly said, "Thank you."

"Yer welcome. Now, get me upright an' tell me what we learned from that thing that almost fried me. We got plenty of work ta do before the next one comes our way."

"Next one?"

"Yeah, I'm gonna guess the big boy I saw at Will's was strike one, the winged Angel was the second, and this thing, well, this has gotta be the hat trick. You, me and Eva got a lotta work to do."

"Eva?"

"Yer kid, Doc. Till I know otherwise, I'm guessin' you two are in as deep as whoever's behind this chit. I'm also gonna take a stab that she's done more a' the armor an' equipment work while you've handled the surgical stuff. So I got the Doc who keeps my universe in line, and his Evil Angel. If you ain't gonna give her a name ta protect her, I am. Eva...Eva Angel. Get used to it."

Delambre remained silent for almost a full minute. When he spoke, he muttered only a word.

"Pestilence."

Cat looked at him, too tired to be patient. The fanatic was up to his old tricks, and he'd just sent a horseman to do away with his greatest competition. Cat turned his gaze toward the geneticist with a sudden renewed interest in scripture. Gritting through the pain of his muscles and the tension of the IV's, he sat upright.

"Pestilence, huh? Let's have a little bible study, Doc."

CHAPTER TWENTY-FIVE

Cat was no scholar in religion. He'd gone through his share of classes in the orphanage but asking him to recite scripture was like asking a cadaver to do the Charleston. He had as strong a chance of reciting a monologue from one of the mandatory literature classes or the so-called Bill of Rights.

Delambre's aptitude for religious reference was far deeper, as he demonstrated. 'And I saw, and behold a white horse: and he that sat on him had a bow; and a crown was given unto him: and he went forth conquering, and to conquer.

'And when he had opened the second seal, I heard the second beast say, come and see.

'And there went out another horse that was red: and power was given to him that sat thereon to take peace from the earth, and that they should kill one another: and there was given unto him a great sword.'

"Technically, of course, Pestilence rises first, though that wasn't the case with our encounters."

"So, the original MH, yer tellin' me that was...War?"

"Yes, and no," Delambre said as he shook his head. "I actually think that was a prototype. I'm not certain it was ever meant to be discovered. Our enemy is chaotic and reckless enough that his first attempt may have prematurely held its audition."

Cat nodded. "Yeah, I remember havin' a ringside seat. That big monkey almost stepped on me." He took a drink and continued. "Corporate Security gettin' rid of the big beast might have ended the story before anyone realized there was more to it. You think this was a good thing for our lunatic scalpel jockey?"

"The MetaHuman's premature death may have instilled a heightened sense of caution in our enemy, though I doubt it, based on his continued behavior. Shutting down

110

his creation was a strategically sound move. Bankrupting his accounts was the logical follow up action."

Cat turned a cold gaze toward the geneticist. "How'd you find out about that?"

"I have access into his account as deep as any hacker you could hire."

The cleaner was off the sofa, his pistol raised. He face heated, and his temper soared. "You wanna explain that last statement, or do I hire yer little girl ta find me a cleanin' service that can get your brains off my walls?"

"I thought you'd respond in such a manner." Delambre's hands were raised in a traditional display of non-violence. "As I mentioned, Catwalk, this alleged religious fanatic and I go back a long way. The image you captured earlier was no coincidence. He didn't craft his Angel of Death out of some distant memory. He did so as homage."

Cat let the barrel of the 11mm drop. "What're you sayin', doc?"

"Our enemy believed he was honoring my daughter by placing her image on the harbinger of death. He knows me. He knows Angela. He even funded my research long before he stole the majority of my studies."

Cat cursed under his breath, reaching back and draining the rest of his glass before facing Delambre again. "So, ta put it in simple terms, you designed the last few things that tried to kill me?"

"In short, yes."

Cat holstered the pistol. He stepped away from Delambre, who breathed a silent sigh of relief. The cleaner looked around the room twice before shaking his head and returning his focus to the geneticist he recently hired.

"Remind me to fire you again tomorrow, Delambre. For now, I need ta know who you think the next religious icon is gonna be. I'm flexible. If I gotta face a six-story Buddha, or a ten-meter Cthulhu, I'm alright with that. I just wanna know how to prepare."

The medtech stared at him, a few moments longer than he had intended. When Catwalk returned his gaze, he couldn't help but ask. "Why didn't you kill me?"

"Cause yer not party ta this, Delambre, and neither is Eva. You got yerself in some deep chit, which is why you came ta me. I get it. You're a helluva team. You understand genetics, what makes people tick and how ta alter that. She's got you whipped when it comes ta cybernetics and operational applications. Together, you're a one-two punch most Universities can't match. I get that. I shockin' get it."

Cat turned his gaze away for a minute. He leveled his gaze at Delambre and nodded, confirming something in his own mind. "You targeted me. You risked yer ass ta find me. You approached me seekin' a partnership, but that wasn't it. That was never it. You didn't come ta me for a job. You came ta me for protection."

Delambre dropped his eyes to the floor. "You were, and are, our best hope for survival."

"Good. So let's start talkin' about the next MH, an' how I'm gonna retire it without losin' any a' my own limbs. I got a date tomorrow, an' no Apocalyptic mofo is gonna keep me from makin' it."

Delambre's sudden confession left a sour taste in Cat's mouth. He hadn't hired the geneticist just to add another victim in need of a savior. He'd thought that Delambre was every bit as sharp as he'd interviewed. After all, the medic's credentials were flawless. Maybe that would still apply if the homicidal maniac crafting MetaHumans wasn't tied so closely to the geneticist. For a few minutes, Cat had considered putting a slug into Delambre and tying up loose ends. The mad scientist would have one less reason to chase him down.

Two other big obstacles impacted that theory. First, his enemy knew that Cat was responsible for crippling his means of payment, as well as murdering one of his prized creations. Second, even with Delambre in the ground, the mysterious scientist would still come after Angel, Eva. As he thought of her, Cat made himself pause.

Maybe investing in Delambre hadn't been such a bad move. The old man was above average, but Eva had shown her skills as one hell of an asset. For everything her father knew of his internal biology, she'd shown equal aptitude for armament, armor, and new ways to integrate his cybernetics. Writing off Delambre would mean writing them both off. That changed things. She added too much value to the equation. He'd continue with the two of them as his colleagues, even if that meant putting his neck on the line a little more than usual. Cat chided himself. It came down to a woman.

Didn't it always?

From his closest bets, Delambre seemed willing to believe that the third horseman, Famine, would be near completion. The elder bookworm seemed positive that the design would be flawed as a result of the creator's limited budget and inherent vulnerabilities in the original design he felt his counterpart had stolen. There was a larger than average chance he was correct. After all, War had shown up out of order due to its creator's lack of control.

It was best to treat their enemy with a loose leash, since there was no way of telling how erratic his behavior, or his creations' designs, had become. The twisted image of the cross, complete with skulls and fire, confirmed Delambre's original theory. The severed right hand of the thing called Pestilence matched what Cat had seen in Will's morgue. There wasn't much left to circumstance.

For now, Cat shuffled all of those thoughts into a folder marked 'secondary chit'. Delilah had called him back, and the H-S sped along the highway to their meeting point. Given that the last time he'd seen the model, she was in shock. He was amazed she would ever contact him. The thought of seeing her again was an instant injection of adrenaline, and he pushed the motorcycle to redline several times on the way. Something about this woman invoked a feeling of pure desire whenever she was near.

He leaned forward, his chest on the tank. A twist of the wrist and the armored motorcycle channeled his desire for Delilah into an easily read kmph gauge.

CHAPTER TWENTY-SIX

He'd programmed in the directions, but with his recent bout for survival and shift in trust with his technical team, Cat couldn't remember the name of the joint. Either way, what was important was getting there and drinking in the sight of the captivating redhead once again.

A blip in his heads-up display indicated he'd arrived at the coordinates. Cat looked up to see a large neon sign promising multiple orgasms by state-of-the-art designed cybernetic humans. 'Better than the real thing', it callously declared. He scowled under his helmet when his comm rang. Undoubtedly, it was Delilah, and she was savoring the small victory of tricking him into hitting the wrong location. Whether she meant to really meet him remained to be seen.

He clicked the line to life. "This is Catwalk, comin' to ya live outside of the Healin' Hands Massage Therapy Center. I'm hopin' this is a joke an' yer not callin' me a walkin' prick."

Her laughter was low and throaty. "I am not inclined to insult those who save my ass. Just thought you might like a challenge."

He was more relieved than he wanted to admit. The sanctuary of the helmet was welcome since he was pretty sure he was blushing. "Any time, Red. So...if yer callin' now, then you must be close enough ta get a kick outta this. Wanna tell me where ta park it?"

"Oh, let me think." The delay made him clench his teeth. "It's called the Java Joint. Corner place, looks like it has one door. Dim lighting. Great coffee and privacy. Remember my directions?"

Cat rolled his eyes, knowing she couldn't see. "I can see it from here. I'll be there in...I dunno, two hours?"

"Two hours," mock disappointment resonated in her voice, "I have two coffees waiting."

114

"Well, I gotta give myself time ta recover from the 'better than tha real thing' multiples that this place promises. I figured you were sendin' me here so I didn't show up ta meet you a ragin' bag of hormones."

"I wouldn't want to do anything to aggravate that!"

"Alright, since the coffee's hot, and the hostess too, I'll head yer way now. Just remember, you were warned bout dealin' with a revved-up guest at yer little party."

"I can take care of myself," he heard her reply and her nails audibly tapping the counter. "Revved up sounds...interesting."

The squeal of tires was the only response as he fired the bike into a burnout, reversing his direction. He'd come a long, long way from the junkyard and the rusted ol' Kawasaki. A cold shower might be in order at the moment, but he wasn't going to delay his chance to share the model's company.

The H-S slid to a halt in under a minute. The engine dropped to a low hum, sounding upset at having to stop so soon. Cat bounded off of the motorcycle, arming its security system. He pulled off his helmet, ran a gloved hand over his hair, and pulled the door to the coffee shop open. Taking one extra breath, he stepped in and took a look around.

Catwalk had seen countless shoots, endless advertisements and a dozen billboards of the model. When he spotted her across the room, they all failed to do her justice. Delilah sported a one-piece jump suit of tempting red leather. Her dark hazel green eyes casually surveyed the small room. Then, her gaze drifted to the door. He smirked in response, trying to exude more confidence than he was feeling. She was a pro at this interpersonal stuff. He had fewer occasions to practice his poker face, but hoped it was holding up alright. He walked toward the woman and the inviting booth, measuring his paces to slow himself down.

"Good eve, would you care to join me?" The auburn-haired starlet gestured to the steaming second cup that sat next to hers. "I presumed to order for you."

Cat removed his glove and extended a hand to greet her formally. "I'm honored."

Her skin was soft in his grip. "Please. Sit."

He leaned down and kissed the back of her hand before realizing he'd even done so. "How could I resist such an invitation?"

Her reaction was a speechless stare, and he again second-guessed himself. The devil on his shoulder poked him with a pitchfork, reminding him to be who he was and not some caricature he'd tried to cook up. He placed the signature helmet in the booth next to him, the vacant yellow eyes seeming to watch his every move. He craned his neck from side to side with an audible crack, unzipped his jacket, and sat down. He eyed the coffee. "An' here I wasn't sure you even remembered my name."

"Mr. Caliber, I wanted to thank you for -- for meeting me. A phone call seemed only cursory. I felt it important to tell you in person." Her voice dipped to a whisper. "Thank you."

He chuckled. "You already thanked me. Somewhere in the neighborhood a' ten times. Right between askin' me who they were and confirming...again...that I killed them."

Her blush radiated from her cheeks downward. She'd been looking into his eyes, and his last words forced her gaze from him.

He raised the coffee in a mock toast and then took a sip. It was better than he'd expected. "So..."

"Ordinarily, I am not so repetitious."

"You never told me why you were at the Shift in the first place."

"Research. I've been approached by a clothing line about modeling their goods. I was hoping to witness their target market without being disturbed."

"I mean this in a nice way, I promise. How much more did you spend buffin' up yer security in the few days after our meeting?"

"More than I should have, I suppose. I ordered an outside firm to come in and run through a security audit. Their consultants installed new cameras and motion sensors at my office and my hotel suite, and improved four-point biometrics for all the 'employee only' sections of the hotel. They were installing some system that correlates all the cameras and detection equipment and alerts the guards when I left. It's outside of my realm of understanding, but I realize how important that equipment is now."

"That's a lotta work."

"That wasn't all. I went weapon shopping. I was told I needed training." Her tone betrayed the thought that she'd been forced to swallow bitter medicine.

His eyebrow shot up instantly. "Nitro City's most beautiful woman went weapon shoppin'?"

Her head tilted. "I can't expect a savior to jump out of the darkness every time a questionable someone approaches, can I?"

He was back in his comfort zone. The pressure on his chest was gone. Instead, he could address areas of his expertise in an effort to build something between them. Gods, he wanted to build something, anything tangible, between himself and the goddess across the damp tabletop. He tipped his head. "Fer the right price, Red. I'll jump outta yer armoire if you want."

Her eyes widened. "I was not thinking of hiring you as a bodyguard, Mr. Caliber. If I take some classes, some martial art or other, learn to handle the pistol that should suffice."

"Well, damn. An' here I was thinkin' I could give up the glorious life I'd made fer myself." He took a long sip off of the coffee. "I can definitely teach any of the things you mentioned, probably blindfolded and drugged."

"Really?"

"I've had a gun in my hand since I could count. I went through years of training in Jeet Kun Do, Aikido, Krav Maga and Kenpo when I got my legs an' started my cop career." He paused, realizing he was marketing himself as some ninja superhero. "Details out the window. I can help."

Delilah's green eyes studied him over the rim of her coffee cup. "You did all that?"

"Yes. No. Let me explain. Most of the initial training is pure programmin'. Think of it as yer first two years a' college pre-recorded and installed into yer brain like software. It's fast and convenient, but it's flawed."

"Instant education is a flaw?"

"Knowin' more than the other guy is alright, until everyone knows the same thing. Everyone with that training knew the same moves, the same combinations, and the same actions an' counteractions."

"That's bad," she replied.

"The second someone knows what I'm gonna do next is my last second alive."

Her face paled a bit at his response, and she suddenly glanced to make sure her cup was still steaming.

He leaned forward. "Lemme just ask you this."

"Yes?"

117

"Did you invite me here to hire me as a trainer in self-defense, or was there another reason you dialed me up?"

"It was to thank you, and to, perhaps to get to know you better."

There, she'd said it, he confirmed to himself. It was a bold question, but if she'd seen him as nothing more than a killer and not the man behind the mask, he'd need to sever ties quickly. He stared at her for longer than he'd wanted. Finally, he nodded. "Good. Cause I can't shoot ta save my ass."

Delilah's eyes grew wide. "You can't? But you're in law enforcement, right?"

He chuckled. "I'm not in law enforcement. I was in law enforcement back east, but no, not any more."

Her wordless nod was enough.

"I'm an independent contractor, an odd-jobs man, what some people would call a 'cleaner'. Usually, it means protection or kidnapping, or on rare occasion, retiring a competitor. In a sentence, Delilah, I'm not always a hero." He felt like drowning simply for saying it, but she was the first woman in years he wanted to be honest with. It was a welcome and uncomfortable change.

Delilah smiled. She didn't bolt out of the cafe. Maybe there was hope after all.

"I could have let some of those attackers live the other night, but in reality, they would have only made life hell for me in the next few months if I did. I killed to send a message, to let people know that I was, and you are, off limits. Does that even make sense?"

"Yes, I suppose it does."

"*Hey, I did just kill a child molester who cost 18 families their children,*" he screamed inside his own head. He wanted to offer some sort of confession or be his own character witness, but it would hardly hold up against the stockpile of darker deeds he'd done. "Tell me about yer recent purchases, maybe I can give you some pointers." He brought the cup to his lips in a desperate move to shut himself up. The fact that it was empty didn't matter.

In a gesture that swam with natural grace, she reached out and placed a hand on his arm. "I won't claim to understand the depths of your work, but I do know what you did to protect me."

She pulled her hand away and made her focus change to her recent purchase. "The salesman called it a 'Glock'. He said it would be easy for a woman to handle."

118

The contact was something Cat never would have anticipated from the runway model. His gaze remained fixed on where she touched his arm.

"Personally, I think he wanted to make a sale, but I let him talk me into buying it. It's in a case at home, waiting for...whatever." She sipped again.

Without looking up, he rattled off details. "Probably a Glock 16, 9mm, ten in the cartridge, one in the chamber, semi-auto capability, not too much recoil but could overheat due to the polymer components of the barrel."

Her comments about the salesman registered with his distracted mind. "Wait, he said what? What a sexist pig. Want me to shoot him in the foot?"

She laughed. "I'll think about it."

He looked up. "Well, my first response involved a Samurai sword and some very sensitive parts. Sorry."

"No, don't apologize. Tell me more...about you...about...you." She ended aimlessly.

"How bout we schedule a little range time? Maybe we can go shootin' together?" He had no idea why he even suggested it. He was a notoriously bad shot, which had led to using the Stinger baton and some of the close-quarters fighting techniques. It had also led to his affinity for the sawed-off shotgun.

"I'm flattered that you have time, and that you offered. Yes."

Great," he said far too soon. "What's your schedule like? I can make some time, I'm sure."

Sure, Cat, right between the religious zealot, the forced physical therapy, the side jobs to pay for Will and his crew, getting a firmer handle on Delambre and Eva and tuning up the bike. There was a 25th hour in the day somewhere.

"How about Wednesday night? Say 8:00? Or is that a busy time for you?"

"If it was busy, it won't be." He grinned. She was amazing, and he was bumbling about low-budget handguns.

"I'll bring the weapon in its case, the ammo, the cleaning kit. Anything else?"

"Well, yeah, maybe one thing."

She looked at him eagerly. "What would that be?"

"You like motorcycles?"

CHAPTER TWENTY-SEVEN

24 July 2022

Every night for as long as he remembers, Leon wakes from the dream to the acrid reality that he cannot soar. He cannot walk. He cannot run. He prays to the god he's read about but doesn't believe in. He prays for death, any escape from the unresponsive body that has become his cell.

Morning comes. His prayers are once again unanswered.

CHAPTER TWENTY-EIGHT

The scientist allowed himself to smile only the slightest bit. It was the first time in as far as he could remember. His latest creation was nearly perfect, though not as perfect as his angel. She is absolute perfection, the embodiment of all a slave should be. She is as she was designed to be, the pinnacle of excitement, the embodiment of loyalty.

His brain reflected on the geneticist, his counterpart, once his friend, the tall man with salt and pepper hair. He remembered learning so much from the man. He'd been the one to preach honor, trust, compassion, such bullshit. It was the technical expertise, the algorithms, RNA and DNA replication and relationships...conversion of man to machine, that the other valued. He provided testimony and tried to convert his counterpart, every time met with an obvious brush-off. Each memory became fuel for his internal fire. It increased the depth of the chasm between them.

He remembered it then, meeting her, the angel, his rival's daughter. She was radiant, succulent, with olive skin and full lips. Her dark hair framed her face, and her eyes were deep and inviting. He remembered every detail of her. He could bathe in the memory of her, and her silent statement of wanting him from her first reflection.

He opened his eyes to look down, the same dark hair gripped tightly between his clenched fingers. He pulled and the beautiful brown eyes glanced up at him. She hummed an inquisition. She was unable to speak. Her mouth, the angel's mouth, was full. Her lazy eyes pivoted up to meet his while she continued to service him...the pinnacle of excitement, the embodiment of loyalty.

He enjoyed the feel of her warm mouth surrounding his cock. She was perfection. His rival's daughter, born again in a new form, on her knees, worshipping him. He closed his eyes, and the image in his mind shattered his focus. Yellow eyes burned through the angel's eyes, the glowing eyes of the cat.

The realization ignited the venom within him once again, hatred for the Cat.

His fingers clenched tighter, and the angel responded with instinctual resistance. Soon, she succumbed, as she was designed to do. In response to her, his hips moved faster, harder. The scientist embraced it then, his hatred of the yellow-eyed, chaotic hitman. The hatred devoured him as a drowning victim. Hatred of it. Hatred of the man. Hatred of the Cat.

He decided then, that he would unleash the Angel on him, in time. For now, she was his. His hips increased in violence. His grip nearly frantic as he pulled on her hair. The angel enjoyed every aspect of it more. She savored him, the way he fucked her face, forced himself down her throat. The scientist shattered between ecstasy and fury as he reached orgasm. He achieved the ultimate pleasure and the pinnacle of hatred.

The angel received his pleasure with hunger as designed. It was one of her core desires. The master's pleasure drove her existence. She accepted it willingly, a gift for all she had become in his vision. Her only other desire was blood, that of the liar, the one who the creator sought dead above all else.

The scientist finished, realizing that his eyes had rolled back into his head as if in a drugged stupor. He exhaled finally, his chest burning. When he released his grip, the angel licked her lips. His pleasure was hers. "You were quite determined, Master. I only hope I did not disappoint you."

The scientist brushed her sweaty hair, removing it from her flushed face, "No, my Angel. You are, as you have always been, perfection. Soon, you will exist for me, with me, without interruption, without corruption, when those who would betray us burn in the flames of eternal wrath."

"Go, my angel. Fly!"

Angelyka burst upward in a combination of ecstasy and pride, flush with the affection of her creator. Her exultant laughter echoed in the room as she ripped skyward, disappearing in a laser-sharp silhouette.

Relaxation should have been his. His heart rate should have ebbed downward, yet venom overpowered anything else he could think or feel. Despite physical satisfaction, he needed death to sate his desires. The geneticist and his bitch daughter could wait. For now, another had stepped in his path and delayed his coronation.

The Cat must die.

CHAPTER TWENTY-NINE

The Honda-Suzuki reacted with trained loyalty at his every command, gliding over the damaged road and between the scorched buildings of Downtown. The perfectly crafted machine was Catwalk's to direct, if only his head could stay as focused. The new stim treatments made his back as sore as any memory, but, in theory, they were more effective than drugs alone. Maybe there was a cure for his botched surgery after all.

He left behind the Shine gangers and the fires, moving southwest toward the more upscale part of town. The establishments here weren't the armored fortresses of Beverly Hills, but Hotel Infinity wasn't in the slums either. He found open freeway for almost ten clicks before the lights grew in frequency again. He scowled, and the cycle seemed to echo his hatred of restraint. The engine cooled beneath him as the mechanical growl silenced in his chest. Like it or not, it was time to drop speed in favor of the caution flag.

The digital readout of coordinates chirped inside his helmet, and Cat arrived in the circular valet area in front of the monstrous, plush hotel. He whistled at the sight. The place was an absolute palace compared to his loft, and the dwellings of his usual clientele. The structure before him boasted more than a dozen individual architectural designs, each overlapping and attempting to control the next. He shook his head at the phenomenon. Hotel Infinity seemed to adapt with every second, shifting in the multi-colored lights that outlined its frame.

The place defied description, and probably logic. Cat patted the gas tank of the motorcycle, anchoring back to what he could feel and understand. He lifted his gaze back to the Hotel, and it seemed different than what he had just recalled. Security through obfuscation or evolution. Cat scoffed. He needed more rich folks on his client list. Too bad this visit was completely personal and not for hire. He could use the paycheck. Sometimes, financial reward wasn't the reward in mind. This was one of those times.

The H-S slid smoothly to a halt near a parked limo. The valet began to approach, but Cat shook his hand, waving the suited man away. "Touch it and it'll explode, Johnny Boy." The valet blinked wordlessly, catching the cred chip in his hand. Cat didn't even break stride, removing his helmet and unzipping his jacket before hitting the first step. He looked up at an expectant and overly courteous doorman.

"Greetings, Mr. Caliber," he greeted in one of the deepest tones Cat had ever heard, "you are expected."

Cat paused, instinctively sizing up the behemoth who addressed him. He hadn't been prepared for the welcoming committee. "I'm expected, huh?"

"Madame DuPree is in the lounge, sir." He pointed the way.

"Hmmm...no dress code?"

"You are her guest." He continued, accenting his words with a practiced polite gesture.

Cat grinned broadly and tilted his head. "Well then..." He walked in, following the doorman's gesture. It was nice to be welcome anywhere, much less a place he'd kill to get into anyway.

He skimmed the room, saw the undeniable form of his hostess, but managed to keep pretending he was looking around. The yellow eyes gave him enough flexibility to hide it if he wanted to stare and not get caught. He thought she might have waved, but at this point, all he wanted was to derail her. The doorman had caught him by surprise, and he was bent on returning the favor.

On a hunch, Cat overacted the comm ringing and mimed answering it. From there, he launched into a loud and boisterous act of screaming at a phantom telemarketer trying to sell him health insurance. By the thirty-second mark, half of the lobby was staring.

He erupted into a stream of profanity, finally slamming the comm shut. Looking up to the crowd of staring eyes, he bowed with the flourish of a Thespian. Gasps of indignation peppered the lobby, and the murmuring began.

"Who was that man?"

"How rude."

"What a jerk."

As he stood up, he leveled his gaze to the auburn-haired goddess at the bar sipping Crème de Menthe. To her deepest embarrassment, he waved and stepped quickly in her direction. She was blushing. Good. She rose to meet him, gracing his cheek with a kiss.

"Good eve, Mr. Caliber," she said in her low, throaty voice, "will you have a drink?" Her face was flushed, and the green in her eyes deepened.

"I would love to, but I better refrain at the moment." Cat raised his right hand in the air and mimed the motion for accelerating the cycle. "I may toss one down when it's just my life at risk, but, well, never with a passenger."

She didn't miss a beat. "Of course, you are my guest. Is there anything else I could get for you?" She set her own glass down and didn't reach for it again.

"A light?"

"My pleasure," From somewhere in the depths of her cleavage she brought out a silver cigarette case and a slender lighter. "Please, allow me."

The cigarette was between his fingers by the time the flame ignited. He inhaled a few times and nodded thanks. "Bring yer piece?"

"My...oh! Yes," she glanced around and lowered her voice to near whisper. "Yes, I have it." There was a barely visible bulge in her leather jacket pocket. She nodded slightly toward the jacket. "I am looking forward to learning."

Cat blew smoke, literally and figuratively. "Awesome, but we have a problem."

She tilted her head. "What problem is that?"

He nodded his head toward the tinted windows. "See that ride out there? That's my custom Honda-Suzuki. I wrenched every part on that overpriced puppy myself."

She turned to have a look. "You have many talents, I see." Her eyes remained on the bike. "That's our transportation then?"

"Oh, yeah, that's part a' the deal. Here's the problem though. Every component on that thing is yellow, black or chrome." He turned to face her with a stone face. "Red will clash. I'm gonna need you to take all your clothes off."

Delilah took a drag off of her own cigarette, watching him without a word. She studied him through dark lashes, as if she was considering his statement as fact. She feigned offense, allowing her cheeks to flush before she spoke.

"Mr. Caliber, I thought you a gentleman. I must have given you more credit than you deserve. I'm sorry that I wasted your time, and I hope you make it off of the Hotel grounds with all your limbs intact." Delilah stood, turning her back on the hitman and motioning to an oversized cyborg at the far end of the lounge.

"Whoa," Cat called, trying to stop her before turning the plush lobby into nothing more than a war zone. He waved a hand quickly. "I was kidding. I'm kidding!"

Delilah stopped, gazing over her shoulder at him. Her eyes glistened in the light. A smile crept across her lips. "Oh. Kidding. You may want to look around. The other reason you managed an exception to the hotel's dress code is me. I think one good turn deserves another. Don't you, Mr. Caliber?"

He'd overstepped his bounds by a long shot, but wasn't that always the case? Instead of antagonizing her, he took a drag from his cigarette. "Look, Delilah, as much as I'd love to see you without that outfit...never mind, that's not what I meant. I mean, it is, but..."

"Well, then, let's assume you've already learned how to control your impulses before they become words. I'm going to pretend that's a skill you've already mastered." She smiled, the embodiment of cool. "Now, Mr. Caliber, if you don't mind, I'd like to have a look at that machine."

He mumbled. "Wow, suddenly a drink sounds like the right solution." He shook his head, embarrassed at his own conduct.

Delilah made a conciliatory gesture. She'd regained her composure and the upper hand.

"That doorman sure is a snappy dresser." The words felt desperate before he ever spoke.

Evenly, she said, "It's his job. What sort of drink do you prefer?"

He balked internally at the horrible shift in subject matter, but it was a desperate move. When she replied right in stride, he laughed. Taking a deep breath and finally exhaling, he replied, "I really just want to get you out on a ride with me. How's that for starters?"

Delilah's smile was perfect. "It's a fine idea."

Cat stood up, chanting the mantra, "You're an ass" under his breath ad nauseum. "You ever worn a motorcycle helmet?"

She gathered up her jacket and began to slip one arm

into it. "I wore one once during a photo shoot. If you're asking me if I've ever ridden a motorcycle, I'm afraid the answer is similar. I've been on a motorcycle, just not one in motion."

"What idiot photographer would ever hide your priceless face?" He wanted to follow up with a qualifying comment like "I'm not a stalker, I swear" but pulled back from further embarrassment.

She looked at him sideways. "One hired to bring out the best in a motorcycle. It seems female models are preferred." There was a touch of the cynic in her tone. "I'd really have preferred an actual ride. But all they did was to polish it wherever my fingers touched."

"Madame Dupree, with you in the shoot, no one on this world or all the colonies would ever know there was a motorcycle in frame."

"You have quite a silver tongue." The flicker of a smile played on her lips. "Will you expect me to remove my prints from your motorcycle?"

"What? No, you can leave prints anywhere you want."

She giggled slightly, the priceless smile crossing her lips in victory. "I'll wear gloves." She drew out a pair to show to him. "Are these appropriate?"

"You'll be holdin' on ta me instead of the bike, but yeah, I think those will work just fine." The thought of her nails against his skin crossed his mind, and he stopped to remind himself of where they were and what they had scheduled.

Her hands gripped into his sides as the H-S left the circular parking area in front of the Hotel Infinity. They crossed the parking lot in under ten seconds, hitting the ramp to the Interstate. He waited on purpose before clicking on the comm.

The H-S was purring along in third gear, somewhere near 100 kmph before Cat tapped the button opening the communication between the helmets. "How you doin', Red?"

"Fine," she replied, about one octave higher than usual.

"Alright, we'll both be okay. There are a few simple rules if you...whoop, hold on." He leaned the bike hard left, crossing two lanes of traffic before returning to avoid a bus held together mostly with duct tape and prayer. One side of its bumper dragged limply behind it, sending sparks along the road. Cat figured he would move out of harm's way before the bumper cut loose completely.

"As I was sayin'," he chirped with the energy granted him behind the handlebars, "there are a few rules."

She held on to him tighter, leaning against the turn with a natural sense of balance. She was breathing hard. "What rules?"

"Three rules. One. Lean the same way I lean."

"Two. Don't put yer feet down without tellin' me."

"Three. Don't cover my eyes or we're both organ donors!" He thought of a few more rules, but left them resounding happily within his skull.

She laughed at his last comment. "I'll behave, I promise."

"Alright. How are you for freeway time?"

"Faster? Oh yes!" She leaned forward, the length of her body pressing against him. Her booted feet were firmly planted on the rear pegs. "Ready when you are."

"Good ta hear. Hold tight...an' I mean tight." Cat gripped the rear brake hard, skidding the back tire around until the H-S was perpendicular with traffic. Delilah looked to their right. Pairs of headlights barreled down upon them from cars and trucks alike. She squeaked as she tugged on his jacket.

Cat said into the comm. "Let's see how this handles."

The rear tire erupted into smoke as he burned out before taking off. She clung to him as if her life depended on it, which it did. The acceleration of the custom monster paid off as they leapt off of the highway ramp. For what felt like forever, they were airborne, leaping off of I-10.

When they landed with a stretch of sparks and an indignant thump, they were smack in the middle of the northbound lanes of the 405. The lights behind them grew brighter, and the sound of horns circled them like a hurricane.

Cat ripped the motorcycle into a 0 to 60 sequence that shook them each to their dental work. By the time they each caught their breath, they were pushing 150 northbound on a completely different highway.

Finally, Cat checked in, "Wow, that was pretty crazy, even for me. How ya doin' back there?"

"Gods...I love it! More!" Her voice betrayed an excitement he hadn't heard from her before. "The fools didn't want me to ride. They wanted the fun all to themselves!"

"Alright lady, hang on tight." The twist of the wrist was like a shot of Shine in his veins. He was feeding off of her responses, verbal and physical. He continued to accelerate, dodging traffic as if in slow motion. He saw every vehicle as a clunky, slow 3-D model, and evaded them with ease, just as when he spent hours on the motorcycle simulator back at St. Patrick's.

"Go!"

By fifth gear, they were nearing 180 kmph, each set of taillights a blur as he erupted past them. This was an enviable goal for Cat. One he'd never attempted with a passenger, but something about her clutching to him drove him to new heights. All he wanted was more. He heard Delilah scream behind him in an unadulterated high. He grinned wider. She'd never been allowed to ride before. He treasured the excitement and focus of the ride. He loved the fact he was sharing it with the beautiful redhead.

Long before he'd wanted to, Cat saw the exit ramp approaching. He'd have to slow down, but there was still some room for fun. "You listenin', Delilah?"

"Yes," she sort of gurgled.

"Good. I'm about to give you a strange request. Don't ask, just obey. I need to you to wrap your legs around me." The ramp was approaching too fast to give her time to understand.

She'd been stretching her neck to look around him and saw the ramp. Almost instantly, out of fear and a newfound trust in him, her long legs moved to curl around his hips. A squeal left her as she locked on to him. He was already gripping the clutch, but not slowing down enough when he felt her legs move. Grabbing the brake, he dove right, his armored knee scraping the pavement. His knee and the foot peg of the bike struck the pavement. A shower of sparks erupted behind them. If Delilah's leg had been behind his instead of around his waist, she'd need a skin graft when they stopped.

The slide continued for almost ten seconds, the length of the spiraling ramp, before they were upright again, heading eastbound on the 101. Cat caught himself laughing before he could decide which boisterous statement to put forth.

She said something, but it wasn't audible.

He chuckled. "Tell me you just said, 'pull over'."

She rasped, "I wasn't that polite. But please do pull over." It was only after he'd come to a complete halt that he realized the trembling in her legs and arms wasn't from the vibration of the powerful engine.

The H-S cut off a random traveler, finding the dimly lit haven of a closed gas station. Sliding under the covered section of the pumps, Cat shut the engine down. Slowly, she detangled herself from him. "I...I need to..."

With his MetaHuman agility, Cat leapt from the bike, landing several feet away. "Take off your helmet." He said as he approached her.

Delilah's shaking fingers undid the strap, and the helmet was off. Her hair cascaded over her shoulders. Her wide green eyes stared at him. "I didn't leave prints, did I?"

Cat could hardly feel a thing through the adrenaline, but he remembered every tint of her skin. His fingers reach for her as if in a dream. He grabbed her hair, pulling her to him. The highway disappeared. Traffic disappeared. Everything disappeared as their lips met.

CHAPTER THIRTY

16 August 2022

Leon's hands are worn. His arms are burning. Not every portion of the orphanage is built for wheelchair access, and he's managed to find some of the hardest areas to search today. An endless rain pelts the window. Trickling shadows form from the dim lights outside. The light falls intermittently on his face, mingling with the beads of sweat on his skin. He closes his eyes, relaxing for a moment, letting the downpour become his soundtrack.

A scream pierces the percussion of the rain, or rather, the reverberations of a scream from down the hall. The desperation lifts the voice into a betraying range reserved for fear. Sucking air in quickly, Leon drives himself forward, his hands on the wheelchair's rims. He pushes forward again and again, each repeated motion bearing several feet of cracked and dim hallway.

The scream comes again, closer, just as high. Leon is sweating harder. His mouth is dry, but this is a sound he knows well. Panic and fear were part of life on the streets running drugs for a gang. He's both invoked and uttered those sounds before. St. Patrick's, however, is a place of peace. That sound…those emotions…don't belong here.

Another determined push forward bears fruit. The wheelchair reaches a juncture, and he sees movement to his left. His dark eyes acknowledge three forms. Two have their back to him. Their movements are aggressive and focused. The third form strikes him with the brilliance of a sunfire. She is slight, skinny, but not muscular. Blonde hair frames her flushed face. Her makeup is smeared. Tears draw the blue eyeliner down her cheeks in black despair. She screams again. One of the boys has her wrists clasped hard together. She stares at him, pleading.

"Hey!" Leon shouts before he even realizes he's done

so. He's always been a scrapper, a dirty fighter willing to do anything to win. He's seen the blonde before. She is a friend of the Asian girl who has been reaching out and trying to mentor him. She's proof alone that hope exists in these halls. Wheelchair or not, Leon isn't willing to let two meatheads beat hope out of a friend.

No one beyond their small clique has even acknowledged him beyond sarcasm. The flame inside says he's going to step in, even if he can't physically step at all.

The two boys turn to face him, dropping the girl in a heap on the floor. The one who held her wrists is obviously in charge. He's enraged. Blood fills his forearms, the veins in his neck, and other areas of his pubescent manhood. He has dark hair, self-cut into a makeshift mullet. His friend has a shaved head, his own work, with amateur tattoos and markings evident from his temples to the base of his skull. They've both invested the majority of their time into building their bodies, not their minds. That's bad news for them in the long run, but for right now, it's Leon's problem.

"What's wrong, too many days till the next issue of 'Gay Teen Monthly'?" Leon chides the pair, his eyes shifting from side to side for a weapon, anything that will help him try to even out the odds. The whole time, he screams inside for the blonde girl to run, to get help, and to make his confrontation worth something. She remains a pile of nerves instead, sobbing against open palms.

"Boy," the dark-haired assailant states, "you just sentenced yourself to a long period of pain."

He strides towards Leon, his frustration determining his motions like an angry puppeteer. His shaven-haired counterpart approaches from Leon's right, a flanking move. It's more strategy than Leon would have given them credit for, and it cancels out a few other maneuvers he thinks of.

Leon yanks upward hard, pulling the pin from the brake of his right wheel. Forcing as much motion as he could muster, he backhands the pin to his right. As accurate as a sniper's shot, the pin embeds itself into the neck of the bald attacker. His cries are hardly human at all as the boy drops to the ground, clutching his neck.

Leon turns his gaze back to the left just in time to see the fist of the dark-haired boy. The bigger boy's strike sends him spinning. Leon seeks to pivot away, bringing his legs underneath his body to prepare for the counterstrike. Reality hits him as his head strikes the tile. His legs will not respond now, or ever again.

He feels the grip on his neck before his head stops spinning. The impact of knuckles against his jaw devastates him again, along with the feeling of the cold tile beneath him. The boy is punching him over and over again, but Leon is no longer able to focus enough on a single blow, merely the continuation of pain from the newly opened wounds. The iron taste of blood is no stranger. The pressure in his mouth and the closing of his nose make it harder to breathe as he feels the dull repetition of the boy's blows.

Every color swarms about his brain as his head rocks from one side to another with the impact. As he thinks of the spectrum, each color becomes replaced with red, the blood flowing freely from his nose and mouth. He accepts that soon enough, only blood red will remain.

Then, without notice, the blows stop.

Leon isn't certain how many breaths he has forced in and out, only that the tile is cold against his battered form. With an effort, he makes himself open his eyes, and only the left eye responds. His right is already too swollen to pass that test. The blurry image bares promise. The dark-haired boy is kicking, trying to voice his retort, but his feet are far off the ground, his form lifted skyward by a Herculean enemy.

"...see you anywhere near Angie, or Leon, I'll rip your teeth out one by one," the savior says, Leon unable to hear the precursor to his message of enforcement. As clarity returns, Leon realizes it's the blonde boy from one of his classes. Even with the blood loss, he remembers the boy's name.

"Bobby."

The boy's form slams the would-be assailant against the wall a few more times before tossing him atop his bleeding friend. The two scramble to their feet, running to seek medical attention for their various injuries. Leon smiles briefly, slumping downward against his sore shoulders. Bobby goes to the attackers' original target, helping her find her unsteady feet. "It's okay, Angie, I promise. You're safe now."

Leon tries to grin. The effort brings pain, and he coughs blood. He puts a name to the blonde girl. Angie is in several of his classes. He struggles to remember the Asian girl's name, but can only think of "rookie", her nickname for him. Maybe hope is alive in the halls of the orphanage. Maybe he's found friends here at St. Patrick's. Then again, he's certainly made new enemies.

Bobby and Angie approach him, with forced smiles and the nervous aftershocks that come from physical assault. Their statements are hardly audible, the walls and ceiling fading away around them. Soon, the image of the pair condenses, swirling away into an ever-decreasing point. Within seconds, the two orphans, the incident itself, and the orphanage that was once his home dissolve into a mere pinpoint.

"You seem far less tense than your last treatment," Delambre remarked, offering an unsolicited opinion of Cat's musculature. The hitman barely heard him, clinging to the memory of being attacked and how he came to meet his fellow orphans. Focusing on where he had been helped him every time he received treatment for his untested cybernetic enhancements. Cat simply stared at the black spot on the floor, the one, which had so recently encompassed the life-altering experience in his mind. Bobby and Angie became siblings his siblings. Together with Mi-Young, the four of them had voluntarily taken the surname 'Caliber'. He was ashamed that he'd almost forgotten the altercation that set the stage for their alliance.

"Guess I just been lucky lately, Doc." Cat offered, reluctantly relinquishing focus on the awakening of his memory. He wasn't about to openly kiss and tell the events of last night's ride. Something about Delilah was both enticing and calming at once. He was curiously drawn to her, and for all he knew of relationships, maybe it was something far beyond physical.

"Well," Delambre replied, "with hardly an ounce of squirming and whining, our session here is done. I suggest you drink plenty of clean water, allow your system to purge its poisons, and focus on your next target."

Cat rolled to his side, stretching his neck in circles.

"You mean 'our' next target, right?" He stood up, shirtless, and grabbed the cigarettes from the tabletop that held his possessions.

Delambre's voice grew in volume but not pitch. "I just told you to purge your system of poisons."

"You told me a lotta things, Delambre. I'll listen ta the ones I think will help me, but right now, after the ride I just took, I want a shockin' smoke."

Delambre's silence was his only response for nearly a minute. "Very well, kill yourself, again. I'm only here to put you back together." His tone betrayed an exhaustion Cat hadn't detected before. "If you've got a target in mind, what do you believe it to be?"

"I was thinkin' about that. If our rogue doc is all you claim him ta be, then I can't help but think he'll pit his Famine against me next." Cat took a long draw, imagining what the doctor would come up with for that design.

Delambre nodded. "He's already shown a lack of adherence to the Scripture. He was willing to betray the Bible for his own benefit. I'd consider that a clear sign that he's more dangerous than any true religious fanatic."

"Good point. His ego means he's willing to scrap the by-the-good-book plan."

"That may also surface in how he customizes the MetaHuman designs."

"This head case has already blown it with his attempts at the Horsemen. I should only have Famine left ta deal with, and his version a' yer kid."

The older man's gaze betrayed an inherent protection and an instant pain. He lowered his gaze and nodded.

"Sorry, doc, I didn't mean it like that."

Delambre strode toward Catwalk, his eyes locking on to those of the yellow-eyed hitman. They neared a foot apart when the geneticist reached for the hand of his counterpart. Without a word, he took the cigarette from Cat and raised it to his lips, drawing in a long and well-experienced taste.

"You're going to kill her."

Cat grinned. The geneticist's sudden theft of his so-called poison made him laugh openly. "Doc, we'll be doin' body shots offa her corpse next time we see her."

Delambre's demeanor wasn't nearly as cocky as it was concerned. He locked eyes with Catwalk for an extended period before bowing his head, nodding and taking another drag.

"For her sake, and ours, I pray you're correct."

CHAPTER THIRTY-ONE

Catwalk crouched in the shadow of a blacked-out billboard, drinking in the view of Downtown Nitro City. The punctured and damaged sign had once flashed a neon invitation to join the Off-World movement. Rising ashes had since coated it in a dead gray pallor, somewhere between gunships and gravestones. The wind pulled it apart in places, causing a rhythmic slapping sound of wood against metal. The seemingly endless rain added its percussion to the creaking of the twisted sign. The invitation to paradise far away had devolved into the hollow wails of a revenant.

Cat took a mental inventory. The shotgun was holstered on his back, the familiar extendable baton and 11mm pistol flanking his hips on his belt. His breathing was steady, and even in the crouch for almost an hour now, his legs betrayed no pain or fatigue. He watched the polished limousine, parked outside of Hydrogen Alley, an up-and-coming establishment that combined custom drugs and even more customized massages.

It was a simple job, one that had come in through a former co-worker back in DC. The blood trail was pretty convoluted; someone's wife's twin sister's husband was having an affair with his co-worker or some such nonsense. In the end, it didn't matter. Cat was supposed to prove it, provide pictures, and give the offending party a scare to set him straight.

The job had been in his data banks for almost three months. He'd almost forgotten about it and would have if not for his recent meetings with Delilah. The first time he'd been hired to protect her, she was being transported in a Daimler-Toyota XL300. The same model limo reflected in the glow of his yellow eyes tonight. The suit who'd hired him for that escort job was just as empty as the one who feigned importance when he entered

Hydrogen Alley 50 minutes ago. Cat made a note.

Empty suits made bad employers, but easy prey.

The setup was actually pretty clever. The suit's female co-worker moonlighted at the club just to provide them with a place to get together. Undoubtedly, he paid in cash, she returned it, and there was no credit trail for the wife to snip out other than the expense of the limo, which was simply a show of self-importance. If Loverboy had been content to take a cab, there wouldn't be a paper trail. Instead, this self-important lowlife allowed a seven-meter motorized model of compensation to lead to his discovery.

Cat had already snapped pictures of both the husband and his whore entering on several occasions. He had her shots in four different wigs and eleven different outfits. The latex nurse was the most frequent. Maybe the suit had something for getting his temperature taken.

They usually handled the affair with discretion. Cat had only managed to gather one set of pictures where the couple had left together. If they'd have bothered to close the moon roof, he wouldn't have had the real damning evidence, but they'd been stoned and careless.

As it stood, the last thing he had to do was to put a little fear in the man. That was always the fun part, unless of course, he was on hand when the wife confronted her cheating man. No two betrayed women behaved alike, but they always shared the same, underlying objective. It was in the execution where they varied. He smirked beneath his masked helmet when the driver opened the door.

Right on time.

Say what he might about ol' Loverboy, he was a 60-minute man, each and every time.

Catwalk leapt from his perch, soaring downward to the pavement. At the last moment, he folded, tucking his head to his chest and rolling forward. His legs and spine compensated for the impact, and he lifted his gaze to the limo. Rain swept down his helmet, dripped from the cat's fangs, and joined the endless flood traversing the street. Cat had studied his subjects and their routine, and he knew every step the suit and his supporting cast would take.

The couple used the same driver every time. He was a svelte boy, a chrome bitch with an artificial tan and slick blue and black hair. He was better suited for fetish model ads than for combat, which is why he always carried the two 10mm H&K's under his tuxedo coat. The door opened, and he crushed the cigarette beneath his patent leather shoe.

With a flick of the wrist, the baton extended to full-length, echoing in the air as Cat launched toward the driver. The young model turned, hands raised in the air instead of reaching for his pistols.

Mistake.

Catwalk landed right next to him, swinging a back fist to the boy's left temple. The force drove him from his feet. The driver's head bounced off of the limo door before he tumbled to the asphalt. He was on the ground in a crumpled heap before the hitman even looked down.

"Fashion over function, boy," he stated to the unconscious form, "ain't always the best choice."

Loverboy emerged from Hydrogen Alley. His eyes were blurry, his walk slightly out of time. Even in the rain, Cat could sniff the Shine sweating out of the suit's pores. The slightest hint of scratched skin exposed itself from just atop his collar. His hair and clothes were askew enough to indicate he'd hurried to recollect himself. The rear door of the limo was open, even without his driver there to hold it for him. He wore the stupid half-smile of over-indulgence as he slid into the limo.

The door slammed against his extended leg, catching him midway down his right calf. He yelped in pain, yanking his leg inside instinctively. The door shut again behind him as he gripped his leg and clenched his teeth. Raising his attention, he slammed both fists against the glass, unaware of the figure that had slid through the moon roof and sat next to him.

"Cognac, Jerry?"

Loverboy sobered up instantly. He turned to see a pair of yellow eyes facing him, extending a glass of the liquor, which had previously meant a precursor to paradise. He bolted backward, his back against the glass. The predator in the limo remained still. "C'mon now, bud, it's not like I can drink it." The humanoid launched at him, its hand crushing his throat against the window. The glowing eyes were a breath from his face. "I'm not even human."

Loverboy flailed an attack, his blows paranoid and uncoordinated. The attacker pulled back, still holding the glass. For several seconds, Jerry's arms struck nothing, just repeating a gesture of desperation. When he looked up, it was still there, holding the glass.

"I'll ask you again, Jerry. Cognac? Isn't that always the pre and post-party ceremony?"

"Why…what…what do you want?"

"Are you gonna drink this, or am I gonna make you?"

"I can pay you…What do you want, man?"

"Last chance. You slammin' this one?"

The assaulted man stammered something unrecognizable. He was blubbering tears already and had probably pissed himself in his drugged and inebriated state.

"Suit yerself." The yellow-eyed figure darted forward, slamming the cognac against the side of Loverboy's head. The glass shattered, showering him in a hail of shards and brown liquor.

The panic cut him more deeply than the glass. He struck out blindly with his legs, covering his face and head with his arms. "Stop! Stop! Come on, what do you want?"

A gloved hand gripped his chin between his covering arms, yanking him forward by his jaw. "Go home. Explain yourself. Be ready for the consequences. If not, I'll deliver the body of your little whore to your office."

The figure pulled him close enough to witness his own punctured face in the reflection of its yellow eyes. "Each of the next ten days, one piece at a time."

Loverboy's head struck the tinted glass as the attacker pushed him backward. His eyes were dazzled. His brain swam in pain. His leg was bleeding through his suit, and there were contusions to his face and skull. He looked down, choking slightly on fear and pain. His attacker was gone.

So was the bottle of Cognac.

He fell forward, his face in his hands. The motion pushed shards of glass further into his forehead and cheek, but the heaving of his chest and the burning inside far outweighed the pain. He choked on his own guilt and anguish. Whatever that thing had been, it had delivered the ultimatum: Confess what he had become, or simply what he had done, and why.

Jerry turned his bruised and bloody vision upward to the night sky. Rain fell down on him, streaking the blood and fear down his brow and into his eyes. It stained the creases of his face, dripping into the fake leather of the limo. There was no sign of the attacker, only the night sky, the stars reflecting down upon him like a mirror of his own guilt.

He reached a shaking hand to the phone.

CHAPTER THIRTY-TWO

The ringing comm promptly ended Cat's dream involving Swedish twin nymphomaniacs and a hot tub. He let it ring a few more times before answering with a sarcastic, "All lines are busy, hold please." Running a hand through his hair, he reviewed the night's events while searching for an antidote to the cottonmouth he suffered.

He'd returned from visiting Loverboy, chilled the Cognac and changed into more comfortable attire. He'd cleaned and inspected his guns, meditated and spent some time upside-down on the inversion table to help his back. After that, he'd made the mistake of checking messages. It took three glasses of the Cognac for him to authorize the amount Will had demanded in his invoice.

Rubbing his face, he returned his attention to the comm. "Checking your news feeds, M'sieu Catwalk?"

"Not quite yet, Delambre."

"Good. I'll wait. You'll want to check this morning's messages."

Cat knew better than to second-guess the scholar. He immediately flipped to his messages. There were two marked as unread. One was from Mrs. Loverboy. It read only, "Thank you."

The second was an encrypted financial statement noting a deposit three times the amount he'd agreed to when he took the case. Putting the pieces together, he returned his ear to Delambre. "What did I miss?"

"Would you like the feed or my version?"

"Surprise me."

A video feed popped over the comm, expanding to full screen before him. The familiar visage of Scoop McEwan provided every sensational detail of a murder-suicide involving a director of operations for an off-world transport firm, his wife, and his mistress. The faces of

143

Loverboy, his blushing bride and his lover graced the screen next to Scoop. The whore was even wearing the nurse's outfit. Cat tried to refrain from laughing but hadn't the slightest hope of doing so. "I can't believe it."

Delambre responded, "So you've seen it. I find your inability to believe such a rash and hostile execution a probable course of action."

"Oh, it ain't that," Cat replied. "I can't believe she paid first!"

They caught themselves laughing at the same time. For Delambre, it represented relief. After all, their last few interactions carried quite the current of tension. For Cat, it meant that the check he'd just stroked to Will wound up costing him nothing.

Cat followed the details with Scoop muted. Loverboy had called home and apologized. By the time he got there, his wife was gone. She'd left a note stating her intent to kill the mistress. When Loverboy backtracked to Hydrogen Alley, his wife engulfed the entire place in flame and nitrous, killing the couple and a dozen of the cleaning crew.

"I didn't know she had it in her," Cat said absently while he watched.

Delambre chuckled on the other end of the comm. "None of us did. As you might say yourself, 'Ain't that a bitch?'"

Catwalk laughed so hard he dropped the comm and ended the call.

The scientist removed his fingers from the trigger of the airbrush. He had drawn an exact mirror image and every pore needed to reflect its intended opposite. The angel's eyes were an exact match, each framed in a delightful eclipse-like black. She remained perfectly still, awaiting his direction. He paused longer than he should, if only for effect. "Open your eyes, Angelyka."

From her knees, she followed instruction, raising her gaze to meet that of her creator. Her makeup was complete, perfect for her on-camera debut. After all, she must appear without flaw in the lens when she ripped the Cat's heart from his chest. The coverage would undoubtedly be present when the latest of the high-profile threats appeared again on camera. The media was always hungry to feed its audience. He would have been remiss if he didn't tailor his creation in the perfect visage for her time in the spotlight.

The scientist brushed the back of his hand against his angel's cheek, and she leaned into his touch as if it was salvation. "Soon, Angel, you will have your freedom to slay our newfound enemy."

"The execution of this target pleases you, my master?" her slightly synthetic voice replied in question.

"Ah, yes, Angel," he grinned, "more than you can fathom."

The construct's eyes flashed with direction. "Then his demise shall serve as my only goal, Master." Her hands closed around his own, the faint outline of painted artwork on her palms.

The scientist grinned, stroking her hair. His thoughts were a step ahead of her as always. He saw not only the assassin's execution, but that of the geneticist and his whore daughter as well. He smiled. "I have faith in you, my dear. I have no doubt you will deliver all that I expect of you."

"When the time comes, I know you will kill the hitman without remorse or hesitation."

The Angel smiled a silent confirmation. She was programmed for exactly that purpose, and her painted face reflected submission to his wishes. She would perform exactly as she had been instructed.

Kill enemies upon direction. Slay any opposition.

Kill the Cat.

CHAPTER THIRTY-THREE

9 September 2022

The breeze shifts intermittently from scarcely a touch to an occasional full breath against his skin. Leon looks out over the scrap yard, savoring the pause in the endless acidic rainfall. The puddles form and grow on the gravel of the rooftop. The air here is cool enough without the wind's assistance. It's quiet. A few stray locks of black hair stream across his face, not quite enough to interfere with his view of the scattering vermin below.

He exhales, the smoke choosing directions as random as scared roaches at the first sign of light. He licks his lips ever so slightly, savoring the acrid taste of the cigarette. Without looking, he extends it to his right, into the nervous waiting hands of his newfound friend. Mi-Young focuses so intently on the cigarette that her eyes nearly cross. She takes it. After all, she promised she would. Rather, she's claimed she already smoked plenty of times in the past.

One inhalation of smoke draws the light on her bold-faced lie. It takes almost 20 seconds before she regains her breath, almost three minutes before she regains her natural color. By then, Leon has taken the cigarette back from her, taking several drags while she restores her demeanor. "What was it you claimed, sis? I remember something about a pack-a-day habit fer a few years?"

She shakes her head mutely. The attempt at a clever retort invokes another coughing fit.

Leon turns his gaze back to the scattering homeless below. "It's a skill like anything else, Dearheart. Hell," he inhales deeply from the cigarette, "even rookies have skills."

The young Asian girl who has mentored him since his admission finally acknowledges that he may know something she doesn't. She waves a hand as if to end the conversation. "Oh, good gods of cement and mortar, Leon. Why would you even want to be able to do that?"

Leon simply takes another drag off of the cigarette, blowing the smoke towards the heavens. "You taught me before, Mi, about focusing on my inner self...J-breathing and such mumbo-jumbo. Your strength is in savin' yourself by believin' in who you are. My strength may be the opposite. Maybe my goal is ta teach you that you can kill yerself regardless of yer position on life."

The black-haired girl stares at Leon mutely. Her intention from the beginning has been to teach him about the points of life worth living. Perhaps, for the first time, he's introduced to her instead the reasons not to.

After a pause, the boy speaks, smoke cutting his lips with each word. "It's who we were, to some degree, which makes us who we are."

The statement slapped him with such accuracy it was refreshing. Catwalk looked at the clock, remembering at the last moment to invert the numbers. The display read 1725, meaning he'd been hanging upside down and meditating for nearly twenty minutes. His legs didn't ache at all, but he felt the strain in his upper body from the weights in his hands. After all, he'd been exercising the practice of J-breathing he learned in the orphanage. Focusing, he curled his body upwards, and his abs and arms screamed in protest.

He slapped the dumbbells back into their mounts in the ceiling and gripped the straight bar. Unhinging his legs, he dropped to the ground, landing in a crouch. The change in blood flow struck him hard. The swelling was visible in his limbs. He remembered the quote he'd made a decade or so ago. "It's who we were, to some degree, which makes us who we are."

Catwalk smirked. Back then, at St. Patrick's, he'd meant that being a ganger had taught him how to smoke. Now, that statement bore even more accuracy. If he'd never been the invalid, he would never have been the police experiment with the cybernetic legs and spine. If he hadn't ever become that cop, he wouldn't ever have come to Nitro. He wouldn't have become a cleaner. He wouldn't have met Delambre, or Eva.

Or Delilah.

Shockit. The realization hit him hard. He would barely make it to pick her up if he didn't move right now. Pain be damned, Cat sprinted to the shower. He had a date and lasting memories or physical therapy would have to take a backseat for the time being.

Within minutes, he was astride the H-S, full-throttle to pick up the redheaded goddess. The cycle answered his slightest lean or inflection of his wrist, just as it was designed. From brake fluid to heads-up display, Cat knew every centimeter of the custom cycle like an extension of his own skin. He found the Interstate and triggered the Nitrous. In seconds, his taillights disappeared into the distance.

CHAPTER THIRTY-FOUR

Cat whistled to himself when he approached the glorious entryway to Hotel Infinity. He caught himself gazing far too long at the architecture and immaculate landscaping. He wondered how many times someone had to gaze on the building before it stopped being impressive. It appeared as elegant as ever, but slightly different. He chuckled. There simply wasn't a more appropriate palace for the divine Delilah Dupree.

The Honda-Suzuki roared to an unwilling silence as he parked it once again near the entrance. Cat dismounted and patted the tank of his obedient companion. The two of them had experienced quite the workload. Returning his gaze to the hotel, he bound up the stairs, stopping to see which doorman was on duty this starry evening.

An enormous man stepped from the doorman's post. His frame suggested that he might spend time as a stunt double for Hovertanks during his off hours. His well-trimmed but full beard made him appear more bear than man. There was no denying that this man was bred or trained to run off the unwelcome guests clamoring to visit one of Nitro City's most sought-after figures. The buttons on his perfectly pressed uniform coat were so polished that Cat caught his own reflection. He fixed his gaze on the cleaner. A white-gloved hand slowly rose to the brim of his cap. "May I assist you, sir?"

Cat popped his helmet off with practiced ease. His eyes rose to meet those of the doorman. "I'm here to meet with Madam DuPree."

The massive protector eyed the strange newcomer with distrust. With a deep, throaty scoff, he opened a small leather bound writing pad and consulted it. "One moment, sir. Your name?"

"Catwalk," the hitman replied. *If this guy mentions that damn song I'm going to gut him right here* he thought behind a gracious smile. "Catwalk Caliber if it's a first and last name thing, you understand."

The bear scribbled something in the pad, most likely a note not to trust this visitor. "Mr. Caliber." He had paused for obvious effect. "Ah yes, Madam DuPree is expecting you. If you'd care to go into the lounge, I'll inform her that you are here."

Cat nodded, then stopped suddenly. "Hey."

The bear tilted his head. "Sir?"

"How much ta see that list?" His grin broadened.

The bear blinked. Otherwise, he stood still as a statue. "The information is confidential, Mr. Caliber, a security measure. You understand."

Cat nodded again. "Sure thing, an' I respect you fer doin' yer job. Just, you know, as a favor, maybe explain to everyone else on there whatever it was about me that made you hesitant the second you saw me. I'd like 'em ta know who else is in the game."

"I will discuss it with Madam DuPree, sir." His white-gloved hand clenched the small book as though it was a priceless treasure. "The lounge is there." He nodded his head.

"Yer a good find, Dudley DeBruin. Your past military experience and more recent cybernetic surgery really make a good combination in a protector. Hell, there aren't many folks, artificial or otherwise, who can boast receivin' the Soldier's Medal. Yer a rare breed. If you ever want ta expand yer portfolio, look me up." Cat had already paid Will to do background checks on all the security staff at the Hotel. With a smile, he headed toward the lounge.

Dudley huffed something undeterminable through his beard as he reached for the comm. His eyes remained fixed on the man called Catwalk while he called upstairs to inform his employer of her guest.

Cat stepped into the familiar lounge, noticing that the bartender and waitress were the same as the last time he'd visited Delilah. Exhaling the tension of squaring off with the oversized doorman, he lit a cigarette. Dudley was big, tough. He reminded Cat of Data, the Enforcer on his cop squad back in DC, except Dudley could put together a sentence without squeezing a trigger. Data was on full-auto all the time.

He whipped his view over his shoulder without meaning to, but the cadence of the heels on the floor was undeniable. Approaching from the far end of the lobby was Delilah, her auburn hair pulled back in a ponytail, cascading onto the leather jacket as red as her lips. As if determined to ruin the moment, the bear named Dudley stepped to her side and shared a brief conversation with her.

The cleaner returned his gaze forward, drawing in more of the cigarette and shaking his head. He couldn't pick up on the conversation, but the quick exit of the doorman indicated he wasn't happy with Delilah's approval of her gritty guest. He heard her heels and felt her coming closer.

"Good eve, Cat" she said. Her low, throaty voice held a welcoming tone.

He stood as she drew near, bowing slightly and extending a hand to the open chair near him. "Whatever you do, don't blame the poor man. If I was Dudley, I wouldn't trust me anywhere near you either, beautiful."

She surprised him with a quick kiss on his cheek before she sat down. "He's very good at his job."

"Yeah, he reminds me of an' old colleague." Cat looked back out to see the form of Dudley watching them both. His inhuman eyes met those of the decorated war veteran.

"I believe you were going to assist me with my weaponry skills."

Her words were a sudden splash of reason, moving attention back away from the doorman. "Yeah…"

She breathed the words, "I am glad to see you."

The grin split his lips before he could stop it. "I'm glad you're here, Delilah. I kinda wish we had all night ta splash down some drinks an' wax nostalgic." He smirked stupidly, her presence grabbing some of the strings that controlled him. "Alas, we've got 15 minutes before our appointment at Trigger Happy Jack's Indoor Range."

Her hazel green eyes lit with a touch of mischief. "Trigger Happy Jack's. I can hardly wait."

"I hope you don't mind. I brought the bike."

Her smile showed perfect white teeth, offset by glistening red lips. "I hoped you would."

The bike slipped to a controlled halt. This ride had been more restrained than their last, though Cat was tempted to drive faster at the slightest contact with his passenger. They had refrained from any overpass jumping or facing oncoming traffic, maintaining a speed under 140 kmph and only executing a handful of multiple lane changes. It was easy to tell that Delilah was still nervous when they finally parked. "Well, here we are."

The neon purple of Trigger Happy Jack's Indoor Range was visible for a hundred meters. It was a flamboyant call to any gun lover who might stumble into its radiance. The parking lot was riddled with potholes, and the paint on every wall within sight was faded and peeling, but the neon displayed as brightly as a dozen spotlights.

Delilah refrained from sharing whatever comment she might have made.

"They're not all this tacky, mind you," he chuckled. "Most are worse."

She couldn't help but laugh softly. "If you say so."

Cat locked their helmets to the motorcycle, grabbing the cases for their weapons. He armed the bike as they walked towards the establishment. The windows and walls were reinforced with grid-sensitive lasers, but the doorway opened automatically. There was little surprise to that set-up once the couple entered the lobby. Guns of every shape and age covered the walls, most aimed at the doorway. At the far end of the sanitized white lobby stood an unkempt man almost as hulking as the protective doorman, Dudley. His skin bore a metallic sheen, and his shoulder-length, black hair was peppered with grey. He wore a faded camouflage shirt and olive drab pants. His right arm was cybernetic with a mount at the elbow. Right now, that mount bore an artificial hand, though that may just as easily have been an auto-rifle depending on his mood.

"Catwalk," he bellowed in a deep voice. "Damn good to see you, boy!"

Without meaning to, Cat brought his hand protectively to the small of Delilah's back. "Hey, Jack, how's biz?"

"Better every time you enter the door, and," the older man paused, "who is this delightful vixen you've delivered to the Eden of Ammunition?"

Cat leaned closer to Delilah, his voice almost inaudible even at that proximity. "He's gonna do the tongue thing. It's not real, don't worry."

From beneath long dark lashes, Delilah studied the man who Cat called Jack. She leaned slightly into the support of Cat's hand on her back. She lifted her gaze to Jack's eyes and then down again.

"Oh, one of those," she barely murmured.

"This," he replied cheerfully, "is my friend De...Donna. Donna MacMurray."

Jack rounded the counter, his arms extended in an attempt to hug his new guests. As he emerged from the comfort of the counter, it was obvious each of his legs had a similar brace to that of his arm. If he chose, he could be a walking arsenal with a few selective additions.

"Welcome to the Crown Jewel of Artillery, the Shiny Buckle in the gun belt of life, the pinnacle of all that is and ever has been shells, explosives ordinance and anything otherwise associated with gunpowder, projectile expulsion and mayhem-inducing technology." Jack bowed deeply, and when he stood back to his full height, he extended his tongue, licking one eyebrow and then the other.

"Good eve," she said simply, with a polite smile. If his behavior had fazed her at all, she maintained the ultimate poker face.

Cat stepped between the two of them, reluctantly letting go of his brief contact with the model. "Jack," he said with an exaggerated degree of surprise, looking at the shopkeeper's legs, "when did you switch out the left leg? That's unbelievable! I thought yer old lady forbid it."

Jacks' gaze turned toward Cat instead of Delilah, the revelation of his marriage darkening the skies of his evening. "Aye," the veteran growled, "She saw my reasoning as I told you she would."

"You mean you just did it and came home with the surgery?"

Jack looked positively admonished for nearly thirty seconds before they both burst into a fit of hysterical laughter. The shopkeeper slapped Cat squarely on the shoulder and then added, "How many rounds do you need today, Boy?"

Catwalk's gaze was on Delilah with an undercurrent of relief. Her eyes were on him before he looked at her. They passed a silent acknowledgement between them. "Y'know, I hadn't thought that through." He leaned closer to her, "Hey, Red, extend yer arms."

"Like this?" Her face soured a bit at the sudden outpouring of aliases.

"Like yer gettin' cuffed," he said, tilting his head.

"Been cuffed before?"

Her cheeks reddened. "I have no arrest record."

He gripped her forearms, squeezing slightly. Leaning forward, he whispered to her, "That is SO not what I asked." Turning his gaze over his shoulder, he released her arms. "100 rounds of 9mm, Jack, an' 200 rounds a' 11mm."

The veteran shopkeeper placed several boxes on the countertop. "Bill your usual, I assume, Catwalk?"

Cat simply nodded, grabbing the boxes off of the counter. He turned to Delilah. "Ready ta squeeze off a few rounds?"

"Lead the way," she replied with a fire behind her eyes.

The couple entered the solitude of the shooting range, lane after empty lane prepped for target practice. They walked past several uniform lanes before stopping. Catwalk extended a pair of noise canceling earphones to the out-of-place beauty. The dampening earphones were simple and functional, if not delicate. Cat removed his jacket, revealing a tight black tank top. Some of the scars of his surgery were evident, covering the skin across his shoulder blades. His legs were covered with a light camouflaged grey and black pair of pants. He checked his midnight-black hair, ensuring it was pulled back into its tight ponytail as he loaded the Glock. He followed by loading a series of the ammunition into a handgun he pulled from his belt.

Delilah slipped the earphones on, studying Cat as he went through his preparations. Her fringed leather jacket was laid aside. She wore a designer brand maroon tank top, beneath it, tight jeans and a glistening silver belt. A silver choker graced her throat and simple hoop earrings were now hidden by the earphones. She stepped closer to watch him load the Glock.

Cat's eyes were focused, loading round after round into the handgun. Her scent was inviting something wild within him. "I am so not looking up right now, because if I do, I will be as useful to you as a holographic crash test dummy."

"Please continue. I am here to learn, O Wise One." There was laughter in her voice and genuine interest. "How soon can I do that?"

154

He handed her a cartridge. "Done already, Donna."

She took the cartridge and looked at him sideways. "Donna. Right."

He looked at her and shrugged with a guilty look. "I didn't want to tell him who you really were an' well, Shockit, I'm not the best at aliases on the spot."

"It's fun to have an alias. Who knows, I might use it elsewhere. So, like this?" She held the cartridge as if to load it into the gun.

His pistol was pointed toward the floor as he loaded it and shifted the safety off. "Here's the deal, Delilah. You have a dual-action only pistol, so as you shoot, the next round will automatically load into the chamber. That means when you pull the trigger, you pull it again for another bullet to fire."

She nodded, listening carefully.

"That means two things. First of all, you don't have to advance the chamber so you can fire faster."

"What's the second thing?"

"Don't play Russian Roulette with it." He winked.

He pulled the chamber back, loading the first round. "I was grabbing your arms to see how long I thought you could fire before you got fatigued." His gaze turned away from her to the paper target some 20 meters away.

"Ah, that makes sense," she nodded.

Cat fired a single shot at the target, a two-dimensional silhouette of a human, its circles scoring higher and higher as they drew tighter. Despite the protective earphones, Delilah flinched. Pausing a second between shots, he fired several more, his body hardly moving.

He set the pistol down, clicking the safety back in place. With the press of a button, he moved the target closer on its automatic track. From a few meters away, each of them could make out the groupings of his shots. Two would have missed. The other six entered anywhere from the left collarbone to the left ear of the target.

Cat leaned back to address her, "I told you I'm a horrible shot."

She pushed the right earphone aside and looked at him. "Could have fooled me," she said amiably. She looked back at the target.

He scoffed. "Alright, let's see how you do, killer queen."

"Sure," she patted her pants. "Would you hold my comm? I'm waiting on a call, but I don't think it would help me in the middle of this shooting thing."

"Of course," he grinned. "Like I could deny you anything."

She flashed the signature grin he'd seen on billboards and vid-feeds for years. Earphone back in place, Delilah stood with legs apart, able to balance on the high-heeled boots without a thought. She held the gun straight ahead of her in her right hand, her left hand grasping her right wrist, and slowly aimed at the target. Her finger squeezed, and she flinched again. Her brow furrowed.

Catwalk pressed the button to advance the target. As it neared, the bullet hole was evident, a clear miss above the target's left shoulder. "Alright, yer on the right track. Hell, you hit the target." He pushed the button to send the target back to the 20-meter mark. "Do this for me," he instructed, moving so that his form was pressed against hers from behind. "I want you to aim for his left hip, right at the base of his ribcage, above his thigh. Will you do that for me?"

Her breath caught. "Yes." She aimed the gun toward the target's left hip.

"Good. Then, after you pull the trigger, take a breath, exhale and fire the exact same shot...until you're out of ammo. Ok?"

She nodded and forced herself to focus on the target. She squeezed the trigger. She squeezed it again. The shots rang, one after another.

The lengths of their thighs were touching, and the majority of her back was in contact with his chest. She leaned into him harder than she had to, and Cat drank in the intoxication of her. A sheer layer of cursory fabric separated them from intimate touch. He lost count of the shots she fired. She squeezed the trigger again. A nearly silent "click" was the only answer. Delilah, before she even knew, had squeezed out twelve rounds of lead.

"Gods," she said softly.

Neither moved for the space of several breaths, remaining pressed against one another in the reclusive range. Reluctantly, Catwalk stepped away from her, pressing the button to draw the target closer. As it drew near, each of them witnessed the results. Delilah had fired twelve shots. With his guidance, nine had struck within two points of the heart. Two of the others were within three points. The only exception was her initial shot.

"I did that?" Excitement boiled over in her voice.

Cat grinned with pride. "Aim low if you know the recoil is gonna drive yer shot upward."

"Aim low," she repeated.

With a broad gin, she looked toward the boxes of ammunition. "Again?"

A smile crossed his lips, mirroring hers. He tapped the call button on the wall. "Jack, we're gonna need some fresh targets down here."

CHAPTER THIRTY-FIVE

"Over two dozen vehicles are now ablaze as a result of the tanker's accident, and countless lives have been lost in this tragic attack." Scoop McEwan's voice delivered the up-to-the-second news with his trademark clarity and definition. McEwan once again provided the play-by-play to the massive loss of human lives with the candor of a ringside announcer at the latest Murderball tournament.

Catwalk was already gearing up when the comm signaled him. "Yeah?"

"Your tone indicates you've witnessed the newsworthy events coming in?" Delambre asked.

"I'm on it."

"I feel I'd be failing you if I did not inform you that some of the stills I've seen include a silhouette identical to the one who tried to murder you at The Cell Block."

"The Angel."

"I've never heard the term used more inappropriately."

"Shock. Shock. Shock. Shock. Shock. The metallic whore who beheaded Midas and nearly did the same to me?"

"Much better."

"Good, I'm lookin' forward ta puttin' an end ta that flyin' bitch." Cat slipped his gloves on, leaping onto the awaiting motorcycle.

"M'sieu Catwalk, I'd advise against a reckless approach to this enemy."

"Got some advice for yer partner suddenly, Delambre?"

The geneticist paused and responded by quoting a writer dead for nearly two centuries. "'There are chords in the hearts of the most reckless which cannot be touched without emotion. Even with the utterly lost, to whom life and death are equally jests; there are matters of which no jest can be made.' Take care, Catwalk. This is no typical opponent. Your life, our lives, may very well rest on your next actions."

Cat stopped, staring at the gauges of the motorcycle, held prison by Delambre's sudden literary obsession. He wanted to say something, anything, to acknowledge the advice of the man who'd provided guidance and mentoring in their short relationship. Instead, he killed the signal, his lips curling into a sneer beneath the mask. Only a few kilometers away, an angel beckoned, an angel desperately in need of being dragged back down to earth.

The scene was everything he'd expected. Accidents piled up at the intersection of Highway 110 and the Santa Monica Freeway, causing a panicked legion of backups in every direction. Cat steered the H-S along the emergency lanes and between traffic, startling parked pedestrians and those who had abandoned their vehicles. He slowed the roaring engine as he caught a glimpse of the murderess streaking through the air in the distance.

Civilians ran by him, terrified, and the usual flurry of law enforcement agents and media formed a semi-circle before him. As he approached, he studied her. Her every attack was performed in clean-cut repetition, almost a figure eight through the air with only a variance at the end when she chose an individual target. The local boys should have picked up on it with their targeting computers, just as he had.

She was flying in a pattern.

Either the programming of this airborne killer was very, very basic, or she was baiting him. Cat grinned, and he could picture her creator patting himself on the back. It was that obvious. She was executing a pattern, intent on catching him when she neared ground level. With each descent, the gunfire and screams increased, and panic flowed outward among the civilians like a tidal wave.

Cat knew patterns. They were predictable and therefore flawed. Any combatant who knew his enemy's next move would be victorious. It drove him to study martial arts instead of accepting a pre-loaded chip that would program him with the skills. Programs contained algorithms, and algorithms created patterns. Predictable. Flawed.

"Alright, ya high-flyin' pleasure model, let's play," he said aloud, even if only he could hear. He pulled the shotgun from his shoulder holster, leveling the barrel at the tail end of one of the nearby CorpSec cruisers. With two blasts, he destroyed the rear tires of the vehicle, bringing the car's rear bumper in contact with the well-worn pavement of the Freeway.

He shouldered the still-smoking shotgun, steered the H-S hard to his left, aligning it with the rear of the damaged cruiser. A distant look confirmed that the Angel hadn't changed her attack pattern. The cleaner exhaled sharply. She wasn't processing the new change in environment.

The H-S struck the police cruiser at a low enough degree to launch it skyward. A second later, Cat and his motorcycle illuminated the skyline. The flashes of a hundred media fired in the air. He drew in a breath and leapt. The hitman pounced from his vehicle, catching the winged assassin by surprise.

Angelyka squealed in anguish and horror as the very flesh-and-blood being she'd been sent to exterminate slammed into her. Cat quickly wrapped a forearm around her neck. The construct's inhuman voice shrieked at him. She changed direction immediately. They took off northbound along the highway. Striking her left wing with the baton, Catwalk held on for dear life.

The angel's flight pattern became erroneous. She smashed into an occasional street lamp or the roof of an abandoned truck. She caught the worst end of the tactic at first. Soon, she corrected, and it was Catwalk who collided with the obstacles. His helmet clanged against a streetlight, then a construction ahead sign. He gripped tighter, focusing on his own breath. Metallic tones rang in his ears.

Angelyka performed a barrel roll, seeking to regain control of her flight. Cat craned his neck upward to follow their flight path.

"Oh, chit," he screamed. His enemy shifted to her right, and the two of them brushed the side of an armored Hovertank in a shower of sparks. With his weight and the near miss, the angel lost control, and the pair spiraled downward.

They banged hard off of a parked rescue vehicle, and Catwalk nearly lost his grip. Instinctively, he gripped harder with his arm around her throat. The duo tumbled and rolled, tearing up pieces of pavement. The black-framed, dead eyes of the angel met with the defiant gaze of the hitman. For an instant, the world disappeared, swallowed by the absolute hatred they shared.

Consumed with one another, they never saw it coming. They smashed through the plate glass windows of Good Samaritan Hospital. Shards of glass embedded into the flesh of the angel and the cleaner as the pair crashed into the Emergency Ward. Cat lost his grip. He bounced several times across the tile floor before he slammed into the nurses' station, his back forced into a bridge. The air left his lungs. White lights flashed in his skull. If he'd been human, his vertebrae would have cracked under the strain. Fortunately, his spine was anything but human.

His head swam. He could make out figures, all moving in slow motion. Some moved toward him. Others moved away. It was a dream, a slow, terrible dream. He coughed and recognized the taste of blood on his tongue. Somewhere in the distance, the sounds of Angelyka's impact indicated that she'd been just as unlucky. Her metallic shriek resonated in his head again. He pushed himself upward from the crash cart, too focused to catch the irony.

And then it began.

It started with one scream. Then panic spread its icy fingers through the room. The personnel and patients reacted in sheer terror. Fight-or-flight instinct kicked in. Scared beings stepped over and around him. They flooded to the shattered glass of the exit. Cat struggled to find his balance. He was pushed side to side in the sea of fleeing bodies. Looking up, he realized he had a moment of opportunity to get the jump on his enemy.

Angelyka hardly raised her eyes from the cold hospital floor when Cat's boot struck the side of her head. She rolled several times, her neck craned hard to the right. Cat sprinted after her. He stomped on the tile floor where she lay. She folded her arms and wings against her body. His boot crushed the tile. He repeated the movement, but her momentum carried her body just out of his range. Cat moved faster, but the Angel was slipping further away. Safely out of range, she rose to her feet.

The Angel spread her wings to gain balance. She reached for anything nearby and threw it in his direction as a diversion. Cat blocked or shrugged off her desperate interference. He kicked aside an empty wheelchair. An empty bedpan sailed past his head. The pattern had worked. Cat lifted his right hand and fired the pistol three times, rupturing the Angel's left wing. Angelyka let forth a howl. The glass of the patient rooms shattered, raining glass down on the hitman.

The angel's fractured wing drew inward. Cat approached, gun raised. Angelyka struck with her opposite wing. He fired the pistol, punching holes in the ceiling. Her blow knocked him backward. Cat landed on one knee, focusing on his injured prey as she retreated down a side hall. He raised the pistol. With a snarl, Angelyka spun to her right, and the outermost point of her right wing fired forward at him. He barely had time to move before the metallic projectile sliced through an IV bag. The blade embedded in the wall next to his head. Saline doused his armor as he stole a quick glance at the sharp spike embedded in the tiled wall. Cat recuperated and digested the new development. She broke the pattern.

That was bad news.

Angelyka had more attacks than he'd guessed. He was lucky to have evaded this round. Had she been on the offensive, he may not have had the split-second he needed. He looked at the metallic spike. It took both hands to pull it out of the wall. It was sharpened to a razor-fine point, but contained no contact poison or other inhibitors. It was designed solely to shred the flesh of victims.

So, there it was. Risk being a dartboard for a deadly, fast MetaHuman, or fall back and figure out his options. Cat looked at the hospital signs.

"Shockit," he spat, the taste of blood still on his tongue. He loaded a fresh clip into his pistol and followed the Angel's trail.

CHAPTER THIRTY-SIX

Catwalk poked his head around the corner, expecting immediate counter-action. Instead, he found only the damaged remnants of another hospital hallway. A lighting fixture swung loosely from one end, showering sparks along the sterile tile floor. This hallway had been abandoned. He stepped forward with a degree of caution, Delambre's words suddenly resonating within him. "'Even to the utterly lost...there were matters of which no jest can be made.'" Hell, he'd carried a death wish for years. Could that artificial reflection of another woman be any different?

He turned left to find more of the same. Hospital beds bent and overturned. He ran video, if only to recognize those too weak or too slow to get out of the way. Scars cut into the walls. Glass and concrete fragments littered the hallway, still no sign of the destructor. This time however, he picked up a few more screams evident in the distance. He increased his pace.

Another left. A right. Another right. More of the same. Each revealed more damage, more victims, and more signs that he was closing the gap. Cat increased his pace, and his heart rate, with each new pathway.

He turned to his right. The familiar sulfur scent of new flame caught his nose. On instinct, he lifted his forearm skyward. The metal spike clanged off of his armored glove. The blade bounced harmlessly down the hall behind him. With a sneer, he cursed himself for not having read the signs. Angelyka stood at the far end of a long hall. Her left wing hung limp at her side, her lips curled in hatred. Her right arm was hidden behind her, her right wing partially open. Cat stopped. She was hiding something.

Cat snuck a quick glance to the left and right. The sides of the hallway were made up of paned glass. The sound

163

that hit his ears made him stop cold. He could hardly make out the silhouettes of equipment, and the increased octave of the crying voices. The angel had led the fight to the children's ward.

Cat stopped. A bead of icy sweat trickled down his neck. He froze. Why? Why now? He'd killed before. He'd killed children before, for a fee. Now, something was different. Those voices weren't just hospital cases. They were children. They were innocent children. Something clicked within him, and Shockit, it was exactly what the Angel had been banking on.

She shook her head, shards of glass showering the floor. "Let's see how you handle this particular challenge, Cat." The tone of his name dug into his skin. Her voice was an intrusion. No, not her. Its voice.

She shifted her weight and turned, opening her wing. Her right arm held a bandaged boy no more than two years old. She grunted and threw the child along the floor of the hallway. The crying boy rolled along the tile. The construct shifted her right arm backward to strike.

Cat sprinted and leapt. Angelyka launched a series of blades from the tips of her right wing. Cat dove. He wrapped his arms around the child. The blades strike his back. One clanged needlessly off of his armor. The other two found their way beneath the mesh, tearing through his skin. Blue flame filled his veins. He screamed against his will.

He clutched the child against his chest. He tried to find his feet, but his body wouldn't listen. He fought the desire to inspect the damage. Instead, he pushed the child into the nearest doorway, out of the angel's line of sight. The blades could remain in his back as long as the innocent kid was safe. With a grunt, he made it to his feet, holding his left arm flush against the doorframe while his adversary watched his movements.

The Angel grinned and tilted her head to the side, seeming less human than any other time he'd ever seen her. "How…interesting."

As he staggered, she reached into the room closest to her, pulling forth three children. Through his haze, Cat saw two girls and a boy, probably a family. Cat regained strength, the blood flowing freely down his back under his uniform. "C'mon Angel, this is between you an' me, not these bags a' flesh."

Her response was a grin and a slight bending of the

light across her inhuman eyes. "If they are so inhuman, let's see how you handle this." Angelyka pressed two bandage-laden children in his direction, clear targets for her next attack.

Catwalk darted forward as she fired the line of blades. With a leap, he blocked several blades and let the others contact the mesh of his armor. Rolling to a knee, he assessed the additional damage he'd suffered. The two children behind him stood, wide-eyed and unhurt.

As the cleaner rose to one knee, merely five meters from his enemy, he saw the final attack he couldn't stop. Angelyka drove the razor edge of her right wing deep into the chest of the third child. Her inhuman eyes stared directly into Catwalk's as her blade drove through the dark-haired girl's chest. Her insult to the cleaner was clear as she spoke. "You are fragile."

Awash in hatred, Cat leapt in her direction. As he did so, she threw the dead girl at him, causing him to grab her and roll in response. He continued to roll past her as Angelyka moved to evade him. She re-grouped and prepared to attack his prone form.

Cat hugged the dead child against his chest, indignant and venomous. He reached backward, and felt the cold steel of the closed elevator doors. Instinctively, he reached up and slammed the closest button on the wall. Shifting his gaze, he saw Angelyka rise to her feet. She began to stride towards him with a self-indulgent smile.

As she neared, the doors opened behind him. Clutching the dead girl tightly, he darted into the open elevator. The angel sprinted forward to catch him. He made out every feature of her disgusting form, just before the doors closed.

The seconds of delay felt like eternity to the construct. She had the Cat at her mercy, and the pause in his assassination caused by an elevator button was inexcusable. Her hatred rose at having missed her chance to slaughter him. When the elevator opened, she grinned. He would no doubt be grieving the child he couldn't save. His humanity made him weak. He was hers to destroy.

The elevator doors opened, revealing a solitary figure. The dead girl stained the floor of the elevator. The hitman was nowhere in sight. Angelyka listened, and when she heard the slightest sound, she reacted. With a shriek, she drove the razor blades of her wing time and time again through the roof of the elevator car. Sparks showered down on her as her metal wing pierced the elevator car. After several strikes, she paused, the holes in the roof offering no return in the form of blood or evidence of human reaction.

Angelyka sneered. She'd expected the Cat to perch above the car, ready for her willingness to bite on the bait of the slaughtered child. Perhaps he had fled her attack, betraying the children in an exercise of self-preservation. She grinned with an infusion to her self-esteem. She enjoyed the taste of his cowardice. Perhaps she'd kill the other children just to give him something to think about. With a smile, she raised her gaze skyward, seeking confirmation that the human had retreated from their encounter.

The elevator roof erupted inward. Angelyka turned her head away from the debris on instinct. Cat dropped from his grip on the cable, slamming his fist into the side of the angel's skull. He landed in the elevator and kicked the back of her leg, forcing her to the floor. Seeking refuge from any other civilians, he slammed the button for the top floor. Angelyka attempted to stand, but Catwalk's combination of kicks and strikes kept her pinned to the elevator floor as the doors shut.

The whining sound above indicated that the elevator was ascending. Reaching downward, he grabbed Angelyka by her neck, pulling her to face him. As they moved upward, he slammed her stunned form against every available wall, his eyes focused on the damage he could inflict on this harbinger of death.

Without any cognitive guidance, he simply swung his fists and steered her form from left to right, again and again finding the flesh-like weaknesses of her constructed body. His blows struck her jaw, the sides of her face, her eyes, over and again as the elevator car rose floor by floor. With every strike, he lost touch with any humanity that existed within him. All he wanted was vengeance on the Angel for the children she had just slain.

Her protests decreased in volume and frequency as he struck her again and again. Slowly, recognition of his physical state found him once again. The acute pain of his shoulders and arms crawled into his awareness. Blood soaked his armor and stole from his arms. His breathing was forced, and every ounce of his inner venom was taxed. He opened his eyes and caught himself by surprise.

Beneath his fists, the tear-filled eyes of Delambre's daughter looked up at him.

"Please...Cat...Please..." she gurgled on her own blood.

Catwalk rose upward in surprise, creating a distance between them. Had he been hallucinating so badly that he'd assaulted Eva? What complications in his makeup could have forced him to such a resolution?

The eyes of the angel at his mercy shifted once again to those of an inhuman construct. The claws rose, narrowly missing his face. Falling backward, he landed flatly as Angelyka fired a series of blades into the ceiling above. As the light and cold of the night air found them, she raised her claws and tore aside a section of the ceiling. Casting one last glance at him, she pushed upward on her damaged wings and pressed into the night sky.

Cat caught her form moving away against the skyline. Extending his baton, he fired the tip in her direction. With a one-in-a-who-shockin-knows chance, the tracer landed squarely against her right wing. He'd be able to track her to her creator's lair after all.

Exhausted, he collapsed to the floor of the elevator, wishing against all he'd known that he could simply replace one...just one...of his actions tonight. He rolled to his right. He brushed the dark hair from the face of the dead girl, his hand feeling infinitely warmer than her flesh. The words caught in his throat, far before they ever found their way to his lips.

"I'm...I'm so sorry."

The pale form of the murdered child was unresponsive and unforgiving as he pulled her close to him, trying with every breath and every tear to reignite any spark of life within her. Unable to justify the death of innocence on any level, Catwalk collapsed on his side in the elevator, pulling the murdered girl's form against his and rocked her in an effort to help her sleep fitfully in the afterlife she'd experienced far too soon.

The tears were unexpected and undeniable. Something inside of him was human after all. In this moment, that something was all that mattered.

CHAPTER THIRTY-SEVEN

10 July 2029

The bizarre man dubbed Saint Taki laughs loudly, setting the tone for their first face-to-face meeting. A veteran of the East Coast scene who fled to Nitro City as the Corporate Militia began wiping out entire blocks in an effort to censor people, Taki established safety out west. He's chosen a handle from those among the original graffiti artists and carries a reputation heavier than an armored hover car.

Tonight, Cat finds himself in Saint Taki's chair, a virtual throne amongst the celebrities of Nitro City. The drugs are far above average, and the connections just happen to come through. Framed with unnaturally high cheekbones, Taki always seems to be laughing, mostly at his subjects, rather than with them. His blonde hair is spiked high, with glowing blue tips. He faces Catwalk, meeting the unaffected glowing yellow gaze of the hitman. As Cat removes his shirt, Taki's response is instantaneous.

The tattoo artist of nearly two decades' fame takes less than six seconds to draw his own verdict. "Chit, man, I can't help you."

Cat raises an eyebrow and challenges him. "Why's that?"

"Man, you got more scars than skin...inkin' you would be like paintin' on top a' someone else's Mona Lisa." Taki powers off his equipment, slapping Catwalk on his shoulder. "You better find a clean slate, man. Your chit is way shocked up."

The glimmer of light and rough outlines appeared within his vision. Waves of time ebbed and flowed before he could register the shapes as human. It was a gunshot to his skull when his eyes began to process details to his brain. Cat nearly vomited at the sudden motion sickness. The dull pressure of a hand registered on his chest, and he dared to focus on the form.

At first, all he saw was the damaged Angel, staring down at him. He tried to rise, meeting the firm grip of restraints across his chest and legs. The pain of a hundred needles stabbed into his back, and he howled in pain. "Cat, please, calm down."

The voice was unmistakably human, nothing like that of the vicious construct. He looked again, and Eva's soft gaze met his. Her hair was slightly unkempt and lines of exhaustion framed her eyes. A weary sense of obligation emanated from her. As he slowed his breath, so did she.

"Eva."

"You've gone through a lot of surgery, and several infusions, Catwalk. I need you to remain as still as possible. That's why you're restrained."

"You don't lie very well."

She turned away. "I knew you'd react that way when you saw me. I wasn't about to have fourteen hours of surgery undone by your gut reaction."

Cat took in his environment. This was the warehouse, the base of operations Delambre had established. "Fourteen hours?"

Eva simply nodded, drawing a cup of steaming tea to her lips.

"How'd you get me out of the hospital?"

She looked out of the window, the orange sun reflecting in her brown eyes. Whether the sun was rising or setting, Cat had no idea. "We paid the doctor on call to pronounce you dead. The news feeds have a great number of pictures of your corpse."

Cat laughed but arching even slightly reacquainted him with the pain in his back. "Did you have to replace anything?" He tried to check for new cybernetics without being able to look at his body. Nothing felt different, but anesthesia had a weird way of invoking that symptom.

Eva kept her focus on the streets outside. "There were a number of contusions, deep abrasions of the Latissimus Dorsi, Teres Major, Trapezius, and tears to the Thoracolumbar Fascia."

"Naturally," he replied sarcastically.

"I also had to re-align a number of your artificial vertebrae. That was an interesting lesson. It's not like your cybernetic spine comes with an owner's manual."

His spine and legs were the result of his involuntary status as a guinea pig back in DC. "Hey, at least I can tell women I really am one of a kind."

"I'm sure they're relieved to hear that."

Cat chuckled. She had her father's gift for rebuttals. He closed his eyes, mentally replaying the events of the night. The memory hit him like a cold rush of sorrow and fear. He laid his head back against the operating table. "That kid...that girl...I got her killed."

"You saved the others," Eva said, returning her eyes to him.

"Call it what you want. They never woulda been in danger if I hadn't wound up there. It's my fault."

"I don't mean those few children in the ward."

Cat looked up at her, questioning her statement. "What do you mean?"

Eva stepped across the open space while she explained, standing next to his bed. "When you encountered Angelyka, she had already drawn the media and local Corporate forces. She did so by going for high-profile targets. That malicious thing had caused the destruction of a shipment of organs to be donated. She, it, then burned a bus of kids heading for a Scientific Achiever's Convention to receive a group award for their kinetic analysis."

"Think it was coincidence?"

"No, Catwalk, I don't. The stats that have amassed so far indicate that of the 47 casualties caused by the combined attacks on the highway and in the hospital, 27 were children." Eva's tone sharpened as she allowed emotion to enter, leaving the statistics behind. "That one isn't like the others. She has a destructive nature at her core. If she had a soul, it would be black."

Cat nodded in agreement. "Pisses you off, doesn't it?"

Eva's response was louder and more heated than he'd expected. "That thing wears my face, my face, Catwalk. Not some artistic mask of some religious rhetoric. You may be prepared to wear the face of a monster, but not me. " She stepped back, shaking her head, "Not me."

Cat shut his mouth instead of attempting to reach out to her. She was a scientist, a medical practitioner, an analyst of anatomy. He was a killer or protector depending on the paycheck. It was a coin toss some nights. He wanted a cigarette or a drink, anything other than to continue this conversation. He hurt enough already. Hurting her wasn't helping.

She bit her lip and stared mutely at the floor while he reassessed his position. Finally, he decided on a different topic. "How much of the surgery did your father perform?"

Eva raised her gaze and something told Cat to look at her. Eva's eyes were tearing up as the words reached her lips. "None. He was gone when I brought you back here."

CHAPTER THIRTY-EIGHT

"So, the scientist has him," Cat exhaled sharply with the last word, his mental focus shifted to how soon he could fight again. If the scientist had been willing to send an assassin out after him, he was certainly willing to add kidnapping to his rap sheet.

"I don't know."

"You said he was gone, not he left. How did you know?"

Eva sipped on the hot tea again, staring at the cup when she withdrew it from her lips. "There were signs of struggle. Things were broken. The lab was damaged."

"Blood?"

She squeezed her eyes shut tightly, the cup shaking in her hands. She nodded. Trying to actually answer him may have sent her over the edge.

Cat started taking stock of resources. He was already mad about letting innocents die in his battle with Angelyka. Turning his back on the geneticist who came to him for protection was an amateur move. "Get these things off a' me."

Eva drew in a breath. "No."

"I'm not kidding."

"Neither am I, Catwalk. You can't run after him in this condition. There are still a number of areas the nanobots haven't completed yet."

"Listen, lady," the hitman replied, the tension rising within him reflected in the increased pain throughout his back. "If you keep me here, your father may not be alive when I find him."

She nodded. "I know."

"Shockit, Eva, I can't let your father down. Let me up." His voice sounded mechanical inside of his head, less human than machine.

"Catwalk, my father and I have discussed this exact

situation countless times. I'm not freeing you until I have an indication that you're in a condition indicative of your rehabilitation."

Cat wrestled against the restraints, his anger growing even more. "Eva, let me out of here. Delambre needs me."

The anger was contagious, and the brown-eyed medic raised her tone to match his own. "Is that how it is, Catwalk? Or is it in fact the other way around? You don't have a damned care about my father beyond what he means to your operations and your bank accounts."

"That's a load an' you know it," he snapped back.

"Is it? Tell me about my father? Tell me about how you interact, for starters."

"That's easy. He gets on my ass every day about smokin' and drinkin'. He's like an annoyin' teacher tellin' me I'm poisoning myself with toxins every time we meet."

Eva darted forward, leaning over him so close their breath shared the same space. "You self-absorbed, goddamned lunatic. You really don't even see anything if it isn't about you, do you? My father has smoked a pack a day for the last decade. He loves a good Scotch, and I've seen him drink military veterans under the table." She stood back up with full eyes. "You just don't get it."

Cat was completely taken aback. How had he missed so much about the man with whom he trusted his very life? "Shockit, Eva, I had no idea. You're right. I've made it all about me, an' I still do. He came to me to help protect you, an' if I let him down, we're both gonna lose someone we need."

Her eyes moved away from him, her response barely audible, "You're not going to lose anything."

"What are you talking about?"

It was years before she spoke. "My father has never been your caretaker. His expertise is on a cellular level. His doctorate is in microbiology and immunology. His passion is research, solving puzzles, finding a cure. He never had more than an actor's part in your treatment and development."

Cat dropped his head back against the bed, the new awareness striking him like a tidal wave. "Christ, it was you…"

She nodded, staring absently through him rather than directly at him. "When you first used that name for me, I nearly broke down the door frames to get at you. I was so insulted, so angered at you. Then, when I calmed down, I realized how appropriate it was. I'd been the one masquerading, putting one face forward while playing a different role the entire time. I'd been the one healing you, while lying every step of the way."

She sighed. "As it turns out, it describes me perfectly."

Cat opened his mouth to protest but the chirp of his comm interrupted him. Eva stepped away, deciding to read the latest stats on the nanobots rebuilding his torn tissue. Unable to answer the call, Catwalk merely laid on the table, pissed at himself for being played the fool. The more he thought about it, the angrier he was for dragging Delambre and Eva into his world. They were safer when they were out there openly in danger. Through him, they'd become active targets, no different than the poor little girl who died in his arms last night.

Cat exhaled sharply and focused on his breathing. Eva wasn't going to let him move and fighting the healing process would only prolong it, likely costing Delambre his life. Instead, he concentrated on returning to harmony with his body. He'd need to heal to be worth anything to the geneticist and his brilliant daughter.

He swore inside his mind. The moment the restraints were lifted, nothing would keep him from revenge on the scientist and his creations. There was blood to spill, and it was calling him with every precious moment.

The words he'd studied in his early cop years rose to his consciousness. His surgery had come with no anesthesia or pain dampening biotech programs. The only thing that kept him sane and effective was the training he'd learned for himself, mental balance and fluidity. What were the master's words? "Empty your mind. Be formless…Be water, my friend."

He closed his cybernetic eyes, drawing deep within himself, the only true destination to which he could travel. The journey within opened his perspective in ways he couldn't foresee.

CHAPTER THIRTY-NINE

15 March 2022

The rain provides the percussion against the window. The creaky boards down the hall mix with the overblown air handlers to provide the harmony. Leon has heard it all before. He nearly has it memorized. Tonight, the melody is different, and it's the one thing he can't control.

His sobs and tears are the dominant melody, overwhelming all other sounds. He was placed in St. Patrick's Orphanage only days before, and he still can't believe where he is, or what he is. The wool blanket is itchy and heavy. The mattress is a cage. The entire place is a prison. Trying to reason with it all, he erupts into a new fit of tears.

He tries to reason with himself without success. Every time he tries to tell himself things will be okay, his perspective is drawn again to his new reality. His legs remain dormant, unresponsive, dead. His eyes close again and new tears crease his face. He wants to die more than anything. He wants release from the cage of the half-corpse he has become.

The yellow light creases his field of vision long before he opens his eyes. He feels the light, the warmth, eons before he can focus. When his dark eyes open, the golden warmth silhouettes her form in the doorway. She is solace, sanctuary, safety. When he finally focuses, she is standing above him, the woman who welcomed him to the walls of this establishment. She smiles down on him, her face displaying the signs of age and toughness she's developed over her years here. "You sound very alone, Leon. Would you like some company?"

He cannot even vocalize a response, settling instead on a nod. When she leans down to him, he clings to her as if his life exists solely in her arms. He buries his head against her, needing the comfort of someone, anyone, a

175

soul who understands him. She brushes his black hair with the softest touch.

"It's okay, my son," she states quietly.

Son. He struggles to remember his parents, any fleeting spark of a memory of either of them. There is nothing of his father, not even the slightest light of a distant dying star. Of his mother, he seems to remember dark eyes, caring eyes…sad eyes. He remembers love and wanting, but nothing more. She is one more unknown, another unrecognized soul in the vast world of dead souls he's come to know.

There is no father. There is no mother. The thought makes him grip tighter to the form of the woman who introduced herself as Sister Mary Cassandra. To him, she may as well be life itself.

As if sensing his desperation, she speaks softly. "Leon, sweet Leon," she hugs him, her cheek resting atop his head, "if you'd like, you can call me Mother."

Leon anchors to her to prevent his very soul from floating adrift, finding comfort in the warmth of his new caretaker. For the first time since his accident, he finds sleep in her arms. In his dreams, he runs faster than motorcycles, he leaps to tenth-floor rooftops, and his eyes glow with the golden glory that provided the backlight of his new mother's arrival.

When Leon opens his eyes, the storm is at its greatest point of assault. The thunder makes the orphanage walls tremble. He hears the pounding of the rain against the window. It echoes in the hallways where the patchwork roof has given way to the rainfall. Mother has left his side. He has no idea how long she stayed by him while he cried himself to sleep.

Her devotion speaks volumes. So much of her finds its way inside of him. His parents are unknown, at best, figments he's recreated out of wishes. After days, and now months in the hospital, they've attempted no contact. They may as well be dead. In terms of Leon's life, they've always been corpses, memories he's created. The orphanage and the orphans within are the only family he has.

A flash of lightning illuminates the silhouette of the wheelchair at the foot of his bed. The peel of thunder follows it within seconds. The storm is directly atop them now, its intensity driving relentlessly down on St. Patrick's. Leon watches the dark spot where he saw the wheelchair a second before.

Another flash of lightning and eruption of thunder. The wheelchair remains in place, an anchor amidst a torrid sea of uncontrolled waves. Leon focuses on the words of his new mother. She was quoting another philosopher, but the words struck true.

'As you think, so shall you become.'

Leon repeats the words as a mantra, his eyes never leaving the spot where the wheelchair rests between flashes with every recurrent streak of lightning. He moves, swiveling the dead weight of his legs off of the side of the bed. His lifeless feet strike the floor with an audible but unfelt thump. He grits his teeth, staring at the intermittent outline of the wheelchair.

'As you think, so shall you become.'

Palms on the bed, he dips downward, then pushes himself back up. He repeats the process again...and again...and again. The wheelchair's silhouette watches him, a mocking ghost, as the subtle burn begins in his arms. Leon continues, the soft fire growing to a heated challenge in his muscles. He has already thought of himself as the one who will exit this prison in search of greater glory. It is time to become that being he perceives.

He counts the repetitions, losing sight of the strikes of thunder and lightning, which cross his gaze. He focuses simply on the dedication and compassion in the heart of his new mother.

He can make out every broken spoke in the wheel, every rusty aspect of the frame of the wheelchair when the lightning crashes again. The fire stretches through his shoulders.

He digests every rip in the vinyl covering of the wheelchair's aged seat and back. He repeats the exercise. The flames devour his upper arms.

He repeats the exercise, finally viewing the wheelchair as an object of his control, instead of the throne, which represents his enslavement. His arms scream. His lungs are adrift in a sea of fire. Still, he repeats the exercise.

'As you think, so shall you become.'

Cat's arms burned, yet he continued to repeat the exercise as the lightning peeled outside, another wave of damnation and depression on the lurkers of downtown Nitro City. His legs balanced atop the tank of the motorcycle as he lowered himself again and again, elbows bent, triceps enflamed with the pain of the repeated motion. So many years ago, he'd taken the words to heart. He'd refused the life of an invalid, living out his days as just another charity case. Instead, he'd become a cleaner, a kidnapper, protector, hitman, extortionist, and killer all in one. He'd done questionable things. He'd associated with the most corrupt and the most honorable of partners.

Anything was better than rotting away in that goddamned wheelchair.

The comm broke his focus, recalling him to the here and now. Reluctantly, he lowered his feet to the ground, then shifted his weight to them. His arms pulsed in inflamed protest. His fingers shook as he clicked on the comm. Dead Air. He'd missed the call.

He checked the comm, and the light indicated he'd missed eight messages. His fingers were still unsteady when he tried to light the cigarette he raised to his lips. Sitting squarely on the floor, he checked the last few days' messages.

Four were from reporters. The first was McEwan, the ace had tracked him down before the rest. Two others followed suit, seeking an interview with the man who took down the angel who had gutted local law enforcement and terrorized school children. McEwan had left another message after the time of Cat's supposed death. He was a true professional, declaring his intentions to secure an exclusive interview, even though the hitman was allegedly a corpse.

Cat laughed at Scoop's tenacity. Shockit, he was good.

The other four messages were from Delilah. The first was nonchalant, almost jovial in tone. "Heya, Tiger. I think you have my comm. I looked everywhere for it, but can't track it down. It's okay. Really, I had the photographer re-route his calls through the Hotel to schedule our upcoming shoot, but if you have it, let me know, k? Oh yeah, by the way, my arms are killing me! You should have said I'd be sore for days, even if we kept our clothes on. Ok, I can't believe I just said that. I'm going. Call me at the hotel. Smooches!"

A grin crossed his face. Her second and third messages

were equally off-the-cuff. She mentioned a follow up date, even jokingly stating that he might need to decide on a safety word if they were ever alone together.

The fourth message bore a considerably different tone. "Cat," with a single word, the rawness of her throat was evident. Her breathing was ragged. She had been crying and could hardly form the words she intended to. "Cat, please pick up…please tell me what I'm seeing isn't true. You're not dead. I know you're not dead." Her voice disappeared for several seconds, returning as a barely audible whimper, "please…"

Seconds passed again, nearly silent other than her sobs. Finally, she returned loudly, "No! You promised you'd be here for me, so, damn it, Cat, you will be. You can't die. What if I need you?" Again, her voice dropped to almost nothing. Catwalk closed his eyes struggling to hear her message with more clarity. Her final words were almost inaudible no matter how hard he focused on them.

"Cat…I need you."

CHAPTER FORTY

Cat rubbed his neck, taking a break from staring at the holo-screens in front of him. Images of Angelyka, Pestylynce, and Wahrr occupied three screens. Delambre's slight smile filled the fourth. He picked up his cup of tea, again, and set it back down. It had long since gone cold while he studied the images in front of him.

"Crazy, isn't it?"

He turned surprised that Eva had managed to enter the room without his notice. She'd traded the lab coat for an oversized T-shirt and stretch pants. She offered him a freshly brewed, steaming cup of black tea. "The end of days has been a prophecy for thousands of years, and here we are, right in the middle of it."

"Some madman's version of it, you mean," he replied, accepting the tea.

She nodded. "It's personal. Maybe that's why I think the whole world is in the balance."

"Who knows, kid? None of us woke up a few weeks ago thinking we'd be where we are today. I never thought hiring yer old man would tie us ta all this." Cat gestured at the screens. He blew out a breath. "The four horsemen? The whole book a' Revelations? Damn it."

Eva didn't reply. She simply sipped at her tea. Cat cursed at his behavior. "I'm sorry. I didn't mean…"

"This wasn't a mistake, and it wasn't an accident. We're here for a reason." She walked around the back of the couch, intent on the screens before them. "So, this is everything you have on the Metas so far?"

"I think so. I have a guy running invoices and purchase orders for me. He's really good. Maybe he gets me a name, or an alias, but I don't think he gets me a real address." Cat ran a hand through his hair. "It's frustrating."

Eva nodded again as she sat next to him on the couch.

"We can make assumptions that my father's former co-worker is the man behind the attacks. We need more. Are you sure this is all you have on these MetaHumans?"

Cat eyed her as she sat next to him. Her behavior was strange. He almost questioned if she might be a Meta herself, but quickly shook it off as he watched her digest data from the files. "If I go over my data, that's pretty much it." He shook his head. "I do have this image from the first MetaHuman." He added the image of the faces on the cross to the holoscreens.

Eva took a sip of tea. "That's pretty gruesome. Ever seen it before?"

"Ever seen what?" Cat lifted his eyes to meet hers.

"That image."

He stood, removing any physical contact they shared. "Yeah, yeah, yeah. This image was on the prototype, but I don't know that it means anything."

Eva set her cup down. "I'd say that's a pretty clear image of the horsemen, and the hell we're all supposed to be paying right about now."

Cat stopped. *The Horsemen.* "I think I see what we've been missing."

"What?"

He shrugged off her response. The warmth of her body next to him seconds ago had been a distraction. He realized all the details he'd missed about Delambre. He remembered the crushing power against his body for being so close to Emory Blake.

"Too close," he muttered.

"What?" Eva rose in protest.

"Too close," he replied. Cat took the images of the horsemen and forced them outward. The faces on the prototype's image attached themselves to those of the known Horsemen. War, Pestilence, and the Angel of Death all blinked back at him. A new file blinked at him with a question mark for the image of identification. The name stated merely "Famine."

Eva stopped a step behind him. "What forensics program are you using for this?"

"I'm not. I'm using a PR campaign." Cat exhaled, mad at what he had missed.

Cat pressed his fingers against the holoscreen, then extended them. The image of each Horseman matched to a different target. War, Pestilence and the Angel of Death immediately found their corresponding MetaHuman.

Famine connected with the big question mark.

Eva leaned forward. "I've seen those pictures."

Cat nodded. "If yer gonna build a giant church, you better convince yer customers that the Endgame is underway. Otherwise, you get no congregation."

"Oh my God," she replied. "I remember now."

The drive through overcast skies escorted him west and north along the shoreline. Catwalk passed Santa Barbara, then Goleta. The potholes and brush that had claimed the pavement of Route 101 reached up to grip at him, desperate fingers of the undead. As the brush thickened, Delilah's desperate words resonated in his head. "Cat, I need you."

He'd come this way before. He vaguely remembered the path when it was pristine and new. A few years of disarray had set the stage for its decomposition. The 101 gave way to a slighter pathway, a single-lane delivery to the opening arms of an ornate church. What a church it had been or could have been. The builders had copied the architecture of the famous cathedrals of Old England, Wales, and the States' National Cathedral. Brick, mortar and marble climbed several stories into the air, a ladder to the heavens. Gargoyles stared soundlessly down at him from the corners. Torn and frayed trappings fought for life against the wind.

A sneer crossed his lips. The faded banners ripped left and right, slaves to the weather. Despite the fading colors and the multiple tears through the fabric, Cat recognized the images they housed. *The Horsemen.* They were the once animated and fascinating images of those who would bring about the visions in John's Book of Revelations. They were beings of mythology. They were beings of legend. They were beings of technology, and Cat had faced most of them in the last few weeks.

Here in the west, under the continuous rain, engulfed in the darkness of self-importance and disregard, the cathedral scarcely contained enough light to honor itself. The mission of its builders had been simple: seek a population to invigorate it as a source of worship and hope. Find the downtrodden people crying for a new beginning and deliver the hope they sought. That mission met instead the imposing cloud of self-righteousness and self-promotion that engulfed this territory and its population. Even before its construction was completed, the church had no prayer of beckoning followers.

It became, instead, the personification of failed religion. It was distant, dark, the hollow shell, which had failed to draw the followers on whom it so desperately relied. Built for hope, the bricks of the cathedral instead piled upward in a hollow denial of faith. The gargoyles, once menacing, now seemed to hang their heads in shame.

The motorcycle drew nearer, rising along the twisted and overgrown pathway. Cat sensed something about the place. He couldn't have been wrong about his enemy or about Delambre. This religious sadist would have chosen the largest and most obnoxious center of attention he could find. The zealot felt he could resurrect anything or improve on its design. Eva was proof of that. Even if it had failed once before, this maniac obviously felt powerful enough to draw attention to his vision again and again. Cat shook his head. It was also deathly quiet and out of the way. No one would suspect that the MetaHumans were being built in a cathedral. He was sure of it now, that the final confrontation lay within those walls. All he had to do was to outsmart the egotist who'd drawn him here.

Lightning flashed in his peripheral vision. Cat blocked it out for a while before finally stopping the H-S completely. He squeezed his eyes shut and counted a few deep breaths. So much had happened in the past few days. For the first time in months, he had a hard time focusing. The thought of Delambre dead drew his mouth into a sour frown. Eva's revelation about how much she truly knew rested squarely between his shoulder blades, and Delilah's words echoed in his skull. The cacophony of voices resonating through his head made him grit his teeth.

The moment of distraction almost proved fatal. A black figure descended on him from the cloud-filled sky, slamming into his side with enough velocity to topple him off the motorcycle. Cat rolled twice, sliding over the gravel and through the brush, nearly tumbling completely off of the side of the cliffs. Debris disappeared into the darkness below. He grabbed at anything he could. Weeds tore to pieces between his fingers. Rocks scattered in every direction. Finally, his hand grabbed a sturdy vine. He heard his shoulder pop as the vine halted his momentum. Suppressing a scream, he looked down. The crest of waves was hardly visible a hundred meters below.

Another peel of lightning flashed through the sky. Cat caught the faint outline of the battered angel circling for a second attack. He made a quick inventory of his weapons. A blast from the shotgun would likely knock him loose, even if he could even draw it in time. So much for a sound defense. He wrapped his left arm several times with a section of the withered roots. His right hand reached to his belt. He snapped the baton to its full length in his right hand. Angelyka gained speed, diving at him again. The moonlight reflected holes in her wings and deep scars along her form. She had not been fully repaired. Her left wing was patchwork.

Blades fired forth from the tips of her wings. Cat gripped the roots and tugged upward. He rolled away from the surface where the blades struck. He pinned himself against the earth. Air rushed by his head. He could hear roots snap as his attacker spiraled upward. She'd come close, but had pulled up at the last second. Angelyka couldn't take him head-on, and with her first strike a failure, she was choosing distance and speed as advantages.

If he was anywhere near the marksman he was supposed to be, the fight would already be over. Instead, the best he could do was to keep her close, get a hold on her and pound every ounce of venom out of the inhuman bitch bent on his destruction. The cleaner stayed low in the underbrush, hoping the pouring rain and the thick of the weeds would create the static he'd need to obscure his enemy's view.

The pinpoint direction of Angelyka's next dive proved his cover wasn't enough. Cat's strategy had backfired. The underbrush gripped his legs, slowing him. The Angel's bladed wings tore through the mesh and skin of his left arm. She lifted skyward again, repeating her circle of flight. Cat leapt backward. He cursed his miscalculation, pulling his legs free from the brush. He sprinted backward a few more meters, and Angelyka shifted her flight pattern. The two combatants gained time to recoup.

The fresh laceration commanded his attention despite his efforts to slow his breathing and maintain focus. He grit his teeth, and though he told himself to relax, his body refused to listen. Angelyka circled for another attack, her red eyes keyed on him. This time, she fired a barrage of blades from a closer distance. Sparks erupted as Cat parried three with the baton, while two others clattered ineffectively off of his armored legs. He forced out a deep exhalation in an effort to balance.

Her powerful right wing caught him in the midsection. The impact slammed him backward and knocked the remaining air from his lungs. He rolled once, twice, again, and again. He skidded to a knee, knocked nearly twenty meters from the angel's attack.

Breathe. Shockit, Leon, Breathe. At the rate she's going, she'll tear you to pieces. Your head isn't in this game, an' that'll mean the death of Delambre and Eva both. The welcome feeling of fresh air crept back into his lungs. Angelyka was circling, apparently admiring her work instead of moving in for the kill.

Amateur move, bitch.

Catwalk chided himself for his stupidity. He wasn't back to full health yet, and he was rushing into a fight he couldn't even analyze. Angelyka was a malicious and miraculous creation. He had barely escaped her last two attacks. Now, he was trying to take her on, wounded. He took small solace in the fact she wasn't exactly herself either.

Alright, Cat, you were almost full-throttle when this fight started. Now you're cut, bruised, and probably bleedin' internally. She hardly has any more wrong with her than what you did to her in the hospital.

The hospital.

The memories flooded his skull. In an instant, he recalled the damage he inflicted on her wing. He saw the fight in the streets, the flight over the police vehicles, the shattered glass as they struck the hospital. He saw Angelyka disappear amidst the swarm of terrified patients. He remembered the fight in the ward. He remembered protecting the two little boys. He remembered the little girl.

The little girl.

Catwalk's eyes flashed, the yellow reflecting in his helmet, as he rose to his full height. He slammed the baton into the ground, collapsing it and placing it back on his belt. Recognizing the angel's pattern in the air, he extended a hand, beckoning her with his fingers. Angelyka circled once more to gain speed then launched herself at him.

Cat once again wrapped his left arm in the vines and

brush growing underfoot. The rain seemed to change direction. The wind bowed to the malicious angel, admitting her form as its master. Her wings cut through the air, the metallic vibration sounding a challenge. She tore through a length of the underbrush as she neared him.

As she drew close enough to feel her, Catwalk leapt, catching her under the chin with his right arm. She drew upward, as she had done following every attack, and he squeezed her neck between his bicep and forearm. On instinct, she rose higher, seeking to shake her rider loose. Cat clenched his teeth and squeezed.

Then, they reached the end of the leash. Cat's grip on the roots with his left arm acted as an anchor. He screamed at the sudden pull against his shoulders, but the grip of his right arm caught the angel's throat. The sudden stop pulled them both backward violently.

A loud crack echoed in the air. It was metal on skin. It was a single beating drum in an open field. It was the neck of the angel in the grip of the cat. She stopped trying to fly higher. She stopped flying altogether. The pair of killers began to plummet back toward the ground.

Cat couldn't feel anything beyond the searing pain in his shoulder. It was more than he could bear. He couldn't remember falling, or the impact, or the effect on the angel.

By the time he caught his breath his left shoulder was ablaze. He managed to open his eyes to look for his enemy, but moving his head only amplified the pain. Looking left, he saw the angel prone on the ground, her wings folded over her motionless form. Somehow, his plan had worked. Angelyka's programming was imperfect, and the thought of avenging the innocent child in the hospital had shown Cat how to exploit it.

Grimacing, he rolled to a knee, his eyes never leaving the assassin. He tried to raise his left arm. He was answered by a white-hot field of pain. He exhaled, paused, inhaled, and concentrated. This time the left arm rose slightly higher before the synaptic refusal. It was muscle, not bone. That was all he needed to know.

Pivoting his hips, Cat swung his left arm upward, shattering the ceiling of pain. There was an audible 'pop' as his shoulder returned to place in its ball joint. The immediate agony was blinding, and he stumbled backward, nearly vomiting from the dizziness. He landed flat on his back on the ground, exhaling a stream of profanity. The rain beat down on him, and he took solace in the feeling.

Deciding against testing his left arm further, he used his right arm to help him reach his feet. The angel, thankfully, hadn't moved. Reaching onto his hip, he grabbed the baton again, snapping it to full extension. He limped toward the fallen form of his assailant.

Angelyka stared mutely forward, her eyes darkening from red to an almost human brown. As Catwalk stood over her, she turned up to him, softening her face. Again, the creature at his mercy identified itself as Delambre's daughter. This time, a tear even creased her cheek as she looked upward at him.

"Please, Leon...I beg you. Spare my life."

Cat felt every moment he'd shared with Eva. The way she'd opened up to him, pleaded for her father's life, and revealed her abilities when she didn't need to. She was brilliant but vulnerable. She was defiant, but unable to protect herself in this brutally violent realm.

And she's never, not once, called you 'Leon'.

The hitman turned his gaze away, moving it to his feet. In an instant, he struck, driving the baton straight into the eye of the creation called Angelyka. The construct screamed loudly, and Cat twisted his wrist, activating the Electro-Magnetic Pulse tip of the baton. With a crackle, the scream of the angel descended to a human range, and then became nothing more than an electronic hum.

Finally, in the continued driving of the rain, the peel of lighting and the percussive thunder, the angel was silenced.

CHAPTER FORTY-ONE

Cat slid down the length of the cliff. Momentum was easy. Control wasn't. For several moments, he was in a free-fall. He knew the feeling well. It was the brief sensation of weightlessness, pushed out of yet another Hovertank to combat some brutal unknown maniac back in the Nation's capital. He landed with a chuckle in the beach sand. He wasn't a cop anymore, but the scenario wasn't all that different. There was an out-of-control MetaHuman threat loose in the city. Only this time, the brain running it wasn't in the same body performing the attacks.

He concentrated on his breathing for several seconds. A direct frontal attack on the Cathedral ensured suicide. A simple heat scan revealed several mines and laser-wires along the road. Either he was meant to die trying, or more likely, he was being directed to another path.

The cleaner closed his eyes, focusing, concentrating, layering and defining the sounds surrounding him. The waves crashed along the shoreline in their rhythmic pattern. The flames crackled far above, a pyre for the fallen angel. The lapping of the tattered banners provided intermittent percussion. Still, there was something else, something stagnant, yet unpronounced. The slightest voice reached his ears. He identified it as a faint but steady trickle of water.

He exhaled and opened his eyes, sprinting in the direction of the waterfall. Cautiously slowing as he neared it, his gaze soon fell upon the source of the sound. A large, jagged drainpipe protruded from the mountainside providing sewage and flood relief from the Cathedral above. The rusted and bent rebar jutted out from the side of the hill. Cat thought of the vampires he'd faced defending Delilah. Hadn't he left their fangs looking about the same?

Cat watched the rats crawl around the liquid flow from the drainpipe. He lowered the thresholds on his nasal sensors. The drainpipe provided a way into the underbelly of the Cathedral, but it was going to be an unclean and gut-wrenching path.

He stopped again to gather the faces of those who depended upon him. He inhaled, cursed under his breath and leapt forward, landing in the muck of the Cathedral's sewers. He made a silent wish that nothing was alive in there. If it could survive in this buffet of defecation, he'd probably be defeated by the stench alone. Shifting the sensors of his cybernetic eyes, Cat again steeled his nerves and set forth into the bowels of the ancient church.

Any sign of light from outside disappeared a few steps into the drainpipe. The rain battered the weathered opening, echoing the metallic ringing until it was impossible to determine the source. The thought of a potential flash flood, natural or triggered, made Cat double-check his environment. A few more steps inside confirmed the feeling he was entering a tomb.

The scent of decay struck him full-force through his dampners and made him halt his progress. The air was heavy and wet, nearly thick enough to chew. It was Will's morgue without the sterility and chemical compounds that burned his throat. This was pure decay and rot. Gripping the baton harder, Cat forced himself to step forward, one cybernetic boot at a time. Vermin and unidentified debris slithered past, occasionally wrapping around his feet and legs as the water deepened.

The faint glow of his eyes reflected off of items in the muck, a scrap of metal, broken glass, cracked spectacles, discarded syringes, and a dismembered cyber limb. Either a few too many homeless had lost their way and sought refuge here, or the nomads had wandered inside only to die. Nitro City had enough lost souls to populate its own off-world colony.

Other things floated by. Some were easily identified; others were the proverbial mystery meat. Cat leveled his gaze on a spot ahead, preferring not to know what it was he was wading through. Soon, with the flooding, water or something like it, began trickling down on him. Despite the armor and insulation, grime bored into his skin.

Something solid and heavy struck Cat's legs. At first, it felt like wood, simple flotsam in the stomach-turning sewage. He turned his gaze downward, looking for a handhold to push the junk aside. It proved to be a mistake. Vacant holes returned his gaze from where the rats had devoured the dead man's eyes. His skin was bloated and chewed, while most of his clothes had rotted into scraps. The dead man's bearded and decaying mouth opened, and Cat heard him moan.

Cat kicked the putrid form aside. As he did, the arm snapped from the corpse's torso, held near the form by the remains of its coat. With an audible grunt, Cat shoved the eroded body aside, backing against the wall of the drainpipe. The dead man's head craned at an inhuman angle, his severed arm reaching back towards the hitman. The groan grew louder, a cry of desperation.

As it floated away, the vacant eyes seemed to plead to him. Even before the body disappeared, it began sinking into the muck of the sewers.

Seconds later, it was gone.

Cat pressed against the wall harder than he intended. His skin bristled in a cold sweat. His hands felt unnatural. He shook his head at the sensation and the hallucinations that circled inside his head. What was he doing here, chasing some madman and his constructs to the farthest reaches of the city? He was nearly up to his waist in rotting bodies and debris and who knew what else. This job didn't even pay. He could walk away any time. He could leave the scientist to his heretic insanity. He wouldn't lose anything.

Except Delambre.

And Eva.

Even if he didn't truly care about Delambre and his daughter, there was more to it. Losing the two of them meant starting over. It was a chance he couldn't afford to take. His cybernetics were wreaking so much havoc with his physiology that he might not have the ability to think his way through problems much longer. Losing them meant losing his best chance at survival.

It also meant losing Delilah.

The dead man's groan still haunted him. He slammed the baton against the drainpipe, creating a loud metal-on-metal clang. Not enough. He lashed out again. Sparks showered down from the metal framework. Again. He bellowed something guttural, screaming upward. The

190

ringing of the impact became a note, a chord, a chorus. He struck the pipe. Again. And again. And again. Until the endless ringing in his ears drowned out the wailing of the dead man. His ears began to ring, carrying pain into the sides of his skull. The pain allowed him to focus, to forget his fear. He stopped, shaking his head and clearing his mind. He lifted his head to strike again, and everything grew silent.

He turned his gaze once more back to the world he had known up until now. He could retreat and spend his days waiting for the next construct to come for him. He turned his back on that path, squaring up and looking ahead. The faintest glow of light graced his field of vision ahead. Something appeared far away. It was either the light at the end of the tunnel, or an oncoming train sent to crush him. Either way, it meant freedom from this horrid swamp.

Cat stepped back into the current of the sewage and walked, step by resistant step, steadily forward toward the faint beacon.

CHAPTER FORTY-TWO

Cat stopped after an eternity in the sewage. The light wasn't coming from in front of him. It was coming from above. He briefly made out the ring of light trickling down. Rusted rungs of a steel ladder beckoned him upward. With a wish for a hot shower and a warm body next to him, Cat reached up and grabbed the nearest rung. The steel held his weight. Thank the maker for small miracles. Cat started to reach upward with his left arm. Pain vetoed that idea. He gritted his teeth and formulated a new plan. Slowly, he balanced his boots on the rungs, and reached up once again with his right hand.

He found a stone hallway leading into darkness halfway up the climb. Using lowlight, his Cyberoptics showed him a room roughly ten meters away. He stepped off the ladder and headed down the hallway. The room he entered was almost perfectly round. The flickering light of torches provided the inconsistent illumination he had seen from the drainpipe.

Rising to his feet, Cat glanced around the room, recognizing it as a burial chamber. Arranged in a semi-circle, seven sarcophagi faced him, moss and algae finding their way atop a few of the carved faces. Behind him, the wall bore the tattered remains of a mosaic depicting some sort of family history. He shrugged it off. The cathedral couldn't hold generations of history. It was hardly a decade old. It could only be more theatrics from the nut job scientist behind the MetaHuman Horsemen.

He focused on the scene before him. Each sarcophagus was precisely sculpted. Its concrete visage more human than the gyrating masses at Liquid Chrome or the Cell Block. As if beckoned, he stepped to the nearest concrete tomb, pulling the brush away. The dead eyes that reflected his gaze were those of the MH he'd battled in the convenience store.

"Pestylynce," he whispered aloud.

The concrete figure seemed to move upon hearing its name. Cat fell back a few steps. The cold stone of the wall stopped his retreat. The odd pokes and prods of the carved mosaic pushed against his back. They each provided more comfort than another go-round with the inhuman he'd fought in the liquor store. He closed his eyes and steeled his will. When he opened them again, the sarcophagus provided no threat, only long shadows. He stared at the concrete face for several breaths.

"Rest in Peace, cop killer."

Gripping the baton as an anchor, he neared the second tomb. Brushing aside the overgrowth revealed the face of Eva, of Angelyka. Wings crossed her form along with her arms, proving that this was the intended tomb of the construct, not the human. Cat drew in a breath. Fear didn't enter him this time. Instead, anger found its place within his MetaHuman blood stream. Had the madmen assumed her defeat as well? Did he put that much stock in Catwalk or did he have another plan for his winged assassin? Angelyka was the most highly developed Metas he'd ever faced. Cat took offense that the madman behind it all would be willing to write off such an adversary.

He tore aside the brush covering the next concrete resting place. The cement reflection was similar to the original MH he'd seen. The face was nearly identical to the one who drew him to this case in Will's Morgue, but the features differed slightly. Wahrr.

Cat stepped back and shifted gears. If the madman had gone through all this trouble, he would have had adapted as time pressed on. Instead of continuing along the semi-circle, Cat leapt to the end. He brushed the muck off of the final cement form. Triangular eyes and elongated fangs defined the corpse's features.

"Son of a bitch," Cat laughed, staring at his own image.

He took a moment to stop and recount the sarcophagi. Seven. That made sense. Sevens were huge in Christianity, he remembered that. Sevens and threes. Four horsemen. The other three? He grumbled beneath his mask. The scientist undoubtedly had his own take on his trinity of enemies...the Father, the Child, and the Unholy Ghost. Delambre, Eva, and...

Cat felt his blood boiling before he even raised his arm. He struck without aim. His first strike cracked the face between its eyes. The second splintered the face into a dozen pieces. The third shattered the concrete and the wooden coffin it housed. Cat looked down. His forearm was embedded in the velvet interior of his intended final resting place.

Shockit, I ain't dead. An' if you got a reservation for me, madman, I'm about ta cancel it.

Cat reached the next sarcophagus, reacting with no surprise at its design. The permanent gaze of Delambre's daughter stared up at him. No wings wrapped around her vulnerable human form. This was meant to be Eva's crypt. On a whim, Cat ripped the cover aside, sending it clamoring against the crypt floor loudly. He tore open the lid of the coffin inside and found relief when he discovered it vacant.

His heart crawled into his throat. The thought of Eva in the tomb forced him to rediscover fear, for just a moment. He looked at his hands and saw them shaking. Had she suddenly become that important? "My father has never been your caretaker." Those were her words. She was responsible for his survival, his humanity. Christ, keeping her safe was his anchor to staying human. He patted a glove against the velvet lining of her would-be grave. He exhaled hard and tried to get his hands to stop shaking.

He raised his glance to the next sarcophagus. The air seemed to leave the room. His cop skills should have kicked in. He wasn't certain what to expect anymore. He should have stopped and revisited the analysis and investigation skills he'd learned in his years on the police force. For some reason, he couldn't tap into that memory, not here, not in this awful place. He forced one cybernetic footstep, then another. He muttered the closest thing to a prayer he could remember.

Cat brushed the dust and grime aside, his heart heavy with expectation. His hands cleaned away the dirt. The face looking up at him was older. Lines set in the stone around its eyes. Cat touched the stone face of Delambre. A laugh choked to silence in his throat. Delambre had offered so many jests, so many threats, so many challenges. It had all been an act. Cat smirked. Maybe Eva was the one with all the knowledge. So what? Delambre was the one who reeled him in and earned his trust. Maybe they'd share a glass of Blevins blend down the road to celebrate that very transaction.

The hitman pulled the lid aside. It teetered for a moment before falling to the floor. When the dust cleared,

Cat found himself staring at a simple, nondescript, black coffin. *Anonymous. This was a simple, everyman's final resting place.* Cat stared at the glossy black paint, watching the faded reflection of his own yellow eyes. Maybe Delambre was the man he claimed to be. Maybe he was just an act. Cat prayed silently it would be vacant. His hand shook slightly as he unlocked the coffin lid. With a deep breath, he opened it.

His prayers went unanswered.

CHAPTER FORTY-THREE

Delambre was paler and thinner than Cat remembered him. It was as if his eternal optimism and faith had deflated. With that gone, the geneticist's body seemed to age by decades. His clothes showed no signs of blood. His bones appeared intact. He most likely faced his death with the dignity he carried in every action.

Cat caught himself smirking. Hell, Delambre had probably told the scientist, his old colleague-turned-lunatic, exactly how his death was planned out down to the finest detail. There was nothing the scientist could pretend to know that Delambre hadn't already surmised. Still, here the clever old fox rested, reduced to a corpse in the underbelly of a hollowed-out cathedral, abandoned and alone.

Delambre, I failed you.

Cat absently straightened the collar and shirt of the dead man, the memories and thoughts hammering down on him. He recalled each of their interactions. He was surprised how much he respected Delambre's sarcasm, sharp wit, and fearless protection of his daughter. Eva. Cat exhaled sharply, laying his gloved hand on the chest of his deceased partner. "I'll keep her safe, Delambre. I promise."

Cat stared at the geneticist's face waiting for some snide but humorous response. The world was silent, distant, meaningless. He could almost see his breath in the stale air.

A slight sound of metal on metal alerted him from his trance like a cold shower. Instinctively, the hitman pushed off of Delambre's chest. He leapt over the sarcophagus and rolled to his feet on the opposite side.

The baton snapped to full length in his right hand, Cat looked up to face his new assailant.

A bizarre creature, hardly more than a metallic

skeleton, returned his gaze. From skull to toes, its body was covered in brushed chrome. Dreadlocked braids hung from the back of its head. Its eyes were vacant, skeletal holes, reminding Catwalk of the dead man in the sewer. Its teeth had been filed to point, providing the creation a feral grimace. Its cheekbones were raised, extending the jaw lower. The head hung at an awkward angle, nearly resting on its metallic shoulder. As it moved, the skull craned to the opposite side, as if the neck couldn't support the weight of its head.

Its body bore hardly any mass. The tips of its shoulders, collarbones and ribcage were sharpened. Its razor claws gripped the side of the sarcophagus where Catwalk had just stood. It gazed at him. A guttural vibration escaped its fanged mouth. It stepped backward and pulled aside the fractured piece of the sarcophagus. The stone crumbled to ash in its hands.

"Famyne."

The being raised the pace of its vibrations, sending out a chittering sound in acknowledgement. Catwalk leapt forward, swinging the baton in a backhand strike. The enemy's skull merely bounced from one side to the other like a rag doll. It swung a claw in response, catching air as Catwalk rolled beneath the strike. He forced a sidekick into Famyne's exposed ribs, above where a human's kidneys would be. The creation bounded off of Delambre's tomb and struck the floor. Cat paused a moment, the light glinting in his cybernetic eyes. Any human, normal or enhanced, should have collapsed at that strike.

It had no organs. This thing was a hardened, sharpened exoskeleton. Cat shook his head. Where was a good frag grenade when you needed one?

Cat targeted his enemy and changed his strategy. He grabbed a chunk of concrete from the shattered sarcophagus lid, throwing it hard at his enemy. With surprising speed, Famyne raised its arms in a protective X-block. The stone erupted into dust.

The dust hung in the stagnant air. Famyne leapt forward, attacking with its claws. Its guttural vibrations spiraled upward, something akin to a scream. Cat retreated, blocking the first strike with his baton.

The second strike glanced off of his armor. Sparks followed. Cat gritted his teeth, silently thanking Eva for her armor design. Famyne bore down on him with a series of strikes. Cat blocked everything he could. He slid or stepped backward under the tornado of metal blows.

His chest burned. His shoulders screamed at the impact of each blow. Famyne closed on him. Faster and faster, the skeletal machine cut at him. The baton flew from his grip, clamoring loudly against the stone floor. He lost count of how many strikes the MetaHuman landed on him. His fingers went numb. Then, his hands. He was running out of room.

Then, he saw it. Every blow was aimed at his head and chest. Fatal strikes. Cat dropped. The impact knocked the air from his lungs. He relied on the non-human part of his arsenal. His cybernetic legs slammed into the skeleton's legs. Famyne fell hard. Cat launched upward and over it, landing several meters away. He'd lost his baton, but it had gained him distance. His arms were burning. His lungs were on fire.

The skeleton rose to its feet as Cat drew the shotgun from its place on his back.

"Enough cuddle time," he scowled, "you gotta die."

As he squeezed the trigger, Famyne threw the baton back at him. It forced his shotgun blast upward. Pieces of brick fell around and between the two combatants. Cat slipped in the debris and fell back against Delambre's tomb.

Leaning on the old man for strength one more time.

Famyne rose to its feet before Cat could. Its head rolled across its shoulders. Its vibrating voice howled at him. It struck first with one claw. Cat managed to block most of the strike with his armored gloves. The second came down. Cat rolled to his left. Famyne's claw buried into Delambre's corpse.

Cat struggled to get his arms free. Famyne didn't attack. It stopped moving. Cat pushed off of the sarcophagus and rolled to his feet. He watched in silence as tubes running along its exoskeleton illuminated in a deep crimson. Delambre's form withered instantly, his skin peeled tightly to his skeleton and then tore apart. Famyne devoured the old man in seconds.

"Holy...shockin...hell," Cat managed to breathe out.

Famyne swayed on its frame, the glow of its veins slowly descending to black. Cat stared mutely as it regained composure. Its skeletal gaze swung around to find him again. Cat's gaze went from Delambre's remains to the metallic assailant. His eyes flashed brightly sending an errie glow about the room. Rage replaced fear.

He heard the echo of a metallic scream, his scream, fill his head. He kicked a chunk of cement in its direction. Famyne brushed aside the attack. Cat dove to his right to create space and distance. He slid between two of the sarcophagi, hoping for time to reload the shotgun.

Famyne's vibrations grew slower, more controlled. Either feeding had sated it or there was something Cat was missing. It spoke to him, offering up something he couldn't decipher. "Kiiiiii….Miiiiii…"

He realized he was holding his breath when he heard the sound of metal on stone. Famyne crawled atop the next sarcophagus. It extended its metal claws against and into the stone. The chant continued. Its head flailed from side-to-side on its neck. It repeated its vibrations, the breaks coming in the same cadence.

"Kiiiiii….Miiiiii…"

The clash of metal on stone repeated again, nearer this time. Famyne dragged its claws over the sarcophagus, leaving deep scars in the stone. Cat gritted his teeth. The hair on his neck rose as Famyne stepped onto the sarcophagus above him. The vibrations repeated, closer now. Cat craned his head. His gaze and the barrel of the shotgun were aimed directly upward.

Famyne extended its inhuman gaze over the side of the stone tomb. Cat's eyes met the holes of Famyne's skull. The pressure built in his lungs. Clenching his teeth, Cat pulled the trigger.

The ringing in his ears made concentration impossible. He felt as if he'd ignited nitrous oxide behind his eyes. He wanted to scream, cry, vomit, anything to relieve the searing pain in his skull. Sparks showered over him as the shotgun shell struck the being directly in its face. He dropped the gun and landed on his hands and knees in the wreckage.

The jackhammer in his head began to subside slowly. He managed to get up on one knee. If that didn't do the trick, he wasn't sure what he had left. He recognized the skeleton's vibrations mixed in odd harmony with the ringing in his head. They were slower, not more controlled, but more…desperate? He stood up, leaning hard against the sarcophagus. One of Famyne's legs rested atop the opposite stone structure. The force from the shotgun blast had blown it backward. It lay still among the debris between two of the sarcophagi. Fighting the noise in his head, he found the shotgun. It laid massive in his hands.

Cat rounded the tomb, shotgun leveled before him. The chrome being laid on the floor, arms extended outward, half of its face destroyed by the shotgun blast. Its right eye and cheek were mangled, and when it saw him, its left eye displayed recognition. It repeated the former vibration, only this time it was slower, almost slow enough to understand. "Kiiiiii….Miiiiii…"

Cat stepped closer, cautiously. Famyne made no motion to defend itself or move at all. A puddle of liquid was forming quickly beneath it. The hitman cocked the shotgun.

"Kiiiiiillllllll….Miiiiii…"

Two steps closer. Suddenly, he understood.

"Killllllllll…Meeee…"

Cat recognized the liquid pooling beneath Famyne. It wasn't the sustenance from its victims. It was brain matter and blood. He nearly gagged at the realization. The creation wasn't a creation at all. It was a MetaHuman ripped from its own form and transplanted into this chrome skeleton. It was a human who could never again be human.

"Kill…Me…"

Tears welled in his eyes as he squeezed them shut. Raising his arm, he could feel and taste the suffering Famyne was feeling.

He pulled the trigger.

The suffering was over.

CHAPTER FORTY-FOUR

Cat arranged a small pyre for what was left of Delambre. He'd managed to ruin the closest thing to a burial the old man could have been given. Fire cleansed the soul or something like that. In truth, Cat didn't want the insects and rodents chewing on the desiccated skin and organs that were once his friend. He burned Famyne's skull, also. That was partially out of mercy. It was also finishing the job.

Catwalk returned to the drainpipe. The familiar flickering ring of light was still visible at the ladder's apex. He pushed his tired arms further up the metal ladder, rung after wet and rusty rung. He reached the top of the ladder, stopping at a wooden trap door. He weighed his options. The shotgun was an option, but shooting blind wasn't the best option when dealing with a mad scientist. Save the shotgun for the scientist. He looped his cybernetic leg around the ladder, inhaled, and drove an elbow strike to the center of the door. It splintered like flotsam. Torchlight flickered in the area above. He shook his head, grabbed the next rung, and pulled himself upward.

If he hadn't spent his teen years in the religious orphanage known as St. Patrick's, the setting would have been alien to him. Instead, he recognized most of the trappings right away. Cat rose to his feet, standing in the center of an expansive worship area. Long, wooden pews lined the room before him, facing an elevated stage. A pulpit stood on one side of the stage, opposite a large statue of Jesus Christ. Cat paused for a moment. Had he even laid eyes on the biblical icon since he left the orphanage? Between the pulpit and the statue, at the midpoint of the stage, stood a large stone altar draped in rich scarlet and purple velvet. The cloth was well-pressed, free from wear and stains. It certainly was a recent

201

addition.

The rear wall behind the altar was nearly ablaze with the light of an amazing amount of candles. Wax dripped down the wall, and the candleholders, an eerie mix of white, black and red. Someone had taken a long time to light those candles.

Someone who was expecting him.

Metallic objects on the altar shimmered in the candlelight. A polished goblet, bowl, and knife reflected the flickering glow of the flame. Cat remembered communion and wondered what spin the madman would put on the ceremony. The faint remains of incense clung to the air. The drapes on the altar were flawless. The same could not be said for the rest of the room. Dirt and grime covered the pews. The hymnals and copies of the religious text were water-worn or chewed on by rodents. A layer of black soot and dust covered the stained glass of the windows. Without lighting, the vaulted ceiling disappeared into darkness.

A confession booth stood along the left wall, the enclosure wherein subjects bared their souls to the holy man, and were granted a task to achieve atonement for their sins. As a cop, Cat had plenty of run-ins with so-called holy men. Usually, these religious figures were devoted practitioners of faith. Other times they were the most deviant wolves in sheep's clothing.

The candles flickered, the result of movement, and Cat shifted, gripping the baton on his hip. A figure rose from behind the pulpit, its face shrouded in darkness, its silhouette backlit by the candles. When it spoke, its voice was clear, and human. "'And every creature which is in heaven, and on the earth, and under the earth, and such as are in the sea, and all that are in them, heard I saying. Blessing and honour, and glory, and power, be unto him that sitteth upon the throne, and unto the Lamb forever and ever.'"

Silence. This had to be the scientist responsible for the manic MetaHumans. There he stood. This was the one who had stolen Delambre's work and offered a sick display of gratitude by creating an assassin in the image of his daughter. Cat knew not to approach. Something in the air was wrong, really wrong. Instead, he waited.

The figure stepped to the side of the pulpit, physically

and figuratively looking down at Cat. "I expect an 'Amen' from the congregation."

"How 'bout a 'choke on a corpse's cock', that close enough?"

The scientist paused. "'Fall on us, and hide us from the face of him that sitteth on the throne, and from the wrath of the Lamb; For the great day of His wrath is come, and who shall be able to stand?'"

Cat took solace in the feel of the baton's grip in his hand as he ventured a few slow steps forward. "Which part are you playin', big brain? Coz from what I remember, the role yer quotin' gets squashed by the Jesus a little later on in that tall tale."

The scientist's body language betrayed tension as Cat spoke, though his voice remained unchanged. "'Salvation to our God which sitteth upon the throne; and unto the Lamb."

Cat didn't recognize the verses, simply that they were verses, and that they represented the end of the world. What was that chapter...Resurrections? Reservations? Repercussions? Something like that.

"Wow, yer like a little plush toy. Do I hafta pull yer string ta get you to throw out useless quotes at me, or is that all natural?"

The scientist lost his composure then, smashing the wooden pulpit aside with both hands. "ENOUGH! You have claimed much of my dominion, but now, you shall taste failure. You shall taste enslavement. You will pray for death."

Cat took a few more paces forward. "I've been prayin' fer the ol' dirt nap fer ten years, pops. I'd lay odds that you ain't gonna be the one ta deliver."

"Be cautious, defiler. My power is far greater than that which you will ever know...Catwalk."

The scientist's acknowledgment of his identity was no surprise. He had a slab with his face on it down below. "Really? Well, seein' as how you ain't got much left a' yer biblical vision, I'd beg to differ." The man stood hardly fifteen meters away. There he was. The psychopath who had led to so many lost lives...to Delambre's death. Beneath it all, he was a raging lunatic, caught up in his own dementia. He was going to be fun to torture.

"You have NO idea at all, do you, Catwalk? Yes, I killed your noble partner. That was simply, as the Good Book says, 'an eye for an eye'. You did, after all, ignite the right-hand man of one of my partners. Though, if you hadn't, we wouldn't be here today, would we?"

Cat gritted his teeth. Comparing Delambre to Hitch was an insult. "Gonna find a victim fer every one a' yer nightmarish creations I managed ta put in the ground, doc? That low-grade work you called Pestylynce? The marionette you called Famyne? That mosquito you called Angel? Face the facts, doc. Yer cancelled...out of biz...retired."

"It's true you managed to best my Horsemen. I had such visions of them, running throughout the city, instilling fear, the contagious chaos so welcome amongst the inhabitants of this neon-clad Babylon we've come to know." The figure bowed his head, nodding slightly as he digested the facts. "That has nothing to do with my reason for calling you here, Catwalk. You are here because I chose to draw you to me."

Cat didn't answer, relying instead on a silent survey of the area.

"Don't you see? You live because I choose to allow it. You stand, attached to those inhuman legs of yours, because I decide so. Every aspect of your existence is merely a thread that I command as I fancy. I control you. I own you." His last words echoed with the chords reserved for poets and madmen.

"I am Messiah!"

"Tell yer story at the pearly gates, chitbag. I ain't got the shockin' time." Cat strode forward, focused on ending any further actions by the scientist or whatever other beasts he'd dreamt up.

The confession booth exploded in a shower of wood and glass. Cat's body slammed into the front pew. Messiah's laughter echoed in his ears...

...until a metallic roar filled the room.

CHAPTER FORTY-FIVE

With half-instinct, half-panic, Catwalk launched into the air. The results were less than stellar. The giant enemy missed taking his head off. It caught him in the midsection instead. The blow knocked him through the air like a rag doll. Cat toppled over the pews, landing in a heap against the far wall.

Consciousness moved from best friend to vague acquaintance. His head wavered between bright stars and pitch black. Breathing was a chore. Crushing pain filled his ribs. His left arm was completely numb. Cat tried to find oxygen and to digest exactly what the hell hit him.

The giant form barreled in his direction. Titan. Cat shifted, layering his body against the floor as if he was part of the tile. Shards of glass rained down on him as the Titan shattered the exterior wall of the Church. The reds, blues, and greens depicting the Stations of the Cross showered down. Without thinking, Cat rolled to his right and leapt over the wrecked pews. The beast brought its fists downward, crushing the stones where Cat had been.

Stars danced in his eyes. He was thankful for the mesh of the armor preventing a thousand cuts in his skin from the glass. The heat of the sun erupted in his chest as air returned to his lungs. He inhaled fire. It spread through his veins. It extended into his limbs, wrapping along his spine, and coursed along his artificial legs. He coughed loudly, his lungs bruised and burning from the beast's attack. Cat slid to as much of a fighting stance as he could muster. His attacker rose to its full height in a display of fury.

The figure was immense, with shoulders flaring out nearly three meters. It flexed its enormous arms, either bicep as massive as Cat's waist. Twisted spikes lined its shoulders and forearms, down to its burly fists. Centered between its broad shoulders, the beast had a head more reminiscent of a Minotaur than a human. Two large, chrome horns curved forward from its skeletal face. Its bottom jaw projected forward, setting its face deeply into its skull. As if in a haze of pure anger, the beast's two red eyes glowed down on him. The Titan brought its hands back to the ground with a crash, pausing a moment before its next attack.

A familiar image was forged in its breastplate. Cat recognized the bizarre translation he'd first seen in the morgue. This was the improvement, the production model of the failed prototype.

Cat breathed its name, "Wahrr."

Somewhere in the distance, the voice of Messiah prodded Catwalk with the annoyance of a fencer's foil. "I heard the second living creature say, 'Come!' Then another horse came out, a fiery red one. Its rider was given power to take peace from the earth and to make men slay each other."

With the oxygen fresh in his veins, Cat bounded aside, avoiding the Horseman's next attack. Pews splintered and hymnal pages fluttered into the air. Cat digested the scientist's words. There was supposed to be an order, a specific procession to the horsemen. Cat smiled that he'd at least caused such a detour to his enemy's plans. The giant swung a massive hand backward, cracking through the remnants of the confession booth. Could this thing be another MetaHuman, another half-breed?

Cat thought of Famyne, the being scarcely more than a skeleton, nothing human remaining, but a brain trapped in a living, moving scalpel. If that polished skeleton could have once been human...

His sympathy cost him as Wahrr caught him with a backhand. A human spine would have snapped in half. Cat crashed along the ground, taking a mental inventory of the damage as he struck the floor and rolled. The enormous beast rose again, throwing the wooden benches aside. Pages from the hymnals, musical professions of faith, flittered about in the air. Cat retreated, struggling to find a strategy.

His thoughts were stuck on the skeleton called Famyne. It died, graciously, as a result of the shotgun. Cat drew the sawed-off, searching for his target as he felt the inviting wood of its grip. He evaluated the position of the trigger, its weight when it was fully loaded with shells. The familiarity was comforting.

Cat reached to lift the barrel. His left arm failed. It was all the Titan needed. It struck him full in the chest. The shotgun disappeared near the back of the room. Cat bounded off of the floor. His body struck one of the support columns. He dropped to the ground. The iron taste of blood filled his nose and throat.

He heard the roar of the attacker, mingling with the nasal words of its director. "Then the Lord will be revealed from heaven with His mighty angels in flaming fire, dealing out retribution to those who do not know the Messiah and to those who do not obey His gospel."

Catwalk weighed his options. Could Messiah see in the dark? Could Wahrr? If they were able to activate low-light vision, then destroying the candles would be a worthless endeavor. The shotgun was now a lost treasure amidst the rubble. So far, he'd simply been helpless prey in the targets of the charging bull. It was exactly the perspective portrayed in Messiah's words, in Wahrr's actions.

Time to change the game.

The oversized MH wasted motion after motion to display its power. It shattered another window with the back of its metallic arm. It then brought its fist downward, destroying two pews. Gripping the baton, Cat leapt forward. Wahrr rose to its full height, crossing its spiked arms as a guard. Catwalk's leap was nothing more than a feigned attack as he landed two full meters short of a frontal assault. The Titan uncrossed its arms. Too late. Cat rolled beneath its form, jamming the baton upward like a spear.

The baton struck home in the left thigh of the beast. Cat twisted his thumb, activating the EMP tip. Blue waves of lightning engulfed Wahrr, extending downward along the length of the baton. Catwalk dropped it, rolling to his feet and sprinting behind the giant. With its systems eliminated, it would be easy pickings. He adjusted his balance as the giant fell backwards, its left leg extended, rendered useless by the Electro-magnetic shock.

Cat reached the raised stage. Wahrr fell onto its back. The impact drove papers, dust, soot, and dirt into the air. He chanced a sideways glance to where he'd last seen Messiah, only to find the scientist gone. Near the pulpit, there was nothing but darkness. The baton was buried somewhere under the giant's form. The shotgun was lost in the black near the room's exit. The candles still clearly burned on the stage despite the new wind from the broken windows.

The air carried new words to his ears. "We eagerly wait for the Savior who will transform our lowly body that it may be conformed to His glorious body, according to the working by which He is able even to subdue all things to Himself."

The words ended, and Cat shifted at the sound of metal on metal. "...transform our lowly body..." He was able to digest the changes to the MetaHuman near him before he realized they'd even happened. Wahrr's armored forearms shifted open, two large auto-cannons replaced the spikes.

Wahrr rose on its one functional leg. Cat stared in disbelief. It had gone from brawler to arsenal at the command of its creator.

"Oh, you mother..." The audible click of loaded guns broke his blue streak.

He sprinted, not looking back. The artificial legs provided him with inhuman acceleration. His surgery provided greater speed, leaping distance and control than any purely natural human. Thanks be to whatever god was in his corner.

Cat landed with a thud on the far side of the stone altar. The scarlet and violet banners wrapped around his shoulders like a cloak. He pressed against the stone. He heard and felt the impact of the bullets against the stone. The goblet and bowl flew overhead, picked off by random rounds. A thousand angry hummingbirds buzzed in his ears. They gave way momentarily, replaced by a steady ringing. Suddenly, the gunfire started again.

Cat cowered beneath the shattering stone. "Focus, man. Find the reason you're here." He drew in as much breath as he could. What brought him here? The gunfire became distant, dream-like. The visions inside his head were far more emotional, far closer.

They'd died before him. Partners, co-workers, department personnel, most of them just part of the job. Others had become personal, so personal he was driven by an appetite for revenge, a need to destroy. That was what he wanted. He wanted it to be personal. He wanted Delambre's death to devour him in flame the way others had in the past. Closing his eyes, he visualized the reason he had come. The result surprised him.

It wasn't the geneticist's death that inspired him. It was Eva's. "I'll keep her safe, Delambre. I promise." His words. His promise. His purpose.

The gunfire subsided. Cat leapt into action. Even auto-cannons required a re-load, and Cat had tried to keep as a count of how long the beast had been firing. He pictured Eva alive, by his side, safe. She was the greatest hope he had for survival. Failing now, even if the beast didn't kill him, would mean death.

The red eyes of the giant beast turned to meet him.

Good boy. Eyes up. Let's finish this.

CHAPTER FORTY-SIX

Wahrr was a weapon of mass devastation. It was crowd control incarnate, fear among the masses, a terrorist attack on two hulking legs. It had already moved to protect itself when Cat had tried a frontal assault. He was willing to bet it would repeat that behavior.

Cat leapt directly at the oversized MH, landing short of its attack by design, instead seeking the coverage of the remaining pews. Wahrr growled. The vibrations whipped debris into the air. The pages of shredded books of worship covered the field of view. A fog of dreck filled the room. The two enemies were snow-blind in an array of fluttering hymns. Its red eyes never even saw Catwalk as he landed close enough to share a breath.

He knew its design, thanks to Will. The crazy ME had nailed it. Much of Wahrr's design was the same as the prototype. The beast's auto-guns were chain-fed, yet at no point in time were those ammunition lines visible that meant they were under the armor, riding the biological lines of Wahrr's physique. He targeted the pressure points. If the beast was an extension of human design, Cat knew where to strike.

He drove his foot upward, into the unprotected right armpit of the enormous MetaHuman. The giant howled an electronic protest. Smoke poured outward. Hydraulic pressure released, along with control. Cat landed awkwardly on his side, but Wahrr echoed his clumsiness. Its right arm became a lifeless anchor. It listed to one side then overcompensated. The giant metal best collapsed on its side.

Catwalk grimaced hard as breath returned, and with it, sheer pain. His right shoulder burned from the impact. Oxygen flooded into his body. He craved more with every breath. He scarcely believed his chest was moving until he looked down. At first, his reaction was relief. He saw his chest rising and falling. Christ, he might make it out of this alive after all.

Then, he caught the meaning of the glowing red triangle moving over his frame.

Catwalk launched himself backward. The fangs of a dozen snakes bit into his arm as he moved. The percussion of bullets ricocheted along the stone beneath him. Even with a damaged arm and useless leg, Wahrr had still beaten him to the punch.

Cat crept along the length of an overturned worship bench, analyzing. If he hadn't moved, he'd be chum. He had evaded the first two waves of Wahrr's assault. He gritted his teeth. A third strike would kill him.

They'd done a good job of trading blows. Cat fought to keep his eyes from rolling back in his head. If Wahrr lost, Messiah would simply make a 3.0 version. If he lost…No. He'd always known he'd die alone. This wasn't about him. He slapped a glove against the side of his helmet. "Kill this thing. She's depending on you."

Wahrr was designed as the hammer of the Holy One, able to exact Justice upon the masses without defense. It was a design of intimidation. It was purely offensive, and its defenses were limited as a result. There was the flaw Delambre had hinted at. All its vulnerabilities were internal, hidden from the exoskeleton, which made it so incredibly inhuman. Cat had found the first vulnerability. It was time to exploit another.

He scanned the diagnostics of the prototype. If the armor feeds were internal, then the answer was easy. A chain is only as strong as its weakest link. Two separate glowing areas in the blueprint called to him.

The shotgun was lost, along with the collapsible baton. Waves of gray and then black closed in on the corners of Cat's field of vision like curtains on a cinema screen. Blood loss and multiple injuries were taking their toll. *Focus, you shockin' fool...for yourself, for Delilah, for Eva.* He shook his head swiftly and bit his tongue to redirect his nerves. Eyes ablaze, Catwalk somersaulted backwards, shifting suddenly to launch a direct assault on the hulking Minotaur.

It raised its responsive left arm and opened fire. Cat couldn't help but recall the memories of the prototype's first attacks he'd seen on the news screen. The screams delivered the sickest harmonies, each and every voice reaching Catwalk's sensors. He heard each desperate cry.

He remembered them all.

The elderly landlord died from a shot to the throat. The noisy neighbors, having recently promised to give it "another shot" quickly died in one another's arms. A single mother of two had no time to scream before her chest shattered under the spray of bullets. The media reporter lost his life on-screen before instantly being replaced by another camera.

Wahrr paused for the briefest of interludes. Cat struck. His gloved fist cracked the lower jaw of the Horseman. The MetaHuman raised its metallic hand to its face, and Cat grabbed its uplifted arm. He planted his feet firmly against the armored chest of the giant. Reaching underneath its left arm, Cat grabbed the hydraulic hose. Screaming at the tension in his tired arms, he pulled upward, tearing the hose from its anchor point. The auto-cannon on Wahrr's left forearm fired a stream of bullets, full-auto, squarely leveled at its own face.

Liquid death erupted in a thousand doses. Before the over-sized beast could even process what it was doing, its head was a haze of shrapnel.

Victim of his own efforts and acrobatics, Catwalk crashed hard to the ground, landing squarely on his left side. He was swearing without sound, praying for the return of control and the ability to focus. The white light of pain overwhelmed every thought. The iron taste of blood and bile invaded the back of his throat. Consciousness and breath required concentration. Just when he thought he'd attained a degree of focus, he turned his gaze upward.

The headless, lifeless body of the Horseman crashed down on him.

CHAPTER FORTY-SEVEN

Ash and smoke joined the fluttering hymnal pages in the air, drifting and covering the rubble of the sanctuary. Long shadows peppered the walls, created by the dancing debris and the flickering worship candles. The ringing in his ears subsided, but the sounds of battle still echoed deep into the wings of the cathedral.

The taste of blood was as familiar to Cat as oxygen, sunlight or starting the Honda-Suzuki. He pushed open the hinged shield of his helmet in time to cough and spit. He should have felt desperate. He wasn't sure he could feel anything.

He was trapped beneath the Herculean form of the dead MetaHuman called Wahrr. Without the ability to move his most recent assailant, he would lose consciousness and die due to loss of blood. He was alone in a dark and desolate forgotten cathedral. Who could he contact, and how? Maybe this was best. Maybe his time had come.

"Time to die alone, just as promised." Cat closed his eyes for a moment. He saw the smiling faces of Angie, Bobby, and Mi-Yung. He feels Mother's grip on his shoulder. It will be good to see his family again.

"'But the fearful, and unbelieving, and the abominable, and murderers, and whoremongers, and sorcerers, and idolaters, and all liars, shall have their part in the lake which burneth with fire and brimstone: which is the second death.'"

A chill crept along his spine. He shifted his weight from side to side, praying for the slightest hint of leverage under the dead weight of the metallic beast. He tried to raise his left leg, then his right. Neither answered his request. He repeated the desperate call to his arms. His left arm was pinned and motionless. His right arm had limited motion and every effort hurt worse.

The flickering candlelight provided a twisted insanity

213

to Messiah's face as he emerged a few paces away. He was exactly as Cat had pictured. His hair had grown to shoulder-length, unkempt and graying, recessing from his skull. His skin was awful, including several wine-stain splotches along his head. His eyes were framed with countless lines and supported by thick, dark bags. In contrast, the lights created long shadows behind him, making the statue of Jesus on the altar seem twenty meters tall.

Even in the dim candlelight, the glow within Messiah's eyes was undeniable. The same glow flickered over the knife in his hand.

"What is there to do with such a subject? Leon 'Catwalk' Caliber…liar, whoremonger, thief, unbeliever, abominable," his eyes trailed to the spot where Wahrr had last stood upright, "…murderer."

"Not a lot a' room ta talk, Doc. I can think of a whole shockin' list a' good people dead as a result a' yer machines."

Messiah grinned, "Nowhere near enough. You set me back months, years! Your ignorant trespassing has cost me so much." He moved his head to an odd angle, cracking his neck. "I had so much within my grasp. There was promise to this place, a new beginning. So much promise…"

Cat mutely watched as the scientist lost himself in his vision. "I created each of them for a purpose, a procedural execution so finely tuned that the creator himself would beg for my knowledge. They were my instruments of destruction…the tools I would use to cleanse this horrific city."

"First, the Horsemen would rain down the hell and horror fitting their names. They would unleash the wave of chaos unseen on earth since the fall of Sodom. Riots, mass murder, sheer chaos so contagious that the vermin of the city would digest one another, leaving only the righteous to remain."

"Then, they would crawl forth from their hiding places, seeking direction, seeking a lord to guide them. 'The meek shall inherit the earth.' These loyal subjects would bow before me, become my followers. A new race would be born unto this defiant nation, this continent, this world of unbelieving souls. The Horsemen would lead this army forward to rid mankind of its infection, its mutations…its hatred. I would lead the cleansing of this entire race."

Messiah leveled his gaze to the trapped hitman. "And then you came and ruined everything!"

CHAPTER FORTY-EIGHT

Messiah stalked forward, step after vindictive step. The shadow of Christ's statue hovered behind him with giant, outstretched arms. Cat pushed again, desperately. His legs were dead weight. His arms were useless. He was bleeding to death. From the looks of it, Messiah was about to accelerate that process.

"This was meant to be the new home of creation, of Genesis. Nitro City, under my guidance, was to become New Eden." Messiah babbled on, each step another descent into madness, another shovel full of dirt on Cat's grave.

"Shockit, I heard you were outta yer mind, but I never woulda guessed you were this far gone. Delambre was right. You think that storybook chit is right an' you put yerself dead center in the heart of it all." Even if he couldn't move, Cat was hoping he'd make the scientist erratic enough to do something stupid.

"I am the heart of it all, cleaner. I am the soul of all mankind. I am He who shall walk the path of righteousness. I am Messiah."

Cat's laughter cut through the scientist's speech like a blade.

Venom coated his teeth, the scientist's eyes grew wild, and his chest heaved. "You dare mock me? You, you're no more than another victim at my disposal."

The hitman's yellow eyes leveled at Messiah. "So shut up an' kill me already, you worthless ball a' skin."

Messiah rose up, baring his gritted teeth. His lips were covered in spit, foaming over from adrenaline or drugs. His eyes were unnaturally wide, unblinking. His mouth was a manic smile as he raised his right hand.

He took hardly a step forward when the church resounded with the shot of a gun.

Messiah looked over his own form, taking inventory.

There were no wounds. There was no blood, no injuries. Puzzled, he looked at Catwalk for an answer.

Cat stole a glance in every direction he could. He hadn't been attacked. Messiah remained unharmed. The ceiling was an indeterminate cloud of darkness. The last pages of the hymnals still scattered in the air. It was all a mystery until he craned his head backward toward the entrance.

A wisp of smoke broke the blanket of darkness by the doors. He saw sleight movement, either a silhouette or his hopeful imagination. He returned his gaze to the scientist. With the tiniest hint of recognition, Leon "Catwalk" Caliber began to laugh.

Messiah stopped cold, observing his victim. Laughter hadn't been expected but given his subject, he was willing to accept any reaction. Catwalk's inappropriate elation caused him to laugh as well. He didn't know why, only that something had made his victim laugh in the face of death. He stopped suddenly, feeling something foreboding trigger his heart more than instinct or revenge.

As Messiah turned around, the statue of Jesus Christ came crashing down on his vulnerable form. He never even raised his arms in protection before the solid stone icon crushed his skull. The sound of Messiah's bones as they compressed beneath the weight of the statue was a symphony of relief to Catwalk.

Cat heard every sound. The pages came to rest on the stone floor. Blood seeped into the stones. His breathing was slower and less rhythmic than he wanted. In the darkness, he heard one slow clicking sound, then another. With concerted effort, he turned his gaze toward the door. He realized the sound was step after slow step in the cavernous church. As her figure reached the threshold of candlelight, Cat gazed into the green eyes of Delilah Dupree.

Her voice was thick with fear and shock as she spoke. "I guess I should have aimed low?"

CHAPTER FORTY-NINE

"The scene continues to unfold here, with one gruesome discovery after another revealed. The death toll rises every few minutes, and with it, we begin to understand the exact scope of this historic event. As the numbers reach us, it is obvious to this reporter we are witnessing one of the most diabolical black market corpse rings in the history of the city."

Scoop McEwan was in perfect form tonight, channeling every fiber of energy and charismatic delivery of investigative journalism he could gather. His makeup was a little off, but it usually was. What really mattered was the gravity he applied to each word.

"Here, in the shadow of what once represented salvation to many Nitro City residents, investigators continue to uncover the remains of a still unknown number of victims. Families of these victims can finally gain closure, thanks to the tip from a city mortician, which provided the location to this gruesome killing field. The bodies of several MetaHumans, and parts of nearly four dozen others, have been discovered, and the excavation is hardly two hours old."

Cat laughed openly as the camera panned to Will, who was shoving microphones away from his face with a practiced effort. Their deal had been simple. Cat, Delilah, and any remains of Delambre were evacuated without notice, and Will got to call in the tip. As a result, Will and his crew got to keep the majority of the seven-digit reward.

"Ow! Hey, c'mon, Doc, you could go a little lighter with that thing," Cat growled from the metal table.

Eva's sigh was growing more familiar. "I'm draining the tissue around your elbow, bone-head. I've treated a laundry list of injuries already, Sternum, Ribs, Clavicle, Humerus, Trochlea, Capitulum, Costal Cartilage,

Capsular Ligaments, Medial Epicondyle, and this is what you choose to bitch about?"

She turned her gaze from the cleaner to the redhead sitting in the chair next to him, her hand resting softly on his head. "Honestly, Delilah, you can do better."

"Hey!"

"Well, she can."

Delilah's laughter was a symphony to his ears. "Well, I know he's good at babysitting phones, at least. It's a good thing I went for the newer line with the global positioning software or…"

Cat replied, "I'll show you positioning."

Delilah laughed again. "I don't know, Angela. There's something about this one worth keeping, I think." Her eyes glistened at him as she spoke.

Eva's hands stopped their procedure, and she turned her gaze to the model. "You know, I think I prefer Eva."

Cat was puzzled, while Delilah remained as gracious as if she was being asked to join a formal party. "If that's what you would prefer, dear."

Eva muted the news feed, leaving the bizarre manifestation of the cross evidence on the screen. With a nod, she began working again. If Cat could jump up and beg her for an explanation he would have. Instead, he blurted out the question. "Why?"

Eva paused for several moments, her eyes traveling across the room to the decorative vase on the mantle that held her father's remains. "Angela was the name my father gave to me, his daughter, his ray of sunshine, his 'guiding light for the future'." A warm smile crossed her lips at the thought of him. With another sigh, it was gone. "It was also the name of that unnatural creation Messiah unleashed on the city. I'd rather not have that invade my mind every time I'm addressed."

"Besides," she said, leveling her gaze on Cat, "I'd prefer a fresh start. We're going to be partners after all."

EPILOGUE

The desert horizon blurred in the heat and velocity as the Honda-Suzuki raced along. For the briefest of moments, it left a shadow on the fallen sign that identified Highway 40. Then it thundered away. Catwalk's chest was against the tank with Delilah holding on to him tightly.

Her voice invaded his helmet's speakers. "I thought you said this thing was fast?"

"Oh, niiiiiice. That was almost convincing, except you're grippin' on me as if I'm yer parachute."

"That a complaint, mister?"

"No way on this planet or any other I'm gonna complain about you holdin' me, Red."

He eased the bike around the obstacles in the road, swerving a few additional times when the landscape was clear. She had asked earlier why he was moving the bike when he didn't need to. His response about knowing where the mines were planted invoked almost four minutes of silence.

For now, the odd pairing, the orphaned half-human killer and the glamorous fashion designer, escaped the city. This was the closest thing to Eden that he could imagine. The feel of the motorcycle brought a peace deeper than mediation or drugs. Delilah's voice woke him from an internal daydream.

"You know every millimeter of this road, huh?"

"Yeah, like I know every millimeter a' this bike."

"Anywhere that's absolutely private?"

He thought for a moment, then answered, "a couple."

"Good, find the next one."

"Alright, whatcha got in mind, Red?"

"We need a little time to ourselves," she tightened her grip on his chest. "I intend to leave marks this time."

COMING SOON

Stay Tuned for more of the Leon "Catwalk" Caliber Series

Coming Soon

Lineage
Mercy Killing
Obedient

For more information, visit Nick Kelly at:
Www.nickkelly.com
Twitter: @Nick_Kelly
Or
Find him on Facebook

A SUREFIRE WAY

J.T. Bock's

An UltraSecurity Novel
PepperLip Press
www.jtbock.com

Available on Amazon.com

Chapter One

Bad guys should never be this hot, Surefire thought before she slipped on the crossbeam hanging high above the warehouse floor.

Her next thought, she vocalized. Repeatedly.

"Shit . . ."

She was running along the rafters, jumping from beam to beam in close pursuit of Raven—the annoyingly hot thief—when her knee gave out. Her outstretched foot missed its landing by inches.

Time stopped. Her stomach lurched and her heart screeched to a halt. For a nanosecond, she seemed to float. But that was only an illusion.

She was falling. Fast. Her heart pumped out a last-ditch beat. She flailed her arms and stretched her upper body, groping for the next beam.

"Oof!" Her chest caught the edge, knocking the breath from her lungs. She wrapped her arms around the beam and hugged it tight to her now throbbing chest.

Surefire looked down at her feet, dangling forty feet above the floor below.

Big mistake.

"Oh, God," she uttered. *I can't fail now.*

"Need help?" Raven called out from a few beams over.

Surefire's mouth fell open. She must have misheard him.

Raven jumped, as if on springs, from crossbeam to crossbeam back in her direction. He stopped on the beam across from her and stood with his head cocked, waiting, it seemed, for her reply.

Surefire's gaze trailed up his body from his rock-climbing shoes to his rock-solid abs.

No, she decided, a transhuman baddie needed a bizarre deformity—metal teeth, yellow skin, neon eyes, a joker face—something. Not a second-skin black suit that showed off the body of a Grecian athlete.

It was way too distracting.

Not that she was distracted one bit. She was an UltraAgent—a trained law-enforcement professional. She was always in control and always focused, and she always completed her mission. In this case, capturing the thief directly across from her.

Her falling had nothing to do with being distracted. Her bad knee had buckled. That was all.

His eyes locked on hers from behind the two holes in his Zorro-like mask, and he asked again, "Do you need help?"

Under her own mask, she blinked, registering his question. Did he think she was an idiot?

Surefire repositioned her arms for a better grip. Anger now replaced her fear. "Isn't this the part when you run away? Or toss me to my death?"

"I can't and won't have blood on my hands," he replied.

"Glad you have some principles. It'll help you in court."

He shook his head as if she didn't get it. "I can give you a hand—"

"Stay where you are." She emphasized each word so he didn't mistake her meaning.

Never moving her eyes from his, she hauled herself back onto the beam, inch by painful inch. Swinging her leg over, she pulled herself up onto unsteady feet but remained in a squat for better balance. She took a deep breath then winced as pain sliced through her ribcage.

Just great. A bruised rib.

If Raven noticed she was hurt, he didn't give any indication. He casually stood on the beam across from her. Over his shoulder, he held the burlap sack containing the statue he had stolen from the museum.

Surefire raised her right arm and aimed the small dart

gun attached to her wrist. She concentrated on keeping her hand from trembling as she locked on the masked space between his eyes.

Then she hesitated.

She couldn't shoot him this high up off the floor. He'd fall, and the priceless artifact he had slung over his shoulder like a bag of dirty gym clothes would crash to the ground.

Surefire lowered her gaze, and the bastard grinned.

"You okay?" he asked, not fazed by the weapon pointed at him.

"I'm fine."

He snorted as if he didn't believe her. Her finger tensed on the trigger button hidden in her palm.

"The police and the FBI will be here any minute." She swallowed to strengthen her voice. "I suggest we climb down and—"

His lips puckered into a kiss before he dropped onto the concrete floor as if it weren't a forty-foot fall but a leap off a balance beam.

Dammit!

Not hesitating again, she flicked her wrist toward the ground and depressed the trigger.

Click. Click. Nothing.

She inspected the tiny dart gun, shook it, and tried again.

Click. Click. Again, nothing.

Oliver was so dead when she got back to the UltraSecurity office. She hadn't had time for a weapons check this evening, and Oliver had sworn he had tested her weapons earlier in the day.

"Having a wardrobe malfunction?" Raven called up to her.

Surefire glared down at him. He stood below her with his hands on his hips and his face tilted up at her. Moonlight filtered through the smudged windows lining the top of the building and cast a dim spotlight on his infuriating grin.

She rolled her eyes. He had something up his tight sleeve, or he would have escaped when she slipped.

Then again, maybe he wanted to see what else she'd mess up.

Hands down, he was the most arrogant criminal she'd been assigned. Not that she had encountered many. He was only her fourth assignment since joining

225

UltraSecurity, known as U-Sec, over three years ago. And the first assignment she headed up since her elevation from rookie to full-time agent. The last two agents on the case had been reassigned. Inferno had lost his cool and seared a museum's storage center trying to stop Raven. They had found the last agent, Tara Kard, tied up on Marie Antoinette's bed at Versailles, a priceless vase missing.

So by now, Raven probably thought UltraAgents were pathetic amateurs, and he had become cocky.

Hence, the not running away part.

Either that or he hoped to win her trust and disable her as he had done to Tara.

Whatever his motive, she'd show him.

Surefire grabbed a metal tube the size and width of her index finger, hidden in a small pouch on her belt. She aimed it at him and depressed the release button on its side. A net shot out but didn't deploy evenly. It drifted onto the ground next to him, a limp parachute.

He nudged it with his foot. "Cute. Should I throw this over my head?"

"That would be helpful."

Surefire sighed. Between the weapon malfunctions and her slipping, he deserved to get away, and she deserved to have her U-Sec badge revoked.

"Nah, I'll let you work for it. I don't want you to think I'm easy." He darted away into the shadows of the aisles.

Surefire spun around, straining to hear his fleeing steps in an effort to pinpoint his location. But the building housed metal crates, which bounced sound around like a pinball, making him nearly impossible to track.

"You know . . ." His voice sounded from down below to her left. Or was it from behind? "I don't think you want to catch me. I'm probably the most excitement you've ever had."

"Don't flatter yourself," Surefire yelled, angrier than she intended.

"Then why all the mistakes? Are you trying to screw up?"

She threw down the empty metal tube with a clang.

How long had she been on this case? Three months. And how many times had she almost caught him? Three near misses. And how often had he tried to provoke her? Three times, of course. Three signified the final strike, the final out—the charm. She had begged her bosses for this case. If she wanted to make a name for herself at U-Sec—and if she wanted a raise—then she needed Raven.

Well, she needed to *catch* him.

She scanned the boxes below for one stacked high enough to jump onto but found none nearby. She was a sure shot and a trained gymnast, but she was only human, well, a transhuman. She hated that label the media used for people with extraordinary abilities. She could hit any target—when her weapons worked. But that was the extent of her talents. Looking down at the long drop to the floor, which Raven had taken with such ease and no broken bones, she wondered whether he was something more than a transhuman.

Most transhumans were gifted with one ability. Very few had two distinct talents. Raven possessed several that U-Sec was aware of. Bullets slowed but never stopped him. He toted off statues weighing three hundred pounds as if they were plastic mannequins. Then, during his previous heist, he had walked through the walls of a sealed vault, adding "phasing out" to his list of talents.

Why he didn't use that skill now, Surefire couldn't guess. However, she was grateful. She was close to capturing Raven or at least uncovering his thefts, and failure was not in her family's genes, as dad loved to remind her.

But first, she needed to find Raven again or at least distract him until her backup arrived. They were late, and Surefire was too focused on her target to question why.

Eyeing the rafter angled just above and to her right, she lifted her left arm, aimed a small compact box secured to her wrist, and shot out a line to the next beam up. The small weighted grappling hook, attached to the end of a cable, spun twice around the beam then latched onto the edge. She tugged on it and the hook held. Her gaze shifted to the floor below, finding the perfect spot to land. The drop didn't seem so frightening when she wasn't dangling over it.

Surefire swung down and dropped onto solid concrete.

The hard landing jolted her body. Renewed pain surged along her ribs. She doubled over as she struggled to breathe past the searing sting. She pulled two capsules from a belt pocket and popped them into her mouth, breaking them open with her teeth. Seconds later, a soothing liquid slid like hot Irish coffee down her throat and to her stomach. The sensation branched out to her limbs and dulled the pain but not her senses. For another hour, she wouldn't feel a thing. These Happy Pills, as the other agents dubbed them, were the best innovation by U-Sec's lab geeks.

She ejected the thin, strong cable from the box on her wrist then heard the click of another hook and cable loading inside the small contraption as backup. Though she certainly wasn't in any condition to imitate Tarzan again this night.

Regrouping, she quieted her breathing. Cargo containers loomed above her. Giant Legos stacked in countless rows. She listened for a footstep, a misstep, anything.

And heard nothing.

Surefire slumped against a crate. If Raven were stashing his stolen goods in this warehouse, as she believed, he wouldn't go far. She considered her options. She'd rather not reveal her position. She'd prefer a sneak attack, but the warehouse was so large the only way to find him was to get him to start talking.

Not the typical protocol, but Raven seemed to enjoy showing off his verbal gymnastics, especially when it came to mocking her. Only one way to find out. Desperate, she straightened up and opened her mouth, when Raven's voice resounded above her.

"Did you do that?"

"Do what?" she replied, caught off-guard.

"Nothing. It's probably nothing."

What the hell was he talking about? Her face cinched in confusion under her mask.

Whatever it was didn't matter. The hairs on her arms stood on end. He was close. Very close. His voice was loud, clear.

"Maybe if you describe it, I could help," she offered.

She eased a small stun gun from her utility belt, pressed her back against the cold steel of the crate, bit her lip, held her gun high in the air, and then—

"Doubtful," his voice echoed loudly.

Surefire jumped back. His voice was too close, like he was speaking next to her ear. She whirled around and looked up. Above and to her right, Raven peered over the edge of the top crate. His lips flashed an oh-too-perfect-smile before he backed away from the edge.

She pulled the trigger to at least graze him. Again, another empty click.

What the—?

She flung the gun down and attempted another tactic—not exactly a typical tactic, but worth a try, since Raven was an atypical criminal.

"Come down here, and I'll show you how helpful I can be." She tried to deepen her voice and make it sexy. "Tried" was the operative word.

He laughed a rich, sultry laugh that she was certain he had practiced to get it just so. "You need to work on your bedroom voice. You sound like a man, and I don't swing that way. Ask Inferno."

"Inferno?" Surefire frowned. "What do you mean?"

"What do you think?"

She mulled this over for a moment then balked, "No way. He's an ex-Navy Seal. You're wrong."

"That has nothing to do with it. Why do you think he burned down the storage center?"

"He lost control. It happens to the best of us."

"Hell hath no fury like a queen scorned." Raven chuckled, and his amusement bothered her more than this conversation, which was supposed to distract him instead of her. He had both men and women bumbling over him. Surefire was certain the same thing had happened to Tara Kard, even if she had never given specifics. Tara had hated turning over the case to Surefire, who assumed it was because she had been embarrassed for having failed. Now Surefire wondered if it were something more.

Egotistical bastard. If sex appeal were another one of his powers, he needed to save it for his cellmate.

Surefire jumped when the crates to her left creaked. She caught sight of Raven landing on another box farther down the aisle before he disappeared. She ran down the aisle and vaulted over the metal rails of a forklift.

Think of something. *Anything* to annoy him.

"Considering your outfit, no wonder Inferno thought you played for his team," Surefire shouted before rounding a corner.

A small crate teetered and swayed above her. She could see Raven's outline against the filtered light.

"What's wrong with my outfit?"

Surefire suppressed a laugh. He actually sounded offended. "Looks like something a mime would wear."

"I'm miming something right now. Too bad you can't see it."

"Come down here and show me."

He coyly changed the subject. "I'm liking your leotard. Doesn't leave much to the imagination. I assume it's for distraction?"

Surefire blushed. Ever since she'd moved in with her sister six months ago, Heather's cat, Prada, saw fit to use Surefire's uniforms as her own special bed. Tonight, Prada had made Surefire's only clean uniform into a litter box, and her backup had been lost by the dry cleaners after a previous Prada incident. So Surefire had had to find a new outfit quick—one that allowed ease of movement—and found her old gymnastics leotard. Apparently, her breasts and butt, though mostly her butt, had grown in the past ten years.

"Obviously, it's not working or you'd be down here taking a closer look."

"The view's just as good from up here," he countered, and Surefire didn't think her face could flush any hotter. "But where did you get that mask? A luchador yard sale?"

She balled her fists. Ditto with the mask. Prada had used that as a hairball receptacle. Surefire had dug out her Halloween costume from four years ago when she'd dressed as a Mexican wrestler. Not a good look, but it hid her identity.

"At least I'm wearing underwear," Surefire goaded him again.

"I did that for you." He skimmed along the windowsills. "Was wondering if you'd noticed."

Her body tensed in frustration. She needed to get Raven down to the floor now, and not for the reasons his tone suggested. Her mind raced through her portable arsenal. She had another weapon that released a net—if it worked.

Damn Oliver.

Instead of focusing on work, he was too busy focusing on U-Sec's newest agent and call center manager, Pixie Chick.

They were going to have a nice long chat about the problems with interoffice dating when she returned.

Red and blue flashing lights skimmed across the dirt-encrusted windows at the top of the warehouse. Sirens grew louder as police cars surrounded the building. She glanced at her watch.

About time they arrived.

Nearly forty-five minutes had passed since she'd first called the police after she spotted Raven climbing down from the roof of the Walters Art Museum in downtown Baltimore.

Outside, car doors slammed shut and hard soles beat a path across the ground. She had five, maybe ten, minutes until the cops gassed the place, which was their preferred MO for dealing with transhumans like Raven. And her. Last time they had given her an assist, she'd almost gone down in friendly fire.

Technically, she shouldn't be in here. Shouldn't have entered the building without backup. The warehouse doors were locked, and she hadn't wanted to lose sight of Raven; she'd had to scale a semi parked underneath an open window to get in.

It was a stupid, impetuous, and ultimately dangerous move. However, she'd assumed the police would have arrived sooner. When Raven had entered the warehouse, she'd known she'd lose him again if she didn't follow. Her bosses at U-Sec had to understand. And if she brought Raven in—no, *when* she brought Raven in—they would more than understand.

Maybe even give her a promotion.

She glanced at her communicator, a secure U-Sec cell phone, clipped to her belt. It was her direct link to the U-Sec office and police. She'd silenced it before entering the warehouse. Usually, a dull green light blinked if there were a message. She unclipped it and looked at the LCD screen. No missed calls.

She had spoken with Pixie at the U-Sec call center before she'd notified the police. Oracle—her sergeant and mentor—should have contacted her by now. Despite the officers outside, she preferred to have someone from her own team as backup. Most officers were not thrilled to work with U-Sec or, as they called it, the Freak Squad.

Something clanged to her right. Just above her, Raven jumped onto another crate and then to another window, possibly searching for a weak spot in the perimeter.

"Give up," Surefire called out to him. "The building's surrounded."

"Never stopped me before."

Surefire kept her eyes focused on Raven. Across from her, the doors rattled.

Suddenly, Raven's foot slipped. He fell a short distance and then caught himself on the windowsill. Pulling himself back up, he wagged his head as if to clear it. "You don't feel that?"

"No," Surefire replied, though she couldn't explain the uneasiness prickling up her spine.

A gruff male voice shouted orders outside. Then the police tried to open the nearly floor-to-ceiling doors with a resounding bang. Surefire edged closer to the doors. Her gaze shot to the iron handles. She did a double take.

The doors were chained from the inside.

Something on the far end of the warehouse slammed shut. She looked up and saw Raven staring in the sound's direction.

She grabbed her communicator and tried to control her nervous fingers as she dialed her police contact.

"Detective Matthews," she whispered into the small phone. She held it to her ear but heard nothing. The LCD screen faded to black. The battery was dead.

She hooked the phone back onto her belt and ran toward the exit to warn the police the doors were chained.

A tingling sensation skimmed across her skin. She paused in mid-step. Vibrations, like a mild electrical current, hummed through her veins. Crates creaked and shifted above her, and the floor started to shake.

"What the—?" Surefire grabbed the handle of a cargo container just as a crack snaked through the middle of the concrete floor. Above her, metal containers shifted and scraped together. Across the aisle, a few wooden crates fell and splintered apart onto the floor. She aimed the rappelling gun on her left wrist, but it was too late. Before the cable could deploy, she slipped and fell next to the fissure.

She sprang to her feet and darted away from the widening crack.

This couldn't be another earthquake. In twenty-seven years, she'd experienced only one in Baltimore a few years ago. And then she'd hardly felt anything while driving on the beltway.

Something creaked above her.

"Watch out!" Raven shouted as he jumped from the window to the top crate and landed with practiced ease next to her. Wrapping his arms around her waist, he tackled her to the ground. He rolled with her several times before they stopped with him on top, leaning over her in a provocative straddle—leaving her breathless.

Surefire's carefully packed gadgets on her utility belt cut into her lower back. She couldn't breathe, couldn't concentrate, and needed to get up. She jabbed both palms hard against his chest, but he didn't budge. A loud rumble interrupted her struggle. The sound rose and filled the warehouse, ending in an ear-splitting crash.

The cargo container she'd been standing underneath seconds ago fell to the floor, sending up a cloud of dust and dirt. The metal sides and corners buckled like an accordion.

Her heart thumped wildly. She glanced up at Raven, who was staring at her with a fierce intensity. Under normal circumstances, she might have been frightened by a criminal looming over her. But she was too shocked from her near-death experience to care.

"Thanks," she stammered.

The side of his lips lifted up in a smile. "Anytime."

She noticed he no longer held the sack. "Where's the statue?"

He shifted, elevating his weight from his left side. He inclined his head toward a crawl space between two containers. "I threw it out of the way—"

With her right arm free, Surefire used her thumb to flick a switch in her palm. A dart ejected from the gun on her right wrist, and she jabbed the needle into his neck in one swift movement.

He raised his hand in astonishment and pulled it out. He frowned at the needle. "This is the gratitude I get?"

She shrugged and smiled smugly under her mask.

"Typical woman."

"Typical man," Surefire countered.

He planted his hands on either side of her. His eyes glazed over as the drug took effect. "My body is going to reject it. I'll shake it off in seconds."

"I had this one made especially for you. You left behind more than a fake fertility statue at your last robbery."

He groaned. His arms buckled.

The floor shook again and started separating underneath her back.

She slammed her palms into his chest. "Move!"

But it was too late.

About the Author

When J.T. Bock was a child, she wanted to be James Bond or Indiana Jones or a vampire hunter or Wonder Woman. Whatever brought her the most action, adventure, and romance while playacting on her stage— otherwise known as her grandmother's basement. Now J.T. has assembled her own team of action heroes, supernatural creatures, and maniacal villains and set them on adventures far from her basement to exotic lands and alternate dimensions.

From a secret location outside of Washington, DC, J.T. conjures these pulse-pounding tales to share with those kindred readers looking for an exciting escape. Her alternate identity enjoys spending time with her workaholic husband and their sidekick rescue dog, traveling to interesting locales, running her graphics business, and enjoying life to the fullest with an amazing group of family and friends and a good glass of wine.

Check out J.T.'s latest adventures and find her by flashing her initials in the sky, opening up her favorite bottle of Pinot Noir, or visiting her website at www.jtbock.com.

ICHI

by N.S. Kelly

Coming October 2013

Chapter One

Crunch. Crack. Bones split.

She knew the sound of bones snapping under the pressure of a predator's jaws. She froze. Her nightly run forgotten. She stopped in the shadows of the building next to her, tilted her head, and listened.

She paused as silence descended.

Her stomach tightened.

Human, animal, or other?

She remained still, hiding, listening, as she'd always done and been trained to do.

Her breathing steadied. She fought the sounds, willing them to not be what she'd thought she'd heard. This was not her battle.

She'd wanted to get in her nightly run without a demon sighting. The long days at the morgue shredded her stamina. A medical examiner's daily routine fatigued her enough without adding in this. She'd been working days on end and welcomed the brief respite. She'd started her run to get rid of the stress, not add more.

No, thank you, Universe, for whatever planetary alignment that was causing such upheaval.

She wrinkled her nose. The rusty, metallic smell of blood reached her as she passed by an alleyway. She sniffed, shaking her head, adjusting to the scent. She suppressed the involuntary urge to sneeze by pressing the tips of her index fingers and thumbs together. The minute gesture gave her something to focus on. She took in a deep breath and exhaled. She'd deal. She'd been made for this. It was her calling.

Technically, she wasn't on duty. Shellie was on tap for this. North America was her domain, her responsibility.

Crack.

Growl.

Wet lips smacked together in satisfaction and repulsion rolled through her entire body. She bit back a physical response and focused on her breathing.

This was work, nothing more.

Her stomach tightened. She listened and then crept forward toward the sounds. She stopped and stilled in the shadows of the building, and her hearing expanded. Her hands curled to her sides. Her spine tightened. A plastic bottle clattered down the alleyway, blown by the wind. Tires splashed through puddles several blocks over. The endless rhythm of go-go music playing in Adams Morgan a mile away pulsed in her ears. The city never rested.

Crunch.

Lick.

Slurp.

Purr.

Growl.

She hesitated, every cell in her demanding a response. Pinpricks raced over her skin. She forced her heart rate to slow as she began to take stock. The local samurai wasn't responding. Shellie was late.

Shellie was never late.

Every bit of her being tuned into the sounds. Shellie either was either ignoring her mission or she'd been called elsewhere. She hoped it was the latter. She heard it all, bad sign.

And then, the scent hit her.

She sniffed again, and odd combination of smells — ashes, bones and baby powder—whiffed across her nose. Demon. Rissu, recently born at that.

She shuddered. She wished no one a run in with a mature Rissu. Baby killers. She'd slain several before. A newborn meant an adult had to be nearby.

Who was calling demons into the Nation's Capital? Did they have a vendetta against the current administration?

Stupid, stupid, stupid.

She would never understand those she'd been sent to protect. They did the dumbest things in the name of power, and calling a demon into being was very, very dumb. Although, DC provided a daily dose of all levels of stupidity. She'd chronicled them through the years. Someday, she'd post them up to some website. Or, maybe she'd send an anonymous article. Her sister Samurai wouldn't kill her then.

Focus, Shia, focus.

The sound of another crack reached her ears, and her body began to hum. She couldn't ignore a demon. As tired as she was, duty called...demanded. Shia cast aside the desire to turn the other cheek and move on because this wasn't her domain. The tenets of the Samurai prevailed. Their code was simple: Loyalty, honor, obedience, duty, filial piety, and, when necessary, self-sacrifice.

Cold energy rippled over her, pulsed in her veins, growing with each heart beat. Her eyelids fluttered. The static from within caressed her skin, escaping through every pore and every hair on her head. The familiar satisfaction of upcoming battle crept into her psyche. The feeling of perfect harmony with her body granted a heightened consciousness only true Samurai achieved. Her swords hummed against her back. Her hands reached back without a second thought. The sound of metal against leather whispered as she pulled the hidden blades from their sheaths.

What other woman ran the streets at night with swords strapped to her back? Thankfully, she'd never had to explain it.

Swords in hand, she rounded the corner, and the alleyway opened up before her. Bricks, trash, shadows. Nothing ever changed in the alleyways, unless you counted the probable appearance of hungry homeless, hungrier rats, or a prostitute turning a quick trick, darkness and night. Demons never hunted during daylight hours. At least, none of hers did. No wonder she stuck to late evening runs.

She moved forward, inch-by-inch. She should have taken up needlepoint or some other mindless, home based activity. There were thousands of things to occupy her body and mind, yet somehow, she still had to be out moving and engaging.

Demon junkie.

That had to be it. All her years spent tracking, teaching, it was a drug in her system. She was taking a vacation once this latest infestation died down or when she found Shellie.

She rounded the corner and saw him. Male, not that she'd ever seen a female Rissu outside a portal shimmer. The males? The spines always showed on the males, deep, dark, spiky, through the clothes, if they happened to wear any. No matter how hard they tried to pass off as human, Rissu never quite managed to keep the spines from protruding from their backs.

"No sir, we don't eat the resident beings on the planet we were just called to." She tsk'd him as she stepped out of the darkness.

The creature before her stopped, hunched over in the shadows of the alley. His head turned at the sound of her voice. Shia couldn't make out the demon's victim from this angle, but she was certain it was dead. The Rissu's claws stilled. Chunks of flesh stuck between its fangs. Blood dripped from its long razor like nails and covered the brick wall before him, sprayed forward like the work of some avant garde artist.

Messy kill.

She wrinkled her nose as the scent of wet dog overwhelmed her.

Oh, thank the stars, he'd started with the four-legged beings rather than the humans. She sent a silent prayer for the lost canine soul and focused on the Rissu before her. He was large for a newborn. Her best guess put him over 6'4", though his weight was impossible to estimate, given the anatomy of his race, top-heavy, a brawler, well muscled and powerful. His claws easily tore through the carcass of his prey, a Rottweiler. His teeth had severed its neck and bones. The thing was famished, and she had interrupted its first meal.

Shia weighed her odds. She'd hunted Rissu before. This one outsized her by at least a couple hundred pounds and over a foot in height. She'd bet he wasn't going to like her much after this.

Oh well, the bigger they are, the harder they fall. Right?

When he turned his massive head to look at her, she struck. Her sword whispered through the night air, intent on taking his head from his shoulders. She cursed under her breath as he moved, the tip of the blade grazing his shoulder rather than severing his head from his neck.

"No sir, be a good demon. This is not your realm." She shook her head at him and sing-songed as she followed his movements. She twirled the sword in her right hand, her wrist rotating the long metal blade as an extension of herself. Her motions were almost musical as she stepped closer, separating the beast from his snack.

The Rissu remained hunched over like a cat, back bowed, teeth bared, eyes lit up, studying her every move from the center of the alley.

He growled.

She smirked. "Bring it, fledgling."

She stepped to the side, preparing for his attack. They never learned. When he launched into her, she switched the grip on her sword. He drove against her, and Shia fell backward under the force. She jabbed into his upper ribs; the hilt of her sword in one hand, the hardened spear hand strike with the other. Each blow found the soft space between ribs, and she allowed herself a brief feeling of success. The Rissu's momentum carried them both deeper into the alley. His weight shifted again, and she shoved hard. He slammed into the wall behind them.

The demon howled in pain as the spines on his back struck cold stone. Shia grinned and rolled out of his grasp. Her foot lashed out, kicking his jaw sideways.

His claws slashed out, nails elongated, sharp and spiky, reaching to her. She bit back a cry of pain as his hand knifed down, catching her across her abdomen.

She clamped a hand over her mid-section. Blood rushed to her center. She frowned as she rolled, coming to her feet in a crouch. She chided herself for the premature assumption of victory.

Rookie Rissu, 1, centuries old Samurai, 0.

"Oh no, demon boy, it's not gonna be that easy."

Ohh, come closer demon...ashes to ashes and dust to dust.

She'd send him back into the alternate dimensions, multiple realities, in pain, and definitely in several pieces. Shia satisfied herself with the memory of sending an enemy into a dimension portal once without his limbs. She wondered if she'd have time for such a ritual before the pre-dawn traffic interrupted her.

She blocked out the pain and switched hands with her sword, watching as the blood red eyes tracked her movements. Back and forth. Back and forth, she played.

She waited.

In the pause between shifting of hands, he leapt.

She darted aside, grasping his neck. She pushed down into the pavement as he tried to overtake her. Her body shifted and flowed, her sword swept out and around in the other, intent on taking his head and ending this fight. He darted to the side and slid past her blade. Her sword tip hit the ground, metal ringing on asphalt. She almost bit her tongue in frustration. Her hand let go, claws retracted as the demon tumbled over and away from her. She didn't need him taking her with him. She watched as the

Rissu rolled to his feet.

She crouched, ready, waiting as he stared down at her. When he dashed towards her, her hand lifted in a block to his shoulder, pushing him past her, she ducked, taking her sword with her as his tail sailed over her, ducking under the deadly spikes. They both rolled, standing off.

The Rissu threw a haymaker at her.

She blocked, arm on arm, the impact resonating through her. Her other arm and sword arced out and over. She sliced down, severing his shoulder from his body and then lifted the blade, turning to slash across his neck.

Slice.

A lock of her hair drifted in the air.

She missed.

The blade swirled around her in a defensive posture on instinct. Losing sight of such a beast for a second could be fatal. She drew her sword back, her eyes shifting through the shadows to catch the Rissu before its next strike. After several breaths, she stood upright, cursing her luck and her performance. The Rissu had executed the only move with worse consequences than blindsiding her.

The demon turned tail and ran.

Shia groaned under her breath. She'd get her run in yet. Rissu weren't the fastest demons in the realms, but they left a good trail. She slid the sword back into place on her back and palmed several throwing stars while forcibly ignoring the pain in her abdomen as her body began to stitch itself back together. The metal stars offered comfort and familiarity as they slipped into her hands. Metal vibrated against her skin.

Her vision shifted and red lights danced across the ground in the darkness.

Demon trail.

He'd darted out of the alleyway. He had made an escape attempt, but she could still catch him. Shia sprinted down the alley, nearing full speed in a few steps. She raced forward, intent on the unholy light along the street.

Her focus shifted to the otherworld. She reached the end of the passage and turned the corner. She collided with something solid. The air left her lungs. Stars danced in her vision, and she struggled to draw in a breath. This wasn't Rissu, far too physical and of this realm.

She forced her need to fight deep down, focusing on the

night.

The figure staggered backward, spinning before stabilizing against a parked truck. A beam of light darted over the ground, over the car, into the sky and then stopped. A flashlight.

A demon wouldn't have a flashlight.

Human.

She struggled to right herself and dropped the throwing stars down her sleeve.

Breathe, Shia, breathe.

She didn't attack humans without cause. She shifted, and she took another deep breath, stabilizing.

The man stood upright, leveling the flashlight at her face. Standing, yet still craving air in her lungs, Shia lifted her hands in self-defense. She blinked, willing her eyes to adjust to the sudden glare in the dark.

It was bright.

It took seconds for her vision to right itself. When it did, she could make out his silhouette against the grey night air, but nothing more. As if hearing her thoughts, the man moved the light from her to his own form. He focused the light on a piece of paper in his hand. Centered on the paper was a black and white picture of a Rottweiler.

He turned the light beneath his face, illuminating him in campfire ghost story fashion.

"Have you seen this dog?" He asked.

She bit her tongue. Hard. If she hadn't already locked her knees, they might have buckled in embarrassment. Oh, gods. Ryan. She took a deep breath, forcing her heart rate to decelerate, demanding her body come back into her control.

"Good evening, Detective Calder." She watched as his eyes widened.

He switched the light from himself back to her, studying her as she winced from the pain of the sudden brightness.

"Dr. Ronin, out for an evening run?" He asked.

Shia dropped her gaze, taking in her black sweats. Not something she wanted to be seen in, but there you had it. Thank the Universe the dark fabric hid the cuts it suffered and any blood loss she'd suffered.

"Yes."

She darted a glance over his shoulder, the red lights still hovered over the street. Had the demon sprinted right past him? Her gaze swept over him, making sure he held no hint of red light. She shifted her shoulders, settling her swords in lower. He shouldn't be able to see them, but she didn't need to take the chance with the eagle eyed homicide detective. As odd as he seemed sometimes, he appeared very aware in the human realm. She wouldn't put it beyond him to notice the otherworldly going-ons.

Ryan tilted his head and followed her gaze for a moment over his shoulder before focusing on her again. "Well, I figured you weren't grocery shopping. Looks like you worked up a good sweat." He flashed the light at her feet and along the entrance to the alleyway. "You drop anything?" The light criss-crossed over the demon trail, which glowed like fire in Shia's eyes.

She wished he'd kill the light, but knew he wouldn't. The glare amplified in her head a hundred times over. She squinted. "Thought I heard something in the alley, but no one's there. Decided I better make up my time." She shifted, torn between letting her eyes drink in his dark form and chasing after the Rissu.

Wait a minute.

Rottweiler?

A shiver raced through her. "You're out looking for a Rottie?"

Please tell her this wasn't his dog she'd failed to rescue.

Ryan nodded, "Yeah, Mrs. Bradbury in Apartment 4-G is missing her dog. She's pretty broken up about it. I figured it was the least I could do to help. Especially because Mrs. Bradbury listens to Joe Cocker when she's upset...and her hearing aide isn't always up to par." He moved the light from one side of the street to the other, checking for any uninvited guests. "Nothing inspires a man to community service like Joe Cocker at a hundred and twenty decibels."

Despite her duty, her lips twitched. Decorated homicide detective way laid by an elderly neighbor and 70's soul-singing icon. Priceless. She sobered. She didn't want either of them finding out how the dog died. The crack of bone in teeth still echoed through her head. She wished she'd found the Rissu minutes before. The four legged should have lived.

"You live nearby? Rottie's stay pretty close to home. I can keep an eye out for him while I run." Over Ryan's shoulder the trail began to dim.

"That would be great. You can't miss him. He's got a collar with rhinestones...something about his resemblance to Elvis. I don't know." Ryan handed her the flier. "Two blocks south of here. Trust me. You'll hear 'I Get by with a Little Help from my Friends' before you ever get in the door. My number's on the flier if you find anything, but I think you have it from the Felder case."

Shia nodded. She knew more about Ryan than she cared to admit even before their cold case, the Felder homicide. She bit her lip as the Rissu's trail dimmed and faded. She shouldn't have let him side track her. She was faster than him. He never would have realized it was her if she'd kept moving. Her entire body warmed.

"What's his name?" She'd replace the dog. She couldn't in good conscience let an old lady mourn the loss of her beloved family member because a demon decided to make him dinner.

This job sucked.

Ryan shrugged. "What else? Joe." He gave her a quick once-over. "You mind me asking something personal?"

"You can ask. I may or may not answer." She'd already delayed too long. She rocked from foot to foot, ready to be on the move again.

"The nation's capitol isn't always the friendliest place, especially in the dead of night, for a good looking girl. You have some pepper spray or something handy?" He half-grinned. "Professional courtesy and all..."

Shia smiled. "Don't you know, Detective, I am a weapon. I run the nights. It's the best time. No one out to stop me."

She wasn't about to reveal the swords, throwing stars or baton hidden on her body. He didn't need the influence. The worst she encountered was a stray homeless or a demon. The demons, well, they were hers to handle anyway. The homeless wandered on their way, thinking she was an illusion. She preferred it that way.

"I'd like to share your confidence, Dr. Ronin. I'd feel better hearing you had some tools to help you stay safe." He unbuckled a small container of pepper spray from his belt. "This is compact. It shouldn't affect your running stride, but it could help in case you bump into the wrong night creature."

Her hand lifted. He didn't know about the other creatures of the night. The pepper spray dropped into her palm. The one detective who she thought would do well in her realm had never questioned her findings. Sometimes, she'd had to reach to explain a death. He worked the cases, focused on the facts. She wondered what he'd do if she presented him with a demon, the

Rissu?

She sighed. He'd never even see it. Few did.

"Thank you, Detective. I'll be sure to return this to you tomorrow, if you stop by the morgue."

He nodded. "Thanks. I have the Huang results to pick up. I'll adjust my schedule. Enjoy your run, Dr. Ronin."

Shia shifted, unsure. Ryan never spoke more than a few words, directed at work to her. He was quiet, but he was out looking for a Rottie who belonged to a neighbor. The Rissu was long gone. She'd have to hunt it down tomorrow. And Ryan? He wasn't of her realm, but one of those to protect who now had a demon in his neighborhood. She'd be sure to keep her running route close by. She didn't want some Rissu munching on him or his elderly neighbor.

"Good luck with your fliers and finding the Rot. I hope she eventually turns the music down, for your sanity." She murmured.

She pulled her hood up over her hair and took a step forward.

She stopped and turned, casting a glance back at him. "Detective Calder?"

"Yes, Dr. Ronin?"

"Be careful of the shadows."

It was the only warning she could give him. She wished she could have given him more. She turned and set out at a sprint on her regular path. She didn't need him asking for clarification. He was one to do so. She sprinted away from him faster than she should have.